RESCUED BY RUIN

LADIES OF THE NORTH

BOOK III

ISABELLA THORNE

Mikita Associates Publishing

PART I

CHAPTER 1

Miss Katherine Westlake sat with her needlepoint neglected on her lap as she looked out of her window with dismay. Her cat, Patches, sat on the chair beside her purring as the creature shoved its head against Katherine's hand, disrupting her needlework. Katherine patted the cat absently.

It had stopped raining, but droplets trickled down the floor to ceiling window pane. The sky was a uniform melancholy gray. What would soon be wheat fields stood with sopping puddles in the furrows awaiting planting. The land was stark as far as Katherine could see in the mist. At the edge of her vision was the forest, just beginning to bud. The thicket was shared between her father's land and the Baronet Drickham, Mr. Ephraim Porter. Her father's land was not expansive, but it was fertile. At least they would not starve, she thought, but they certainly would not prosper either.

Prosperity, in Katherine's estimation was only found in London, and she was many long miles from London, a full day's hard riding according to her elder brothers, Andrew and Harry Westlake, who made the trip often and even her younger brother Arthur managed to go into the city for school. The trip was two days for a lady in a coach, and that was when the roads were clear.

Katherine imagined the city glittering on the Thames. Once she had dreamed that she would see it and dance at London balls. She even hoped that she would be able to procure an Almack's voucher and meet the sophisticated London gentlemen who frequented that establishment, but that had not happened; would likely never happen. Such things were only fairy stories told to children. Women such as herself did not get vouchers to Almack's. They did not marry Princes or peers. They married within their station, and her station did not allow for such lofty goals, especially with four younger sisters for whom her father had to provide.

Katherine poked her needle into the fabric and realized with her inattention, she had put it in a knot. With a sigh, she pulled the needle loose from the thread and tried to pick the knot loose with the tip of the needle.

Patches annoyingly tried to help. With a sigh, Katherine put her on the floor and she headed to the kitchen in a huff, where no doubt the cook or one of the maids would provide her with a bowl of cream much to Father's complaint that if the cat was full of milk, she would not hunt vermin.

Katherine looked back at her needlepoint. She would be happy to sew her own clothes if only she could go to London. She was actually reasonably good at the fine work, although she generally liked reading novels better than sewing. Nonetheless, she would work her fingers bloody if only she had a chance to go to London, but she knew, in reality, there would be no Season for Katherine or her sisters. There would be no trip to London at all. The truth was, the city was a day's ride away, but it might has well have been on the moon. She was not going to get the Season she had hoped she would. Her family simply couldn't afford it. When she first dreamed of a Season, she had not understood the monies needed to finance such an operation. Now she did.

It took a load of gold to outfit a young woman to catch a husband in London, both to pay for the material and labor to make the gowns for each day—sometimes as many as five changes of clothes--and sometimes even to weave actual gold threads into the gowns. She knew that now, but Katherine didn't want a gown with gold or silver trim. She just wanted the pleasure of a Season. She wanted to laugh and dance the night away like some heroine in a storybook.

Katherine paused as she finally got the knot out of the silk thread in her hand and put the end in her mouth to moisten the frayed edges of the thread so it would fit through the eye of the needle. She re-threaded her needle and sat with it suspended above the delicate work.

She just wanted a moment of excitement in her intolerably boring life before she settled down to become an intolerably boring wife. Was that really too much to ask? Apparently so.

She had tried to convince her father that if she went to London, and married well, it would help her sister's chances for a good marriage, but he had not deferred to her wishes. Instead of paying for a London Season, her father had chosen Mr. Porter, a steady but uninspiring baronet here in the area of Halthaven. It was convenient that the baronet's land was adjacent to her father's. At least Father said it was convenient. Katherine found it *intolerably inconvenient*. It was very hard to avoid someone who lived in such close proximity.

Mr. Porter did have the dubious title of baronet and was reasonably well off, but he was just so uninspired. The problem wasn't his lack of a proper title, or hair or hygiene. The problem was that he thought the height of excitement was a new crop of wheat poking through the ground, and with planting time approaching, well he was positively ecstatic. Katherine could not fathom it. There was a longing in her soul that would not let her be still and docile. A part of her knew she would make a terrible wife for the country gentleman. He was so stolid and she itched for adventure. What did they possibly have in common?

Her sister, Lucretia, who was less than a year her junior, had purported that opposites attract, but Katherine felt no attraction at all for the gentleman. She would positively perish of boredom; living and dying just a few miles from where she was born.

Harry, her elder brother had no such constrictors on his behavior. Oh, how she wished she was born a man. Harry spent much of his time in London, doing as he pleased, but of course, she could not join him at the bachelor flat he shared with several other gentlemen. Such things were simply not done; at least they were not done by proper ladies she thought with a wry smile. There were a few who denied convention, like Mary Wollstonecraft, but Katherine would not do such a thing to her sisters. Her being so wild would positively ruin their chances for any match at all, and although she didn't like it, she was cognizant of propriety.

It started to rain again as Katherine put her needlework aside and traced her finger in the condensation on the cold window, making a heart and wishing she had some romantic knight to take her away from the dull life that she lived. She thought about Colonel Markey with whom she had danced at a party some months past, when he had journeyed to Halthaven with her brother Harry, but she had not seen him since. His interest was apparently fleeting.

KATHERINE REALLY COULD SEE NO WAY OUT OF THE situation. She would probably marry the dull and dreary Mr. Porter and raise his tedious children, possibly with the aid of a nanny, after all the man was a baronet. He would be able to afford *some* servants. But still, Katherine longed for something more. There was nothing more for a girl born into minor gentry who could not afford a Season, unless perhaps Colonel Markey returned. He was ten years her senior and not a prince, but at least he traveled with the army. She could see the world if she married such a man.

Presently, her younger sister Lucretia peeked her head into the room and Katherine turned. "Katherine, cook has breakfast on the table," she said. "It is going to get cold. What are you doing?"

"Just wool-gathering," Katherine said. "I shall be there directly, Lucy." She poked her needle into the fabric to save it.

"Dreaming of London again?" her sister asked coming into the room.

Katherine nodded and smiled, putting her musings behind her and hurrying to join her family at the table. "I just hate to marry and end all chance of seeing anything of the world."

"Ephraim Porter is a good man," her sister said, "And so handsome."

"I suppose so, in a brutish sort of way." Katherine was not convinced. Even Colonel Markey had a very masculine form and she preferred a more genteel sort of gentleman. Not a fop of course, but someone with a more refined bearing.

Her sister shook her head as they approached the table where their parents and her younger brother Artie were already seated. Her other sisters, Dora, and Georgie joined them presently. Josephine was absent.

"Good morning," Katherine greeted as her father stood and nodded to her as if she were a lady. She curtseyed to him as she was taught, but she would never need to use all of those etiquette lessons here in this backwater town.

Isadora, the youngest of the siblings giggled at Katherine curtseying to her father, but Georgianna poked her. "Soon enough we will all be curtseying," she said.

"Not me," Jo interjected as she joined them at table, and snatched up a hot bun. She looked a bit windblown and Katherine suspected that she had been riding with Artie this morning. Jo hated anything fancy or feminine, and would have come to the breakfast table in breeches if Mama would have allowed it. All of the sisters knew that Artie let her ride his gelding astride, but Mama was completely unaware of Jo's rather masculine proclivities. Her sisters kept her secrets. After all, wasn't that what sisters were for? Brothers, on the other hand, were alien creatures.

"Where's Harry?" Katherine asked. In a rare treat, her elder brothers were here in the country, visiting from London and although Andrew was quiet, Harry always brought adventure with him. He was closest with Katherine and Jo, although he doted on young Dora.

"He has gone shooting this morning with Andrew and some friends," Father said.

"And you did not wish to go with him?" Katherine asked since Father liked to spend time with his sons when Andy and Harry graced them with their presence.

Joshua Judd, the single footman they employed, helped both young women into their seats as Jenny, their maid of all work, set the dishes on the table. They didn't even have a footman to serve them, as Father said women were less expensive to hire due to the tax. They did have several maids, but for just once in her life, Katherine did not want to have to pinch pence. With four sisters and herself, that seemed unlikely.

"Your Father's gout is bothering him this morning," Mother put in.

"It's this blasted rain," Father complained.

"Your father and I were just discussing you, Katherine," her mother said.

"Me?" She questioned cautiously as she lay her napkin on her lap. What would her parents need to discuss? She thought the marriage to Mr. Porter was a foregone conclusion.

"As the eldest, you will of course, marry first," her mother said.

"I thought perhaps you were in need of a holiday, Kat," her father interrupted as he spooned an ungodly amount of sugar into his tea and topped it off with nearly half a cup of cream.

"A holiday?" Katherine gaped at her father who made the offer with unbelievable nonchalance. He winked at her and brushed a hand over his rather magnificent mustache. She wondered what he was planning. Katherine let her glance go to her mother, who was sipping her black tea with a pinched look on her face.

"Yes," Mr. Westlake shrugged. "I've been thinking some time away might suit your nerves, Kat."

"My… nerves?" Katherine stuttered. The last thing that she wanted was to be sent away so that she could return with a better acceptance of her requirement to *fulfill her duty*, as many ladies were oft expected to do. "My nerves are fine," she said flatly. "I will do my duty, Father." She lifted her chin slightly.

"See, Oliver" Mother interrupted, "I raised an obedient daughter."

But Father held up a hand stopping Mama's addition to the conversation. "I'm aware, Mildred." And then speaking directly to Katherine, he said, "I know you will, Kat, but this whole marriage business has put you out of sorts. I am aware that you hoped for a London Season, and I'm sorry I'm unable to give it to you. To any of you," he added to the other girls.

"I understand, Father. I'm not a child."

"Of course not," Father said, while Georgianna slouched with a sour look on her face.

"You spoil her," Mother muttered under her breath, and then addressing her younger sister. "And sit up properly, Georgianna." Mother switched seamlessly back to berating Katherine. "A husband will not be so amenable to your every wish, Katherine. He will want a biddable wife. You know that is so, Oliver."

"Is that what I got?" Father asked with a chuckle. He paused, eyebrow raised, and Mama sniffed. She apparently got a whiff of the girl at her right. She looked suddenly at Jo. "Josephine, do you smell like a horse?" she asked, with her nose wrinkled.

Now, it was Jo's turn to slouch in her chair and bury her face in her breakfast. She mumbled something about an early morning ride.

Meanwhile, Father turned back to Katherine.

"Are you saying that Katherine is not to marry Mr. Porter?" her sister, Lucy, interrupted.

Artie, who had finished the food on his plate, waved Mr. Judd over for more sausages. Mr. Judd complied and Artie tucked in. Katherine often wondered if her younger brother would have Harry's lean body or end up more portly like her eldest brother, Andrew. So far, he was thin as a rail.

"He is saying no such thing," Mama replied to Lucy.

"I can say my own words, woman," Father snipped banging a hand on the table, making the tea cups rattle. He took a breath and continued with dignity. "I received a letter from my sister Portia."

"Heaven forbids! She's not coming here, is she?" Mama asked, fluttering nervously.

"I like Aunt Portia," Jo put in valiantly, but she was summarily ignored, so she went back to eating her eggs.

"No," Father said. "Portia is in London and says she must stay there. I am not sure what keeps her there though. She does not say."

"Well, good," Mama said.

Father raised an eyebrow.

"London," Katherine breathed longingly.

"I'd like to go to London," Georgianna added.

"In any case, your Aunt Portia is at her old school," Father said ignoring both of their comments. London was an old argument. "There is no room for you there at Portia's; either of you. But Portia writes that your cousin Anne is with child. I'm sure Anne could use some help, and she wants for companionship, since her husband is still in London until Parliament closes for the summer. You haven't seen your friends in Northwickshire in an age, Kat. I thought you could use a change in scenery. It's not London, but—"

"Oh Father, thank you," Katherine said impulsively standing and throwing her arms around the man. She kissed him on his whiskered cheek. "I would love a change of scenery." More than that, her cousin Anne was always into some mischief. She was sure that marriage hadn't changed her that much, especially not marriage to Edmund who was often her partner in crime.

"Are we all going?" asked Georgianna with a bright smile. "How lovely."

"Absolutely not," said Mother.

"Perhaps," said Father.

Mama frowned.

CHAPTER 2

To Katherine, the thought of escape from Halthaven was like a sip of spirits that can warm from the inside out. Northwickshire. Her father was well aware that Katherine's favorite cousins were Anne, Eliza and Suzanna Albright. Well, she supposed Anne was an Ingram now, but the Albrights, had been for generations at Aldbrick Abbey. What she would give for an afternoon of Anne's free- spirited advice. Since the lady was soon due to give birth, Katherine could be a help to her, and she knew Anne would have some advice about marriage. She was sure of it. Katherine would trade anything to be there instead of here.

"We should start packing right away," Mama said, "if we are to be sure to arrive before Anne's baby. Portia did not say when she was due."

Katherine's excitement was somewhat dimmed with the thought of her mother accompanying her, but it was better than staying here.

"Mother, do we all have to go?" her sister, Lucy asked. "Couldn't Harry or Andrew take her?"

"May I be excused?" Georgianna interrupted putting her napkin off of her lap and standing. "I want to pack."

"No," Mama said stopping the speculation. "And you most certainly are not going. You have your lessons and a birthing is not the place for a young girl. You will stay here with Nan. You and Dora and Artie," Mother said addressing Georgianna.

"I'm only a year younger than Susanna," Georgianna complained putting her lip out in a pout. "I want to go."

"I don't know why you would want to go, Georgie," Lucy added with a most unladylike snort. "It will be a long miserable ride."

Katherine looked from her mother to her sister, hoping that her sister could convince her mother to stay home. Her sister, Lucretia, was such a homebody, and the most like their mother. Katherine knew Lucy would have much better luck convincing their mother if she stayed out the conversation entirely. Still, even if her mother went on the trip with her, Katherine could not complain. Her father's concern was ever for her happiness, and she had, after all, been begging these past weeks to go to London. Northwick was a step below, but still better than home, and Father had already decided. Mama would not cross him.

While her sisters Lucy and Georgie pouted and cajoled her mother, for different reasons, her father spoke to Katherine. "You could pass the family christening gown to our darling Anne, and when you return, perhaps you will have a grasp of it all."

"A grasp of what?" Katherine wondered aloud.

"Of life," he smiled. "You shall see your cousin Anne and the other young people about it—living life fully—with their own homes and children. Both Anne and her friend Emily are married now. Even that hoyden Henrietta has found a husband if rumors are to be believed. You'll see that those stories, those books that you read, they're fiction. They cannot represent reality. They are falsification and imagination. Such things… aren't real. When you come back, it might all make sense."

"Or not," Lucy muttered, and Katherine kicked her under the table.

"Nonetheless, it's a start; you see?" Father said.

Katherine nodded eagerly, happy to agree with her father's evaluation. Anything that got her out of the house.

"Of course, I will go," Katherine succumbed with an obligatory nod so that her father might suspect that she was taking this sabbatical with the severity he hoped. "After all, dear Anne is in need of help."

Georgianna crossed her arms and sulked.

"How long will you be gone, Mother?" Isadora asked somewhat plaintively.

"Not long at all dear heart," her mother said to her youngest daughter who implored her with wide dark eyes.

"You know, Lucy is right," Katherine added. "You could stay here with Dora, Mother. Father and Harry could take me."

But Mama was already shaking her head torn between going on the trip and trying to salvage Katherine's near engagement with Mr. Porter.

The truth was, Katherine had longed for an escape for weeks. Months even. Father had not been wrong in that. In fact, he was far too often observant of his eldest daughter's needs. Mama would be cross, but only because she had so neatly arranged for Katherine's anticipated betrothed to visit so that they might solidify their engagement. It was all but settled. Not yet public, but only because Katherine still could not bring herself to make her official acceptance.

Mama reminded her that Mr. Porter was a baronet and he would likely not wait around for many more months. Besides, it was doubtful that he was in want of a silly wife who put such stock in fiction.

I'm not silly. Katherine thought in the recesses of her own mind. A lady must have a hobby and interests. Why not books? Just because she had no care for music and only a passable singing voice didn't mean that she should relegate herself to the corners of entertainment. On the other hand, perhaps it was all the better if Mr. Porter did not wait for her.

. . .

In her mind, Mr. Ephraim Porter was entirely too good. He was a good man of good family and good position. He was born late to his father's second wife when the baronet, his father, was elderly. Mr. Porter was already involved in the running of the southern borough and he was well enough in personage for any moderate lady's needs. It was all too straightforward. Was that a proper complaint? She wondered. Most would want to understand exactly what was expected of them. Mr. Porter had laid that all out quite firmly. The sheer boredom of it terrified Katherine. Was she unnatural in that she wanted surprise in her life?

As Mama said, he was settled. Yes. As settled as an old man although he was only a few years older than Katherine. She could not garner any enthusiasm for the match. Katherine could not help but feel the lack of passion. He was too pleasant. Too easy to please. It had all been too simple, and too entirely uneventful.

One afternoon, following an agreeable dance at a public ball, Mr. Porter had asked to call upon her and then, from there, it had all progressed as it ought. Meaning, there had been nothing particularly outstanding about it. There were several meetings, some tea, and a carriage ride which included a clammy grasp of the hand that did nothing to stir her senses. She was only glad he had not tried to kiss her. There was nothing romantic, at least not from Katherine's perspective. Nothing risky, nothing exciting. Ephraim was good. He was such a *good* man, she had no complaints, even though she had doggedly searched for one. She longed for a complaint that she could lodge against the man. There was none. He didn't drink. He didn't gamble. He went to church on Sunday and everyone said what an upright man he was. The man was a virtual saint, but even her own father could see that there was something, some adventure of some sort, which had been lacking from Katherine's secluded life.

If not London, she thought, then perhaps she might get a taste of adventure in Northwickshire. She would help Anne and Anne would surely help her.

"It's settled then," Father said. "We will depart for North-wickshire by the end of the week."

Georgianna continued to pester her mother to go with them. Jo didn't care one way or the other, and Dora cried that she would miss Mama terribly. The house had become positively intolerable. Consequently, even though the weather continued to be cool, Katherine took every moment to escape the house.

Today, the clouds parted from the spring rain, and Katherine took the time to go to the abbey on a charitable trek. Lucy came with her.

"What about London?" Lucy wondered as the sisters walked the long trek back from Halthurst Abbey. "I thought you had your heart set on an adventure in the city? Have you given up that dream?"

"I have not, but I am trying to be realistic," Katherine said, shivering in the spring breeze. They had just deposited their donation of food for the month in two sizable baskets and the girls were relieved to be free of their burdens on the return journey. The road, which had washed away several years before, was still not accessible by anything but foot traffic. There had been talk of repair, but Katherine quite suspected that the Abbey enjoyed the protection of the impassable lane, especially since there was a private access through the Baron's wood that suited all their other needs.

"I asked Father," Katherine said in a breath. "He said that Northwick is a large enough town, but not so large as London that he has to send an army of servants to protect my dignity. I suppose, he meant my virtue."

Lucy chuckled as she rounded a puddle in the road. "We don't have an army of servants," she said. "I do wish I could stay here."

"I don't see why you can't. Perhaps Father will let you stay with Nan."

Lucy turned up her nose at that thought. "I'm not a child," she said.

"Well, what about Marietta? Perhaps you can stay with her. After all the Baroness Halthaven is above reproach. Why don't you ask?"

Lucy was gob smacked. "I couldn't do that," she said. "I wasn't invited to the Baron's home."

"Oh, pish posh. Ask Marietta. I'm sure she will be glad of the company and Lady Prudence will not mind. I'm sure she missed the clatter of her own sisters around her especially with the change in the weather. She will like the company after being so cloistered all winter."

Lucy became thoughtful, and Katherine fell into her own feelings, speaking at last about her coming adventure. "It is true that Northwick is not so large as London, but there is a shopping district and a square."

"Lud," Lucy scoffed. "Halthaven has a square."

"Barely," Katherine laughed. Though the village had, in truth, grown throughout the years, it was still miniscule compared to its northern neighbor. "Northwick is…" she paused in thought. "Well, I suppose it has the potential for adventure for which I have been longing." Quickly, before her sister could respond, she amended, "Don't tell Father that I said such a thing. He thinks I am going to right myself, but I can feel deep down that I am on the cusp of a new me. Someone new is blooming, someone more glamorous and more free than I ever could have been here."

Lucy looked at the denuded trees still stark with the late spring chill and snorted. "It is not yet the season for blooming," she said. "Anyway, what do you expect to find there? A prince?"

"Maybe," she ventured with a twinkle in her eye.

"You have a betrothed. Or near enough. Katherine… Mr. Porter is so good to you, to all of us, and he has a title."

"Baronet," Katherine said with distain.

Lucy put a hand on her waist. "And who do you think you are, putting on airs, Kat? Queen Charlotte? Or one of the princesses? Do you think to marry a duke? Do not be ridiculous."

"Of course not," Katherine said. "I only want a bit of adventure before I wed."

"And you would risk the wedding in hand, for some imagined lark? Are you mad? Mr. Porter is such a good catch." Lucy's words trailed off and Katherine looked at her younger sister who was biting her lip in consternation, her ears turning red beneath her bonnet. Likely that was from the wind. Katherine went back to wool gathering.

"He is handsome, don't you think?" Lucy asked after a while.

"Who?" Katherine asked.

"The baronet, of course," Lucy said exasperated. "And he has money and a title. Why would you risk all that?"

"I'm not risking that at all!" Katherine cried.

"Aren't you?" Lucy asked.

Katherine huffed. "Mr. Porter will be here when I return, if I choose. He hasn't moved a smidge since his birth," she retorted. "He isn't going to surprise me now. Anyway, I'm not going away for a scandalous romance or tryst, Lucy. I won't be ruined, only perhaps more worldly in a decent sort of way. I will have experienced the finer things. I will have taken a moment, dined with a Duke and Duchess, attended a real ball without more than half the guests all related to one another and only one eligible gentleman among a dozen ladies." She paused. "I am simply breathing before I take the leap." Katherine grasped her sister's hands in her own glove-clad ones, "Lucy, we aren't *actually* engaged. Father understands. Why can't you?"

"And if Mr. Porter finds someone else?"

Katherine sighed. "He won't."

"But if he does?"

"I wish him love."

Lucy was silent for a long moment. "I just think it is unfair to Mr. Porter, with all he has done for the family," she muttered. "That's all. He doesn't deserve the disgrace."

"There shall be no disgrace," Katherine objected. "All I shall do is visit our cousins. Revel with the beautiful Anne, and see her new baby once the child is born and perhaps return with some vigor to my life. They have such grand parties and acquaintances in Northwickshire. You know Anne's dearest friend, Emily, is a duchess now with a grand hall and a finer guest list than the baronet would see in a year's time! What fun they must all have."

They walked a short time in silence, navigating mud puddles, and then Katherine added, "For just a little while, I will be a part of that. Then, when I settle for this thing called marriage, it will be with ease. I will have lived, just a little bit. I will have my memories and I will be ready for marriage then. I will have lived my adventure and tasted the sweetness of life."

"What adventure are you hoping for?" Lucy kicked at a clump of nettles that had blown into the path and stared at the bits of green that poked through last year's leaves. "Oh

Kat, I fear rather than be sated, you shall become drunk on this new sweetness of life."

"Of course, I won't," Katherine laughed. "Perhaps I shall help to usher Anne's firstborn into this world, giving me a new perspective on the fragility of humanity. Certainly, more than what could happen here in Halthaven. I've been here my entire life and experienced… nothing."

"Nothing?" Lucy breathed. "What an outlook. Am I nothing, then? What about the rest of the family?"

"I don't mean to belittle what we have shared," Katherine amended. "Any of us."

"Don't," Lucy shook her head with a soft smile and stopped Katherine's apology with a slight raise of her hand. "I understand that there is something in you that has always longed for more, some wanderlust. You and Jo, most especially, and certainly Harry. Why that urge has overpassed me, I have no idea, but I am glad I am not tormented by such things. I only hope that you can go… and return… without causing damage to the life that you have constructed here."

"Father constructed," Katherine teased but she could see that her joke was in poor taste. "Or perhaps, Mama." Father had always been caring in his efforts. He had arranged the best marriage that he could, and Lucy was right, it was nothing to scoff at.

"Your books," Lucy cringed, "your histories and novellas are… not… real…"

Katherine waved away the words. Her sister sounded like Mama now.

"They aren't real," she admitted, "but they come from something. From some reality."

"They are imagined."

"No," Katherine argued. "Perhaps, in a way. I understand that they are fiction. I understand that it is not the average expectation of life. The nightly balls, mystery and exotic travels are likely embellished, but they come from something. There is some kernel of truth. Why I was just reading Miss Austen's new book. To find someone like Mr. Darcy." She gushed.

"I didn't like him," Lucy declared haughtily. "He has his nose so far in the air, he is like to drown when it rains."

Katherine chuckled at her sister. "So you finished the book then?" Katherine asked.

"No," Lucy admitted, and Katherine signed.

"It's just a story, Katherine. It's not real."

"I KNOW THAT," KATHERINE ADMITTED, "BUT IT IS exciting to consider that a man of such worth might love someone like me."

"You are fooling yourself," her sister said. "What do you expect to find, Katherine?"

What? I have no idea, she thought, and then on the tail of that thought came the next. When had her younger sister become so stodgy, she wondered? "Just… the idea that you never investigate… that you accept that everything exciting is merely a figment of the imagination is an impossibility…"

"I do not," Lucy contradicted. "I just find different things exciting I suppose."

Katherine could not believe that there was nothing more to life than that which she had already experienced. She could not settle to the course that had been made for her. At least, not until she had had a taste of something more. Her brother Harry would understand. Jo would understand, and perhaps even young Isadora, but Lucy and Georgie were firmly grounded in reality.

"Then, what lies ahead for you?" Lucy asked in a droll tone.

"I don't know." Katherine repeated. "I have yet to see. However, I feel that there is something more for all of us… if we expect it. If we go looking."

"We? Oh no," Lucy said through clenched teeth. "I don't have your sense of adventure. So, what if I don't go looking? Am I just bound to obscurity?"

"No, darling. Of course not." Katherine knew not what to say for Lucy had never longed to go anywhere, certainly not outside the bounds of their quaint village. There was even a time when Katherine wondered if Lucy would join the nearby convent. Such popery made her grimace. "Your story, I am certain, will find you, Lucy."

"Then why must you go? Won't your story find you here as well?"

Lucy's argument was well-rounded and Katherine had no better answer than, "I don't know. I only know I must go. I am suffocating here, and the thought of marrying without having first lived..." She shuddered. "I don't love Mr. Porter, and you are right. He is a good man. He deserves someone who can love him. If I go on this holiday, and find that this really is all that life has to offer, then..."

"Then you will marry Mr. Porter?" Lucy said.

"I suppose," Katherine said with a sigh. "As you say, he is a decent, upstanding man. He would not mistreat me, and I have no cause to complain except for my own sensibility. My spirit longs for more, Lucy. I wish I was going to London, but Northwickshire will have to do."

"Then go with my love," her sister planted a kiss to Katherine's cheek. She seemed to have given up on being cross. Katherine was sure that her irritability had merely stemmed from the impending boredom that must occur in her sister's absence. "I hope that you find your amusements and discover that they are not so different than what you have already known. Perspective makes life exciting, not a search for some unknown adventure."

"Perhaps you are right, sister dear," Katherine nodded, but she could not believe it. She was certain that there was some secret trove of pleasure, of happiness, that one had only to set out to possess, and it would be theirs. Halthaven, she was certain, had such joys in short supply. Every day was measured and predictable.

Things happened as they ought to with hardly a surprise to be found. Except for the one time the town was in a tizzy about that stranger who appeared suddenly and managed to get himself shot. It turned out he was a dangerous criminal or some sort of brigand, and really, in the end, everyone was relieved that the man was no more. The story only held sway for a few months anyway, at which point the news turned over to the Baron's engagement to Lady Prudence, another outsider who in time became one of the most beloved ladies of the neighborhood.

Lucy had always been close with the Baron's charge, Marietta, even though Lucy was several years her senior. Marietta, meanwhile adored her new Aunt Prudence, who brought adventure to the small town.

Katherine hugged her little sister, knowing that she would not be lonely with Marietta as her friend. Katherine thought it interesting that both the most dangerous and the most romantic moments in Halthaven history had occurred when outsiders had come to town. Halthaven itself, half a day's ride from the North Road, was singularly boring.

It seemed that Halthaven was immune to excitement. That had been the starting point of her theory. One could not count upon strangers and excitement coming to Halthaven. It just didn't happen often enough. If one merely journeyed to a new location then new things *must* be set into motion, she thought.

Northwickshire was no London, but it would do. Perhaps cousin Anne might even introduce her to some progressive women in the town. She had been reading Mary Wollstonecraft's books which purported the most amazing idea that it was only education which separated men from women and that women could be equal to men in every way if they were educated in the same way. She wondered what Miss Jane Austen might think of such an idea.

She knew, even her progressive father would roll his eyes and say that it was best she not concern herself with such ideas. A husband in his right mind would not want a progressive wife. She had never asked him outright, but Katherine suspected that Mr. Porter was firmly in his right mind. It was most unfortunate.

CHAPTER 3

The next day after discussing the particulars of their departure with her mother and father, Katherine started preparing for her journey to Northwickshire. She had two trunks opened by the foot of her bed; the leather recently rubbed with mink oil by the scullery maid, gave off an odd smell. The trunks were empty and Katherine's bed was heaped with evening gowns, ribbons, scarves and dresses. Unfortunately, not one dress in the enormous pile was this year's fashion. Several were several inches too short and a bit tight in the bust. She put them in a pile for Lucy.

"I am going to look like such a dowdy country miss," Katherine complained as she considered what to take with her. "No! Molly. Take those ones away. They are awful, and that too," she said of a puce jacket which had faded from the sun to a pale purplish brown that closely resembled the shade of a day-old bruise. It now matched absolutely nothing.

Molly complied and brought several more dresses from a third chest, lying them also on the bed for Katherine's perusal. Katherine threw up her hands in despair. She expressed her dissatisfaction with an unladylike snort.

"You will look lovely," Lucy said as she bounced on her sister's bed among the dresses, petticoats and ribbons. "I like the green one." She pulled it from beneath some others causing most of the pile to topple to the floor.

"You can have it," Katherine said.

Molly hurried to lift the pile of dresses back to the bed, and as she reached for them, several scarves fluttered to the floor. A broach rolled under the bed. Katherine reached to help her, just as her mother entered the room.

"What on earth are you about, Molly?" she asked aghast that the maid was crawling around on the floor. Luckily, she did not see her daughter in the same state.

"FORGIVE ME, MISTRESS," MOLLY HAD QUICKLY DROPPED into an apologetic curtsey, "But this was out of my hands."

Katherine hoped that she could stay hidden behind the bed, but in the next moment, Mama realized that Katherine was also on the floor and began berating her.

"Katherine, stand up at once! What on earth are you doing crawling around on the floor?" Before her mother had the chance to chastise her further, Katherine held up a broach which was now quite covered with dust from the neglected area beneath her bed. She could not fault the staff for that as she quite often waved them away when she was reading, and they wanted to clean. Perhaps they would clean while she was gone.

“Here it is,” Katherine said holding up the offending object. She coughed and blew away the dust from the object.

"What is it this time, Katherine?" Mrs. Westlake had inquired in her thin voice then added as Katherine tried to help Molly right the pile of clothes which was in danger of toppling again, "Let Molly be; she knows your needs thoroughly,"

"I was merely helping," Katherine protested.

"Then stop helping and let her get on with it."

“It’s no trouble,” said Molly, pushing the pile of clothes to the middle of the bed.

“Exactly,” her mother said. “Molly has the issue well in hand.”

“I mean, Miss Katherine is no trouble, ma’am,” Molly said trying to mitigate the issue.

Her mother bit her lip. “Katherine, when will you learn to be a lady? Crawling around on the floor. Indeed. I expect such things from Jo but you are older. You know better.”

“But Mama.”

“A woman is regal. Serene.” Mrs. Westlake had put her foot down as she clapped her hands as if dismissing all further discussions at once.

On any other day, Katherine would have taken issue with the interference, but at present, her mind was occupied with their impending journey to the Northwichshire and her joy could not be breached—just the thought of it filled her with excitement. Her mother could not take that away from her. Father had already sent out riders to inform Cousin Anne of their impending arrival. By the morrow, she would be out of this little town and on her way to Northwick. If only she were leaving her mother behind as well, the trip would be perfect. Nonetheless, she could not help smiling from ear to ear as her mother berated her for her lack of ladylike decorum.

By the time the sun rose high in the afternoon sky, Molly had her luggage packed and ready by the front door. The footman commented that the trunks were uncommonly heavy, but that was possibly because Katherine had packed more books than clothing. Mostly, that was because her gowns were all three years old or more, not because she couldn't bear to leave the books behind, although she knew Anne was not really a reader and she wanted to be sure she had something to entertain herself in the evenings.

For outings, she thought perhaps she could wear one or two of Anne's old dresses. At least they would be from last season and not three years past, she thought. Besides, Anne had to have bought something in London during her Season, and that was not so long past. Katherine judged everything from London would be better than the simple items made in Halthaven. Even the seamstress in Northwick was superior to old Mrs. Shaw, who had arthritic fingers and was half blind.

Meanwhile, Lucy had begged and cajoled until Mama agreed that she could stay and have a holiday with her friend Marietta. This loosed a cacophony of complaints from her other sisters to either go or stay. In the end, Josephine, who was only a year younger than Lucy, was to come because she was on the cusp of womanhood, although no one could tell that from her actions. More than likely, Mama was afraid to leave her behind unsupervised. And Georgianna was to come because her tantrums could not be borne. Mother staunched Dora's tears with the promise that they would be home soon, while insisting that each of the younger girls only bring one trunk each. They were not packing for a long stay. Katherine was quite certain that Georgianna had more than half filled Jo's trunk with her frills. Jo would be happy with only her riding clothes which had to be packed in the trunk only because mother would not let her wear them on the journey. Nor was she permitted to ride to Northwickshire. "You will ride in the carriage like a lady," said Mother.

Mrs. Mildred Westlake put her foot down as she clapped her hands as if dismissing all further discussions at once. "A woman is regal, Katherine. Serene."

On any other day, Katherine would have taken issue with the interference, but at present, her mind was occupied with their impending journey to Northwickshire, and her joy could not be breached—just the thought of the holiday filled her with excitement. Her mother could not take that away from her. Father had already sent out riders to inform Cousin Anne Ingram of their impending arrival. By the morrow, she would be out of this little town and on her way to Northwick. If only she were leaving her mother behind as well, the trip would be perfect.

The Westlakes packed the carriage carefully because it was decided that they must leave immediately at the break of dawn if they intended to reach Northwick by the nightfall. They all went to bed early, but Miss Katherine Westlake couldn't sleep for the excitement that filled her breast.

That night, she allowed her thoughts to drift towards the matter of marriage to Mr. Porter. It wouldn't be such a trial to marry the man if she would be able to live first, she told herself. This trip to Northwick heartened her. At least she would have some adventure. Perhaps she would fall in love. Perhaps she would find a totally different suitor in Northwickshire. Her mother had been incessant with her recommendations of Mr. Porter. If she heard one more time how proper the baronet was, she thought she would scream.

Katherine knew that even the heroines in the novels she read were not above social etiquette and familial obligations, but she hoped that in Northwick she would have some freedom. She plumped her pillow as she considered. She wished her mother was staying home from their holiday. Father and Harry could have escorted her, but now that Jo and Georgianna were going, the whole trip became a production.

Mama would make dictates to all of the girls which meant that she would treat Katherine like her younger sisters. Katherine despised the idea of her mother dictating her life down to its last detail. If it weren't for her father's favorable opinions, she would have hated life as a whole, but now she had something to look forward to in Northwick. She was sure that Anne would see her point of view, although she could probably not really help. Such was the lot of women.

Oh, there was nothing for it. She would have to endure. Actually, her sisters Josephine and Georgianna would be helpful for completely opposite reasons. Georgianna would engage Mama, and Jo, well, Jo would be Jo. She smiled at the thought. That could be to her advantage.

Katherine rolled over in her bed and looked out of the window. Molly had forgotten to close the draperies, so now, as she lay under her cotton sheets, she could see the full moon hanging in the darkness. She hoped tomorrow would be a clear day. She so hated traveling in the rain, but still, she was going on a holiday. It was not London, but it would have to do.

Katherine mulled over thoughts of the journey and an uncertain, but exciting, future danced in her dreams her as she drifted off to a peaceful slumber.

THE JOURNEY WAS MOSTLY UNEVENTFUL. KATHERINE HAD studiously ignored her parents' squabbling. Instead, she had spent the duration of the first day of her journey with her nose buried in the latest volume of *Lady Gabrielle's Gilded Gala*, a tale told in series in one of her magazines. In the story, the heroine is tasked with hosting London's finest event of the season. In its pages was everything that Katherine longed for… elegant ladies, captivating culture, and London's finest entertainments. Just when the rural Lady thinks all is lost, the wonderment of London comes out in full force to remind her that nothing falls short when members of the Ton show up. In the previous episode of the periodical, the young Lady had been taken under the wing of an eccentric Dowager Marchioness whose days were filled with the finery and merriment of London's most dashing aristocrats. Lady Gabrielle had visited the theater and museums. She had been gifted an extravagant gown sewn by the finest Parisian seamstresses, who were covert English loyalists, of course, and had even taken several turns about Hyde Park with gentlemen whose sole purpose was their companion's innocent enjoyment.

Katherine had sighed and clutched the book to her breast. What a life, she had mused. What a wonderful, fantastical life. She had never been to London, but she dreamed of it often. She had it fully pictured in her mind. The streets glittered with finery. She was sure the air was pure and fragrant. It never smelled like horse manure or muddied pathways the way the busier parts of Halthaven could. The residents were always at their best with nothing to want. Of course, a part of her whispered that it could not be entirely true. She had heard whispers of the poorer sections of the bustling city, of clandestine rumors, and individuals of nefarious intent. Some even said the dust of coal filled the air in the winter, but she didn't think it would be so terrible.

After all, the smoke of wood fires filled the air in the country. She rather enjoyed the smell of a wood fire. Anyway, ladies weren't to think on upsetting things, and therefore, she would not. She punctuated the notion with a nod to herself. That surely meant that if one were to visit such a place as London, then a Lady would be guarded from any unpleasantness as well. The seedier sides of London life would not exist in Katherine's dreams and, she was sure, would not dare to coincide with the realities of those of genteel breeding.

In Halthaven, the poor folk lived right in the center of it all. She'd never felt snobbish of them. They were to be expected. They were a workforce needed to man the expansive country estates, and gratitude was their due. Katherine had often given them charity, and they seemed kind enough in return, but London would be different. She was sure of it. London was a place where dreams came true, where everything, even the streets, glittered in gold.

They were well into their journey for five hours on the second day when Katherine noticed the winding pastures and greenery so reminiscent of Halthaven had given way to the lush forestry of Northwickshire. Some of the deciduous trees had not yet gained their summer leaves and stood stark against the sky, but the pines sheltered them along the road and broke the cooler wind that swept across the land as they traveled north. Here, the coming spring was only a promise.

Many of the trees were only starting to bud, but some spring flowers poked through the cold soil signaling the end of winter and giving the drab wet landscape a bit of color. Several forsythia bushes grew along the roadside. The hardy shrubs produced their spectacular yellow flowers, but many of the branches were still in bud, awaiting warmer weather.

The group had stopped to refresh themselves and the horses several times, and Katherine wasn't anxious to return to the carriage, but Father urged them to hurry so that they would reach Sandstowe Hill before nightfall.

If her father's hunch held any merit, they were nearly to Northwick. Anne had sent word that she was at Sandstowe Hill, her husband's relatives' home, rather than the new Ingram estate which Edmund's father, the Viscount of Kentleworth, had purchased for them. They would be staying at Sandstowe Hill for the visit. Anne had said in the letter that she had not been feeling well and didn't want to be alone with only the servants. Edward's Aunt Agnes had invited her for a visit, and truly Aunt Agnes was more like a second mother than an aunt to Anne. Katherine was a little surprised she had not gone to her own mother at Aldbrick Abbey, but she supposed Anne got on with her mother about as well as Katherine got on with hers.

"I'm surprised she didn't go to Aldbrick Abbey," her mother had noted as well, but Katherine just smiled a secret smile.

"Anne considers Edmund's Aunt Agnes like a second mother," Katherine said.

"A girl wants her mother nearby at such a time," Mama said, but Katherine made no comment.

ANNE HAD ASSURED THEM VIA LETTER THAT EDMUND would be home soon and that his Aunt Agatha and Uncle Cecil, the Earl and Countess of Stratton, were excited for their visit, but Katherine was a little disappointed. She had hoped to see Anne's new home, and she had hoped with Anne alone she would have more freedom. Now, she had yet another chaperone with Edmund's aunt as well as her own mother, which of course, was bad enough. Still, Katherine did understand that Anne had not wanted to be alone with only the servants while her husband was in London, and although Anne did not say why she was not at Aldbrick Abbey with her mother, Katherine only had to look at her own mother to guess. Anne had never had a close relationship with her mother, Katherine's Aunt Caroline and Father's sister. Katherine supposed Anne was too much like Father's other sister, Aunt Portia, although Anne would be loath to admit it.

They left the outskirts of the town behind, and if memory served her right, Katherine could swear she glimpsed the twin spires of the Sandstowe Hill ahead, up on the hill for which it was named. Within the hour, they should be at their destination.

"It's getting cold," Mother complained. "We should have stopped at Northwick and found refreshment."

"The weather has been nothing but pleasant," Mr. Westlake remarked as he folded the periodical he had been reading throughout the journey. This was an old argument. Katherine's father hated the heat, and her mother hated the cold. They kept the servants busy tending the fire, one way or the other.

"At this time of year, we are lucky it is not raining." Father raised his eyebrows at his wife. "I told you it would get cooler as we drove north. You should have worn your Spenser jacket.

“I have the carriage robes,” Mother protested as she paused in her crocheting. “I can barely feel the thread, and my toes are cold with this constant damp.”

Katherine and Jo, who had worn their sturdy boots rather than slippers, were quite comfortable, and Katherine was sure that Georgianna was too excited to complain, but Mama’s eyes flashed in anger.

Mr. Westlake countered ever so nonchalantly. “You insisted on wearing silk even when the Earl would have accepted you in a woolen dress just the same. You know Cecil is a fine fellow.”

Katherine breathed in sharply, knowing that her father had forfeited the peace of the carriage with just one insensitive remark.

“So, you blame me for the English fashion?” Mrs. Westlake turned sharply towards her husband, yarn and crocheting forgotten.

“No, darling,” Mr. Westlake let out, finally realizing his earlier blunder. “I just said that there was simply no need—"

“Do not *darling* me,” Mrs. Westlake warned. "You have already filled Kat's head with all sorts of ideas."

"I did no such thing!" Father protested, but it was in vain.

"My patience runs thin as it is—"

NEITHER HER FATHER NOR HER MOTHER WAS WILLING TO let the matter go, so the bickering continued for the better portion of a half hour. Both of her brothers, Harry and Andy, had ridden on ahead, and Katherine was ready to scream. “I wish I could have ridden with Andy and Harry,” Jo muttered, annoyed, while Georgianna waxed poetic about the countryside, although Katherine found the spring scenery still rather bleak.

"We have arrived!" the coachman announced, finally cutting off her mother’s diatribe.

CHAPTER 4

Immediately after, their carriage's door opened, Joshua Judd, their footman, stood at attention, waiting to help the ladies disembark. Behind him was another gentleman who had just come from the stable with her two brothers, Harry and Andrew. He was tall and exceedingly good looking. In fact, except for a small scar that parted his eyebrow, he would have been perfect, but perhaps that scar made him look more down to earth. Without it, Katherine might have been looking at some dark angel. She dropped her gaze, lest she be considered forward for staring so.

Mr. Westlake extended his hand to help Mrs. Westlake out of the carriage despite their earlier squabble. As the couple reconciled in hushed tones and exchanged hasty explanations, the gentleman behind Joshua stepped forward, filling Katherine's view and taking her hand to help her from the carriage. She immediately felt a fit of vapors coming on. She had never been touched by a man except for her father and her brothers. This was a strange experience that culminated in a rush of energy unlike any she had known. It went from her gloved fingertips to her heart as surely as Cupid's arrow.

Katherine's brother Harry, who had just come from the stable area where he had left his horse, did the introductions. "Mr. William Singer," he said, throwing propriety to the winds. "May I present my sisters, the Misses Westlake in order from oldest to youngest: "Katherine, Josephine, and Georgianna."

As her sisters curtseyed to the gentleman, Katherine feasted her eyes on the handsome man. He had a strong jawline and piercing, dark eyes that seemed to look directly into Katherine's soul. She wondered briefly how he had obtained the scar on his eyebrow. It was disconcertingly close to his eyes, which sent a jolt through Katherine at the thought. His lips were full and inviting. *Why on earth was she thinking of his lips?* She admonished herself and looked at her shoes, her stout boots worn for the road, and wrinkled gown. She realized she must look a fright. A hand went to her straggling hair that had crept from beneath her bonnet, but the gentleman appeared not to notice her dismay or her disarray. At least, he made no comment.

He moved with a confident grace and took her hand in his. Katherine caught a light scent of musk and sandalwood and a hint of spice, perhaps from his travels abroad. She felt her heart flutter as he spoke her name.

"Miss Westlake. A pleasure, I'm sure," the gentleman said in a deep melodious voice as he bowed over Katherine's hand before turning to Josephine and then Georgianna.

"Reserve your judgment, Sir," Father muttered as he collected Patches in her basket. Mother elbowed him in the ribs as he handed the cat in the basket to Katherine, and for once, Katherine could not be concerned with her cat. Her attention was all for the man in front of her, who seemed to take in every bit of her disarray.

Josephine's eyes were already on the stables, and Georgianna twittered like only a young miss could. Katherine watched as the handsome young man turned quickly away. Truthfully, she was anxious to get inside and refresh herself. The last few miles of the ride had been interminable, and she needed the retiring room. She didn't feel refreshed enough to meet anyone, most especially a handsome gentleman. She was so fagged to death; it was a wonder he did not think her one of the maids, or perhaps he did.

WILLIAM SMILED AT THE WESTLAKE SISTERS AS HE greeted them, but his attention was all for the eldest. The light of the setting sun silhouetted Katherine's features perfectly, causing a tinge of auburn highlights in her dark hair that would not be readily visible indoors, and her rumpled gown could not hide the ample curves of her body.

William couldn't help but stare, entranced by her raven-haired beauty. She cast her eyes downward in an effort to break away from his gaze and tucked wayward curls behind an ear while stealing shy glances at him from beneath incredibly long lashes—no doubt worried that he would judge her disheveled appearance harshly due to the journey.

He did not, but he did study her from head to foot. He could not help himself. Although she had donned sturdy boots for travel—evidence that there was much resoluteness within this delicate beauty—William still thought she looked divinely charming in her rumpled attire. It brought to mind things best left to his own private sensibilities.

He took her gloved hand in his naked one, feeling a wave of energy flow between them which made him rigid with the sensation as he bent over Katherine's hand and met her dark-eyed gaze. His senses were alive with what seemed like a magnetic pull towards her that could not be denied or extinguished. He caught an enchanting scent emanating from her—an outdoorsy musk blended with some flower long lost on the trip, but William found the co-mingled fragrance completely intoxicating.

In fact, he found everything about her intoxicating. He liked that she looked somewhat disheveled, as if she had just awakened from sleep. Her tousled hair and wrinkled gown did nothing to dampen her beauty or his attraction to her. He felt a strange flutter when he beheld her, feeling as if his soul was being reconnected with something he had taken for granted or perhaps never knew. Her presence was certainly unmatched by anything he had previously known, and as if she too felt the power of their attraction, her cheeks blushed a delicate pink.

Although he should admire the lady's modesty, he could not help but notice that her body was made for loving. William felt something stirring inside him just from the power of her presence. He wanted to take her in his arms and pour out all that he was feeling.

Instead, William forced himself to take a step back and attempt to normalize the situation, but it was no use; all rationality had left him at her touch. Still, protocol must be kept despite his undeniable anticipation for whatever this visit might bring forth in the time ahead.

As much as William hated having to turn away from Katherine and attend to Josephine and Georgianna, it was necessary in order for him to hold onto any semblance of composure in the present moment. His senses still raced with what had just happened between them, but he would not give in to his commonplace mind. These ladies were not some bit of muslin. They were Anne's cousins.

He took a deep breath and composed himself. If he were to be a gentleman, perhaps it would be best if he avoided Miss Katherine Westlake entirely.

THE EXCEEDINGLY HANDSOME MR. SINGER DROPPED HER hand like he couldn't bear to touch her. He turned away so abruptly the action bordered on rudeness, and Katherine had to reevaluate her estimation that he was attractive. Discourtesy was never appealing.

"Anne will be waiting," the gentleman said as he turned and led the way towards the front door without even a backwards glance. The ladies followed, Katherine's hand going self-consciously to her hair, which she tried once again to shove under her bonnet. She must look affright. She supposed the haughty Mr. Singer was not used to ladies being in such a state. Well, she did not care one whit what Mr. Singer thought of her.

Lady Anne slid to a halt in the front doorway just as the amused butler opened the hand-carved wooden door of the front entrance.

"Come all!" she cried. "Aunt Mildred. Cousins. I am so excited for your visit. It has been an age."

The manor came to life as Anne and her sister Suzanna rushed to greet them. Anne had returned to Sandstowe, her husband's uncle's manor, the previous day from a short trip to her parents' house, which was an easy ride even in her delicate condition.

"Do let me in!" Katherine's mother laughed as she placed a kiss on Anne's forehead. "Such a lovely gatekeeper, but we are chilled with this windy day, and we shall tell all once we can warm our fingers at the fire. Can you believe this weather? It is supposed to be spring."

"It is spring," groused Father. "Cool and rainy. You are lucky you are not drenched to the bone."

Mother turned to engage him.

"Where is this husband of yours?" Katherine asked Anne as she pulled off her outdoor bonnet. Her dark curls were mussed from the ride, and she wondered if she should have braided her hair like Jo and Georgie had done. They looked considerably neater than she did, she was sure.

"Edmund is still in London," Anne said, "but he promises to be here within a fortnight so long as he can sneak away from his father. Alexander has also promised to come home to Emily, so between them, I'm sure they can give the Viscount Kentleworth the slip. After all, they do have the excuse of wives who are enceinte."

"Emily too?" Jo asked.

Anne nodded.

Mother gave her a dark look and shooed her and Georgie from the conversation. Katherine laughed, and Jo refused to budge, but Suzanna, with childlike excitement, herded Georgianna off to the music room. "Caroline and Claire have their lessons," she confided and then whispered conspiratorially, "My mother is the same way," she said.

"As if we hadn't seen the stallions…" Jo added.

"Josephine!" Mother said with a sharp look, but neither Jo nor Suzanna was quelled. Suzanna left the room giggling, but Jo was determined to stay and visit with Anne, or perhaps it was to vex Mother. Katherine had no idea.

Katherine gave an exaggerated sigh and along with her mother made a quick trip to refresh herself.

"Do come in and sit by the fire," Anne said. "It is still a bit cool and damp with the rain, so I kept it lit, but the weather promises to clear soon, and we can go for a ride."

"In your condition?" Mother said with a cluck, but Anne ignored her caution.

After Georgianna was herded to the nursery with the younger children, and Mother, Katherine, and Josephine were seated, Anne looked a question. "Where is Uncle Oliver? I saw him but a moment ago."

"Uncle Cecil caught his attention from the carriage, and they have slipped away to plan a hunt, I am certain," Harry said with a chuckle. Katherine realized her favorite brother was leaning against the door lintel and watching the ladies with a practiced eye. The handsome young man she had just met, Mr. Singer, was beside him. His frank perusal of her caused her to blush.

"In this rain! I will not allow it." The stout Lady Stratton, who had been bubbling with excitement to greet her guests, now stepped into the hall with a countess' authority. She sent a footman to fetch her husband post haste.

"I promise to set them straight," Harry said, heading out with the footman. "Come along, William. Let's leave the ladies to their chatter." But Katherine knew her elder brother was more likely to cause mischief than prevent it. And what about Mr. Singer? she wondered. What mischief might he cause? Or would he be as stuffy and unyielding as he appeared?"

He hesitated a moment in the doorway and then, without a polite word to the ladies, followed Harry from the room.

Anne's Aunt Agnes was all countess as she instructed the butler to tell the gentlemen to come inside and have a brandy in the library while the ladies took their tea in the parlor, unless they would wish to rest a while first.

"Tea would be heavenly," Mother said, while Aunt Agnes continued to fret over the gentlemen out in the rain.

"Oh, Aunt Agnes, let them be." Anne laughed. Marriage and love had brought a lightness to her person that had not been there before. "You know how they are."

Katherine had wondered if her cousin's new life would distance her from the others but soon found that they all settled into their usual places as if not a day had passed.

"You shall not bring that animal to tea," her mother warned as Katherine opened Patches' basket. The cat leapt up upon her lap.

"She is just feeling insecure," Katherine said. "It is a strange place for her." Katherine petted the animal soothingly, and soon the cat was purring.

"I don't mind," said Anne as she reached out to pet the creature. "I have told Alex that I want one of the puppies when his bitch next whelps. The latest litter will be Lucky's get, likely his last. The dog is getting up in years. Alex has had him for an age. I told Emily we should keep two puppies for our children." She laid a protective hand on her stomach.

Katherine preferred cats to dogs, but she did not argue the point. There was something eternally calming about fur beneath one's fingers. She sometimes felt they understood their owners much better than people did.

Tea was poured and cakes were passed to each guest. The girls, Katherine, her sister Jo, and cousin Anne, as well as her mother and her Aunt Agnes gathered around the warm beverage and settled in to share the news. Eventually, Patches grew brave enough to jump down and explore, but she did not venture far. Although cats were supposed to be independent souls, Patches stayed

Katherine listened in silence as the tale of love was told. Anne described their courtship and wedding excursion with excited detail. Each meal, place of lodging, and activity was cataloged and repeated for the ladies' plea-sure. After a while, Katherine tucked her legs beneath her and patted her lap until her favorite feline leapt back into the nest she had created in the folds of her skirts. The calico spun in a circle before it tucked its legs beneath it and wrapped its tail with an affectionate brush around her wrist.

Katherine rubbed one thumb between the animal's ears until the telltale rumble began from deep within its chest. If she closed her eyes, she could imagine herself on a romantic journey with some handsome rogue that had swept her off her feet. Their blissful union would be punc-tuated by a visit to all of England's most fashionable haunts. She would be the talk of the Season, the most envied lady in of all London. Katherine daydreamed, fancying herself as happy and in love as her cousin Anne and her new husband, Edmund. That, of course, was not to be her fate with Mr. Porter. She hoped that Colonel Mackey might visit. Although he had visited Halthaven and her brother Andrew on occasion, the Colonel's family lived not far from Northwick, and he would likely be here if he was home from maneuvers.

"We will have to see it, Katherine. It sounds like something out of a dream." Her sister Jo's voice broke into her thoughts with the mention of her name, and Katherine stammered as she realized that she had not been following the conversation.

"See what?" she asked.

"The paintings…" Ann spoke slowly as if to feed her the answers she lacked. "You would be entranced by the masterful artwork, some of which, I would dare to say, your sister Lucinda's would best by far. Lucinda decided not to visit?" Anne added, just now noticing her absence. "I hope she is not unwell."

"No," Mother said. "You know, she is such a homebody."

Anne nodded. "I understand."

"Daydreaming?" Aunt Agnes murmured indulgently to Katherine.

"As always, our Katherine is lost in her fantasy world of true love and perpetual happiness," Mother added with a dry laugh, but there was censure in her voice.

Four pairs of female eyes turned to examine her as Katherine blushed with an admission.

"Katherine," her mother placed a tentative hand on her shoulder. "At some point, you shall have to start living in the present." The words were soft, but there was derision in them.

"Oh, but Mother, I was." She sighed. "It is only that Anne's story was so beautiful that I could not help but imagine it for myself, for each of my sisters." She glanced at Jo and clasped her hands together, but a small paw reached forward to pull her fingers back to their task. "How romantic to start your union with a view of the city. I can think of nothing finer." She resumed petting her cat.

Anne laughed and agreed. "I should have noticed that you would see nothing but the city."

Nonetheless, Anne was not offended that her cousin had drifted off into her imagination, since Katherine had often been caught about her own musings. In fact, Katherine's mother often cautioned her that no reality could ever live up to the world that she had crafted in her dreams. Although she was determined to settle for nothing less than the truest of love, she did not feel unrealistic in her expectations. Romance she desired, but all could be achieved with ease if she found the right pairing. She was sure of it.

KATHERINE SMILED AS SHE SIPPED FROM HER CUP. "I WANT nothing more than a home in London," she said. "I do not think that is too much for which to ask." She glared at her mother.

"There is more to a man than where he lives," Aunt Agnes purported, but she, of course, did not know about Mr. Porter.

Katherine nodded and made a concerted effort to listen to the rest of the conversation. Anne and Edmund seemed to be the perfect couple. The childhood friends had almost discovered their love too late to be saved, but now they seemed immensely happy and were expecting their first child. Katherine muffled a sigh as she thought about the romance that had unfolded for Anne over the past months, a romance that her own life was sorely lacking with the staid and gloomy baronet.

ANNE SMILED, PLEASED WITH THE EFFECT OF HER recounting. "But I believe that a gentleman need not be so grand. There are more important things."

"What is most important, in your opinion, Anne?" Mama asked. Katherine knew that Mother was angling to get Anne to settle on the worldly attributes of title and coin since Edmund would inherit his father's Viscountcy.

Anne paused, her eyes twinkling brightly as if she could barely contain an inner joy. "He must also have faith that I will make the right decisions even when he does not fully understand them."

Katherine chuckled at the thought. She knew, from Anne's descriptions, that Edmund was perfectly happy to leave most of the important household decisions to his wife, but Mr. Porter was not one of those. Unfortunately, most men would not feel so magnanimous.

"Shouldn't you leave those decisions up to the gentleman?" pressed Mother, interjecting just the attitude that Katherine deplored.

Jo scoffed, and Mother shot her an angry glance.

Aunt Agnes took up the conversation with some aplomb. Since everyone knew that Aunt Agnes and Uncle Cecil were still mad for each other, even after all these years, her comments had the weight of a tried and tested opinion, and all gave their attention.

"I HAVE FOUND TRUE GENTILITY IS WHEN A MAN WHO IS considerate and empathetic appreciates my efforts without asking too much of me or expecting me to be something I'm not." She paused, thinking. "A man with strength, honor, and passion that takes care of others as if they were his most prized possession. A husband who finds contentment in the simple moments of life, but then," she said carefully, "the wife, must answer in kind."

"But what about adventure?" asked Jo, voicing one of Katherine's many conflicting thoughts.

"Adventure is important," Anne agreed, but Mama shook her head, disagreeing vehemently.

Anne looked to her Aunt Agnes for advice, but Katherine was sure she had heard this same diatribe from her mother ad nauseum. She could repeat it verbatim and did not need to hear it yet again.

"A good husband should be fair flush in the pockets, ambitious, and driven," her mother said. "He should be looking for ways to make life better for his family. He should want to provide for them financially and ensure his family's safety while also maintaining their dignity."

"Oh, pooh," said Anne. "Dignity is overrated."

"Says the woman who chased off a suitor with a fireplace poker," added Aunt Agnes.

"Anne! No!" said Mother, wide-eyed.

"That is a story I want to hear," said Jo.

"Later," Anne promised with an eye towards her Aunt Mildred, who looked about to have apoplexy at the thought.

AUNT AGNES INTERJECTED WITH THE SENTIMENT THAT most suitable gentlemen of the Ton were prominently outgoing and forward thinking; kind yet firm—never too strict, but caring for those around them just as much as their own needs.

Katherine smiled at this storied image, but with her heart full of hope for herself and each of her sisters, she lost herself in daydream, picturing herself dancing beneath the stars at Almack's or strolling along Hyde Park with an ever-attentive gentleman by her side…

"What of you, Josephine?" Anne asked of Katherine's sister.

Jo shook her head and spoke on the subject of husbands. "Well, I would not marry a man who doesn't like to ride."

"I'm sure you will marry whomever your father chooses," Mother said, but Jo went right on speaking without a breath. "The finest husband would be someone active and handsome, and he must—" she fixed her mother with a glare. "He *must* be able to ride like no other."

"You've forgotten music and dancing," Anne quipped.

"I categorized that under active," Jo explained. "But yes, I shall take note."

The two of them giggled like school children, and Aunt Agnes chuckled too.

"Agnes, have some propriety," Mother corrected her contemporary, but Aunt Agnes shrugged.

"Oh, Mildred, there is no harm in wanting to ride well together," Aunt Agnes said. "That does make for a more enjoyable marriage, I'm sure."

At Mother's frown, Anne buried her face in her teacup, her color rising.

"I-I mean, you should fit," Aunt Agnes corrected, causing Anne to snort her tea.

At Anne's blush, Katherine's own color rose.

"Oh, dash it all," Aunt Agnes said. "We are talking about horses."

"Are we?" Mother asked with a bite in her tone.

"Whatever were *you* thinking of, dear Mildred?" Aunt Agnes asked archly. She blinked her eyes innocently, and Anne dissolved into laughter, sputtering with mirth.

"I don't see what is so funny," Jo groused.

But Aunt Agnes simply nodded her head in sage agreement. "My dear Anne, you've spoken wisely and given us all food for thought on husbands," she declared, which they all agreed upon before resuming their tea while Jo fumed about being left out of the joke.

“Do not concern yourself, little one,” Aunt Agnes interjected with a twinkle in her eye. "All these qualities are important, but don't forget the importance of having common interests or hobbies that both partners enjoy doing together or separately. More importantly is a common vision for the future. This will ensure many happy hours together with your husband.”

“Yes, because otherwise, he may spend those hours with a mistress,” Jo remarked.

“Jo!” Mother was scandalized. It was clear that Mother was at the end of her patience.

CHAPTER 5

Luckily, Anne rescued the situation from devolving into further debauchery. "Oh, I nearly forgot. It's a bit early, but I have gifts!" Ann announced with a flourish, interrupting Mother's censure of Jo.

"Oh, gifts? For Mothering Day?" Katherine asked.

"Yes," Anne said as she reached into her wristlet and pulled forth several small pieces of folded fabric. "We don't have many flowers blooming yet here, but I could not forget my dear aunts." She peeked into each small package before passing the treasures to their recipients.

Each elder lady was presented with a small brooch wrought from the finest gold.

"It is so delicate!" Katherine's mother exclaimed. "I am afraid to break such a beautiful piece."

"Oh, do not worry, Aunt Mildred," Anne said. She pressed her Aunt Agnes and Aunt Mildred to test the brooches by adhering them to the gowns. Despite their fragile appearance, the jewelry was made with skill and held firm as Anne clipped one of the items to her Aunt Agnes' dress.

"It is lovely, Anne," said Agnes, examining the item and then hugging her niece. "You are such a sweet and thoughtful girl to remember your childless aunt on Mothering Day."

"You are as much a maternal influence as my own mother," Anne said with sincerity.

Aunt Agnes had been given a dainty gilded rosette, and she was busy examining the workmanship.

"I gave my own mother a pearl surrounded by three small stones to represent each of her daughters. Edmund found it at a jeweler in London," Anne said. "A German fellow who, according to Edmund, said that each month is represented by a particular stone."

"How interesting," said Jo.

"I do hope we will see your mother this visit," Mrs. Westlake said. "Oliver was looking forward to seeing his favorite sister."

"She wanted to be here to greet you, but she is down with a megrim," Anne said. "Eliza and Father had words, and Mother took to her bed all this past week. Well, it is a long story, best left alone." Anne shrugged and gave the small silver apple to her Aunt Mildred, effectively changing the subject.

"Did these both come from London?" Katherine asked as she examined her mother's gift. "Isn't it exquisite, Mother?"

Mrs. Westlake nodded.

The cat in Katherine' s arms pressed forward to see if the tiny apple was indeed edible.

"Look at that, Patches," Katherine held the brooch out for the calico to press her nose against. The cat deemed the item unworthy of its interest and began to lick her paw instead.

"Anne, you shouldn't have," Mother exclaimed as Katherine helped her mother to fasten the brooch.

Nonetheless, the ladies thanked Anne heartedly and exclaimed over the beauty and perfection of her purchases.

"Soon, you shall be celebrating your own Mothering Day," Mother said to Anne.

Anne blushed lightly since the condition of her pregnancy was barely showing and rarely spoken of in polite company. Perhaps, Katherine thought, it was because being with child was proof that the woman was no longer a maiden, a topic that was taboo in circles of mixed company, but here, with only ladies present, it was less circumspect.

"Do you think Edmund will bring you something from London?" Jo asked.

Anne shrugged. "Most likely, but knowing Edmund, he will have completely forgotten my condition and will comment I must be eating too many sweetmeats when he sees me." She laid a hand on her slightly protruding tummy, "All the while feeding me chocolates and sweetmeats!"

The elder ladies laughed.

"So it is with gentlemen," Aunt Agnes said. "Boys at heart."

"Oh, no," Katherine teased. "Jo and I were just speaking on the road here about Edmund in just that manner. We are sure, Anne, that you have done wrong by us."

"How so?" Anne asked.

"How might any of us find a gent to marry more beloved than Edmund? He is so sweet. You have set the standard above our reach."

"Is that so?" Anne laughed. "Only a few months ago, I do recall sitting with my mother and sisters while they complained about his unsettled ways. Edmund's reputation has been quite improved since our union. I assure you that any gentleman of upstanding virtue will do well to join our family."

"Yes," Katherine agreed, "but none shall have the many years of history and friendship that you have enjoyed with the Ingrams."

"Then you shall begin the years anew," Mother assured Katherine with a nod to Jo. "I am confident that you shall each find the joy with which Anne has been blessed. That is my greatest wish."

Katherine had some doubt that her happiness ever entered her mother's mind when she settled on Mr. Porter for her husband, but she said nothing to the contrary.

"It is the wish of every mother," said Aunt Agnes. "And every aunt," she added with a wink. The ladies shared their joy as they teased Jo about the necessity of finding a beau who would be able to keep up with her on horseback.

"I understand entirely," Anne assured her.

"Oh dear!" Jo pressed her hands to her cheeks. "I had not thought yet about such things."

"Only think how wonderful it will be," Mother said.

"Wonderful? Frightening!" she quipped.

"Jo thinks the only sweetheart she needs is her gelding," Katherine confided to Anne.

"Well, he is quite the sweet goer," Jo added, and they all laughed.

"I understand entirely," Anne commiserated with Jo.

Mrs. Westlake shared her wisdom on the matter. Though her advice was old and well known to her daughters, it was the first time that any but Anne had listened with fervent interest.

All of a sudden, the prospect of their impending marriages felt real to Katherine. She was reminded that her father had sent her here on holiday to prepare herself for that task.

Mother, meanwhile, asked Agnes about upcoming events, the eligible gentlemen of the neighborhood, and the best methods for determining the character of such prospects. Aunt Agnes gave her questions considerable thought, while the girls listened, but Katherine knew this conversation was not for her. Her fate was set with Mr. Porter.

"Oh, Patches," Katherine whispered to the sleeping animal. "How shall I ever find a man to love me as much as you?"

"Katherine!" Mrs. Westlake snapped. "You tease, but if you put half the effort into securing a husband as you do dreaming, you would have a real man staring back at you rather than that creature."

"Do you mean Mr. Porter, Mother?" Katherine smiled in the sweet way that always softened her mother's heart. The effort was in vain.

"Father made it very clear that we must be wed in order of age," Jo said, explaining in confidence to Aunt Agnes. Truthfully, Katherine thought her mother had browbeaten Father into that dictate. "Georgianna and I have a pact," Jo continued. "She can have my gentleman, and I will wait for hers, or perhaps Dora's."

Her mother groaned. "Josephine, does that mean you are going to be as troublesome as your sister Katherine?"

"Probably moreso," she quipped.

"Do you think that you are incapable of securing your match so that you are prepared once your sister weds? Or have you so little faith in Lucinda that you shall insult her beauty with your procrastination? And what of Dora? Must she wait forever for you and Katherine to get your heads out of the clouds?"

"My head is not in the clouds, Mama. Just Katherine's," said Jo.

"No. Yours is in the barn," Katherine baited her sister, but when she saw that her mother was genuinely upset, she calmed her. "Please do not fret, Mama," Katherine's teasing expression relaxed as she realized that her mother's anger was the result of fear for her children. "I am sorry. I assure you that I consider the matter of my marriage with great weight. I know you do not think so. I only tease because I must keep a joyful heart. If I think too long on Mr. Porter, I shall despair."

"Katherine—" her mother began, but Katherine interrupted. She would have her say.

"I know that Mr. Porter is your and Father's choice for me, but you also know I have yet to meet any that catch my interest. I assure you that I shall not allow the opportunity to pass if love does present itself."

"Love?" said her mother.

"What of Colonel Markey?" Anne pressed the back of her hand to her forehead and pretended to swoon. "He has always taken a preference to your company, Katherine. Tell me, are you all smelling of April and May? Is that why you have come to visit in Colonel Markey's neighborhood?"

Katherine laughed and wiggled her nose against the cool snout of the cat. “Me? In love, Anne? No, but Colonel Markey has all the makings of a suitable husband,” she admitted, “though he is away too often to be ranked as anything but a passing acquaintance at present.”

“That pleases me to hear.” Mrs. Westlake grasped her daughter’s hand and gave a soft squeeze. “All of my daughters are so beautiful; I cannot imagine that you shall not each have a fortunate match, but I cannot wish an army man for you, Katherine. He will be away so much of the time.”

“Would that Mr. Porter was away so much of the time,” Katherine muttered.

“I am sure you do not mean that,” Mother said.

“I am sure I do,” Katherine replied.

Unable to sway her daughter, Mrs. Westlake turned to her niece. “Tell me about your new house,” she urged Anne. “I hear it is very fine. The Viscount Kentleworth gifted it to you on the day of your wedding.”

“Yes,” Anne began to explain, and Mrs. Westlake questioned every statement. She requested a detailed inventory from the grounds to the table settings of their newly acquired property and waxed on about how generous Edmund’s father, the Viscount, was to gift it to them. She lost no opportunity to mention the title.

If it were not unutterably rude, Katherine would have snuck her worn novel from her bag and put it under the low table that sat near the arm of the settee. As it was, she had to make do with her own imagination. The others had settled in with their needlepoint, Susanna and the younger girls joined them, and the visit settled into a normal routine, but Katherine could not be bothered to find her own sewing, which was still packed in her trunk as far as she knew.

As the conversation happened around her, Katherine allowed her mind to wander. A masked gentleman at a ball in the opening of the London season was particularly aloof but interesting. She teasingly removed his mask and revealed the scowling face of Anne's cousin, Mr. Singer. She gasped with the thought and immediately conjured another: a charming, well-inlaid fellow who professed that he had loved her upon first sight of her unparalleled beauty. In addition, there was an intellectual with fine ink-stained fingers, who wooed her through pages of romantic letters and had a secret fortune that was sure to impress her mother, and of course, there appeared Colonel Mackey, who was so smart in his uniform, truly a swell of the first stare. Father pulled him aside for a serious conversation.

Katherine imagined all sorts of fantastical meetings. She knew that the moment when she met her true love would be a memory that she could look back on with pure pleasure for the rest of her life, a story that she could share with her children and grandchildren about the proper way to meet a husband and how to cultivate a life-long love.

Why did that thought bring to mind Mr. Singer's smoldering gaze? She shivered with the thought. It should not be so. He was abrupt to near rudeness. He had stared at her appearance with obvious distain. She would think no more of the popinjay.

Her imaginings entertained her, brought joy to her heart, and mitigated the thought of marrying Mr. Porter. There was nothing that a lady looked forward to so much as the chance to meet her one great love, and Katherine imagined this meeting with true alacrity.

Patches stood and rubbed her head against Katherine's chin. She murmured sweet nothings into her fur until the cat settled down once more. If she could be this content in the future, then it was guaranteed to be a happy one. At present, Mr. Porter was far away, and she was happy to keep it so.

CHAPTER 6

A dinner was to be held the next week at Innbury Manor, the newly acquired home of the Ingrams. This party would be the last before Anne's confinement. Katherine learned that Edmund had come north along with his friend, Alexander, the Duke of Bramblewood, and the most prominent couples in three adjoining counties had been invited to make a boisterous party of sixty-two.

"Surely, you are not going to entertain," Katherine's mother said to Anne. "Not with your being in a family way?"

"No one but close family knows about the new arrival yet," Anne said, laying a hand on her slightly protruding belly. "We will keep it our secret." She laid a finger against her lips, and Mama could do nothing but frown. "I will ask you one favor, Aunt Mildred. Might I borrow a pair of your silk slippers? My feet seemed to have outpaced my middle in the growing," she said with despair. "I cannot get my foot into any of my slippers!"

"Oh, that is the way of it," Katherine's mother said, and the two of them began discussing the state of being enceinte and the like. Katherine let her mind wander to more pleasant thoughts.

The following week, the ballroom was set with tables to accommodate the crowd. Katherine gasped at the splendor of her cousin's new home and the ease with which the lady had arranged the event. Anne confessed that the Duchess of Bramblewood, her dear friend, had helped. "You will meet Emily tonight," she promised Katherine.

"A duchess!" said Katherine.

"Oh, do not be intimidated," Anne urged. "Emily was my dearest friend long before she was a duchess. She is Edmund's sister and like a sister to me. We grew up together and have too many secrets to be formal."

Katherine nodded and tried to quell her nervousness.

A quartet sat in the corner, playing a soothing melody that drifted in and out of the dozens of conversations that were being held between new and old friends. Later, the tables would be cleared to allow for dancing and cards to provide the entertainment for the evening.

Outside, it was cloudy and threatening rain again, but Katherine did not care about the inclement weather. So cozy was the atmosphere that she felt at once that the group was neither too large nor too small. It was a perfect introduction to the society that would have been in London if family matters had not drawn them home. This was likely as close as she would get to London.

Katherine settled into her chair at dinner and was pleased to see many faces that she recognized although she had not been introduced to all. The Duke and Duchess of Bramblewood sat not four seats away, and she even spied Colonel Markey at the far end of the room. He was so smart in his uniform. Anne's mother and father, the Lord and Lady Aldbrick, had arrived, but Eliza was conspicuously absent.

The tables had been placed end to end in two rows that stretched the length of the hall. The voices were cheerful, and there was a raucous laughter coming from a group of young ladies who had found some gossip to entertain themselves. Lady Aldbrick was scolding the group for their lack of propriety, but none of them looked shamefaced, and Katherine realized her brother Harry was right in the thick of it, grinning from ear to ear.

Katherine's brother Harry and Edmund, Anne's husband, left the group and strode across the room to his wife, taking her arm to escort her to dinner. Harry looked about for a partner, but Katherine snagged his arm, and he escorted her to the dinner table.

The Countess of Stratton, Anne's Aunt Agnes, sat at Katherine's right, beyond Edmund, and her brother Harry sat on the other side of her, but he was engaged in making one of the previous young ladies laugh.

Katherine turned to interest the Countess Stratton in conversation. Her pinched curls made her appear severe at first, but her wide smile and wrinkled eyes drew Katherine in at once.

"What a lovely gathering. I am so proud of my niece," the woman commented as she raised a finger to call the footman for more wine. "Some for you, dear? A party such as this calls for more than that cup of tea you have been sipping. You know, Anne has a wonderful selection of wine. It is the perfect addition to dinner."

Katherine blushed and raised her eyes to her mother, who sat across the table. One nod and a small smile granted approval before Mrs. Westlake returned her attention to an old friend with whom she had been chatting.

"Yes, please," Katherine replied to the countess, who called over a footman with glasses of wine on a silver server to give to the diners. Katherine took a glass and sipped delicately.

"You know," the countess said. "I was telling my husband what a pleasure your visit has been for me."

"Where is the earl?" Katherine asked.

"Oh, he and William are about," she said dismissively. "I'm sure they will be in to dinner shortly. Neither are sociable souls, but tell me, how have we not seen more of you in our fair town? You are a lovely young lady."

Katherine flushed, murmured her thanks, and focused her attention on the glass in her hand. Although the sisters often received compliments on their features, their mother had done her best to ensure that they were not vain about the matter.

"Ah, do not be shy, child." The woman laughed. "I am old and unencumbered by the rules of propriety. I do as I please, you know."

"That is a great boon for a woman," Katherine said, thinking that her own moments of freedom were limited.

"That depends a great deal upon the man you marry," the countess said.

"Indeed." Katherine took a rather large fortifying sip of her wine as dinner was served. "Mother has plans for me," she said glumly, "but do tell about your estate. I am most interested in the Northwickshire countryside and the specific town of Northwick."

"Well," the countess said, settling in for a story. "Although much of the area is farmland, there are extensive lands a bit further north which provide most of the wool and leather for local tradesmen. Winebury. Do you know of it?"

"No." Katherine shook her head. "Is that part of your husband's entail?"

"It is not," the countess said. "And the house has been closed for lack of a mistress these past months. Oh, I suppose it is going on two years now. She passed during the influenza outbreak during the winter past."

"I am sorry," Katherine said. "I expect she was a relation of yours."

"Yes, by marriage, but well-loved," the countess replied, her face momentarily thoughtful.

Katherine nodded as she considered the sad tale. She tried to mask her features before the lady noticed, but the soft sigh and hand that covered her own told her that she had failed in her attempt.

"It must be so sad to lose family. You have my condolences," Katherine added.

"Thank you." The Lady patted her hand. "Katherine was her name," the countess said, "but she was known here as Kate. She was beloved, but many lost loved ones to the flu, and there is naught that we can do to bring them back. We have recovered from the misfortune, now, as much as one can."

"In any case, I intend to enjoy this party." She waved a finger under Katherine's nose. "I'll not have your long face or pity dampen either of our moods." She winked, and at once Katherine felt buoyed by the lady's optimism. Despite her troubles, she was a positive force that refused to be bested.

"Then I shall ensure that you do just that." Katherine tapped her glass against the other lady's, and a soft chime sealed their friendship.

"Excellent!" The countess smiled as she finished her wine and waved the footman over for a refill. "My nephew would like to say that I am in need of a chaperone." She winked as she raised her glass to signal for more wine.

"Are you?" Katherine giggled.

"Without a doubt!" The elder winked again, but in addition to the wine, the footman supplied them both with venison in a mushroom gravy and boiled potatoes with fresh parsley that was grown in the herb garden and dried for winter use.

The meal passed in much the same way. The witty repertoire of the Lady Stratton kept Katherine laughing until her sides ached and she was forced to wave away several glasses of wine before she was served a lovely chocolate confection.

Next, the party moved to the parlor for tea and conversation while the servants cleared the dining tables and put out small circular settings that would serve for cards if any wanted a reprieve from dancing.

Katherine tucked her new friend's hand into the crook of her elbow and led the way.

"My, what a fine gentleman you make," the countess teased.

"Ah, My Lady," Katherine played along, "I am honored to be of service. My only wish is that I might draw your attention for the duration of the evening. Might I have permission to remain at your side?"

"Oh heavens, no!" the lady laughed. Her face turned serious, and she caught Katherine's eye with a piercing gaze of dark eyes beneath her greying hair. "You shall do no such thing."

Katherine revealed a pout. "Whyever not?" she argued. "I have not had such fun in ages. Is it so wrong to pass my evening with a new friend?"

"When your new friend is an ancient lady filled with dust and creaking bones and you a young miss of great beauty, I would argue against it."

"Nonsense." Katherinesaid. "I should have no greater pleasure."

The countess looked heavenward and expelled a dramatic sigh.

"Get you to the dance floor, child, before all the handsome gents are taken," she said.

Katherine turned on her heel and faced the woman with her arms crossed beneath her chest.

"Do you not enjoy my company?" she pressed. Her expression dared the lady to slight her.

"Oh my!" The woman roared with laughter. "You are a spirited thing. I am quite taken with you."

Katherine smiled. She had not once heard herself called spirited; stubborn or contrary were the adjectives most used by her mother.

"I have no use for dancing." Katherine offered her arm once again and continued to lead her friend down the hall. "My husband is already chosen, so I do not see the point in causing myself grief. Josephine shall have fair pick of the eligible bachelors. I shall do nothing to distract from her attentions." She whispered in a conspiratorial way that hinted that this had been her plan all along. Though it had not, she relished the excuse to remain out of the spotlight.

"Then you will not dance at all?" the lady asked.

"Perhaps…" Katherine swayed her steps and hummed one of her favorite songs. "After Jo makes her choice. She is very particular and has no patience with fops. It shan't take long for her to sort through the lot."

"What a fine sister you are." The lady watched Katherine from the corner of her eye as if taking measure of her character.

"Do not give me so much credit." Katherine smiled. "I love my sister dearly, but I will not deny that you have been a fortunate distraction this eve. Else, I might have been forced to submit to my mother's will and make practice of my overt flirtations."

The ladies found a cozy corner in which to settle. They were soon joined by Jo and Susanna, who Lady Stratton declared just as wonderful as their sisters.

"You must call me Aunt Agnes," she insisted. "I know you are from the opposite side of the family, but I have been Aunt Agnes to all of the children in the area."

"Children," Susanna said in mock outrage.

"Oh, you are all children to one as old as me. I love having you all come around since I have not ventured more than a few miles from my home for many years, and I must say, I do not regret it."

They assured her that they were glad to make her acquaintance and promised to visit for a picnic in the summer when the fields were in bloom.

"Miss Katherine," a male voice behind her spoke with a hesitant tone. She turned to see Colonel Markey looking down upon her with a shy smile. His proffered hand hung between them, and she glanced down at it with a sudden tension in her throat.

She had not seen the Colonel in months. She had waited for this moment with great anticipation, and now that it had arrived, she could not deny that she was nervous.

He requested her hand for the opening dance. Though the event was not a ball, dancing was to be one of the many activities available to the guests. Katherine had not intended to begin so soon.

She could hear her sister and cousins murmuring their encouragement at her side. They too had discussed the gentleman's return at length. The countess was watching her with a knowing grin, as if she were surprised to see such overt attention that Katherine had not hinted at during their previous conversations. Not, Katherine reminded herself, that she had any reason other than hope to lay claim to the Colonel's attentions. He was handsome as a man ten years her senior could be and had only ever been kind to her, but what placed him high in her esteem was that he had seen the world, and he had told her brother Andrew that he liked traveling. If she married a man who enjoyed travel, she would not necessarily be relegated to stay in one place, although a husband did have the right to leave his wife behind in the country. Colonel Mackey did seem to like her company though, and she hoped that if she married the man, she might be allowed to travel with him.

She placed her hand upon his palm and allowed him to lead her toward the ballroom. Several other couples were ahead of them, and the rest of the party would soon follow behind to sit at the card tables that lined the room.

She noticed that the Earl of Stratton had finally found his way to his wife, and they were conversing with their heads close together, giggling like newlyweds.

"Are you enjoying your holiday?" the colonel asked Katherine. Now that they were away from the watchful eyes of Aunt Agnes and her sisters, his confidence increased.

"Yes," she replied. She informed him of the excitement of the parties and ball that filled their social schedule now that the cold and rain were diminishing.

"Well, you cannot prove it by today," he said with a grimace.

She smiled up at him and asked about his social schedule. She hoped to see him again at another party but was disappointed to see his face scrunch up with distaste.

"It has not had a pleasant past few months," he revealed. "I would much rather have been here," he murmured. "The rain and cold here would have been mitigated by happy company. Rain and cold on the continent with… well, that is a dreary subject, and we will talk no more of it. Suffice to say, there is no joy to be had in it. However," he altered his tone with a sudden cheerfulness, as if he had realized that perhaps the depressing conversation was not the best subject for a party, "I did procure two very special dolls for my nieces while I was away. Never have I seen two faces so alight with joy."

"How thoughtful of you!" Katherine exclaimed. Upon their last meeting, she had learned that the colonel had a sister with two young daughters. His commitment to his family was one of the aspects that she liked about him. She too had a great love for her family. She was close with her sisters and wished whomever she might marry would have the pleasure of that same bond and understand her own.

"It was nothing." He waved away her praise with a modest grin.

"Yes, well…" He turned to face her as they settled at the end of the short line of couples that would begin the dance. "Perhaps next year I shall have more happiness."

She turned her head to disguise the blush at his comment. Perhaps he had meant the statement as a general wish. Yet the affection in his eyes told her that perhaps he had meant to imply that he might one day soon have a family of his own for which to return. She could not say that she was disappointed that he meant to reveal this desire to Katherine.

Perhaps Colonel Markey intended to make his intentions known sooner than she had anticipated. That would be all to the good. Although he was away often with his regiment, he also traveled to London and the continent. There may be a chance for adventure at his side. She gave him a dazzling smile.

The music began, and Katherine allowed herself to be swept away by the dance. The dance was too active to allow for much more conversation, and that was a shame. She wished to press the colonel for more details about his dream of a future. Perhaps that future would one day be hers, if she could shake the presence of Mr. Porter, and she was curious to know what a future with the colonel might entail.

By the time the song was over, the entire party had gathered in the ballroom. Katherine watched Anne and her new husband take each other into their arms, and each looked upon their lover's face with such passion that Katherine had to turn away from the private moment. Their love was enough to fill the entire room with happiness. She wondered if the mildly pleasant feeling that raced through her veins when she looked at the colonel would grow to be just as vibrant and steadfast. The more time that she spent with him, the more she was beginning to think it possible, but would he offer for her before she had to accept Mr. Porter?

"You dance beautifully." A wavering voice drew her attention to a table that she had been in the process of walking past. She looked down to see Lady Stratton seated alone.

Katherine apologized for having overlooked the woman, who assured her that she had intended to blend in behind a set of large fronds in order to sneak in a nap.

"I am quite awake at the moment, however." The Lady patted the seat beside her and indicated that Katherine should sit down. "A short rest is more than enough to rejuvenate this old piece of horseflesh."

Katherine smiled and joined her friend. "I saw you dancing with your husband," she noted. "I must say, you light up the room."

The lady beamed.

"And who was that gentleman that you paired with so well?" Lady Stratton asked.

Katherine felt a rush of heat stain her cheeks, and there was no mistake that the countess had taken note of her response.

"That is Colonel Markey," she replied with as steady a voice as possible.

"You fancy the gentleman?"

Katherine shrugged. "Maybe one day," she admitted. "I have had little chance to know him, as he is often away, but what I have seen is certainly beyond reproach."

"A colonel's wife can travel with him," Lady Stratton observed.

"Oh, no," Katherine exclaimed. "I would not be so presumptuous as to…"

"Tsk." The old woman stopped her. "Of course, you have considered it. All ladies must."

Katherine nodded. To admit that she had thought of the prospect of life as the colonel's wife was more than she had even discussed in open conversation with her sisters. The countess certainly had a way getting to the point.

"He looks upon you with great admiration," Lady Stratton continued.

Katherine shrugged once more. "It is no matter," she replied. "Many years might pass, and the colonel should not be to blame if he were to choose one more readily available."

"But why should he?" the countess questioned.

"I am all but engaged," Katherine recounted.

"Engaged is not married," the countess said. "Why, ask the Duchess of Bramblewood if you doubt me."

Katherine noted the lovely young couple dancing and wondered what story was there.

"Quite the kerfuffle Christmas last," the countess confided. The vicar was incensed, but of course, the duke would not bend, and what with the Scotsmen, what could he do? The vicar had to acquiesce. So, there you have it."

Katherine nodded, completely confused over the whole story, but she smiled nonetheless and asked brightly, "Shall we find a game of whist to join?"

"A deft maneuver," Agnes laughed. She replied that she took no pleasure in cards. "I would much rather sit about and observe the creatures around us. There is much to be learned from the observation of human nature. Do you not agree?"

Katherine laughed and settled into her chair to join the elder woman in a game of guessing what intrigues and conversations flowed about them.

"Ah, see there?" Lady Stratton nodded toward Katherine's brother Harry and one of the young women he had engaged earlier in the evening. They were laughing and whispering over a paper she was holding. "The young miss and her secret lover are forming a letter to her father begging that they might be married. If Papa should refuse, they will spirit away to Gretna Green this very night and bind their love over the anvil, forever to be blessed in happiness and shunned by her father."

Katherine threw her head back and laughed with every fiber of her being.

"One of that pair is my brother," she explained. "And an unknown lady. And although he may be trying to woo her, I doubt they will away to Gretna Green. Harry is not ready to be leg-shackled by any means."

"Ah well." Lady Stratton shrugged. "Now, that I note, the lady, I believe, is the Dowager Duchess Mayberry's daughter home from finishing school. Her father passed these many years ago, and I do doubt that Belinda would turn a blind eye to Gretna Green. She keeps her children on a tight rein, although the Dowager may still be visiting her sister in London, so her daughter has some freedom, I imagine. No doubt she chose to come home at this point entirely because her mother was out of town. Oh, well. The romance was grand while it lasted, was it not? Shall we try another?"

Katherine chuckled, and they played the game for a short while, Agnes creating fantastical tales of intrigue, love, and revenge, while Katherine provided what she knew to be true about the guests in attendance.

The pair roared with laughter until they were interrupted by a tall gentleman with piercing dark eyes and an eyebrow raised in question at the older of the two ladies.

PART II

CHAPTER 7

Katherine was quite sure she saw the gentleman on the day of her arrival, and she had not been able to banish him from her mind. That was a silly thought, she argued with herself, for the man looking down upon them was not one that would be easily forgotten. No, her heart leaped in her chest. He was handsome—one of the most attractive men in the room—but he had paid her little attention since her arrival, and indeed seemed put off by her slovenly appearance that first day. It seemed a shallow observation to Katherine, and she would not mark it. If the gentleman put so much emphasis on her neat appearance, she wanted nothing to do with the man. She was on the whole a neat person but found such excessive fastidiousness tiresome.

"Your tea, as requested." He spoke with a drawl as if he knew the trouble the older woman was like to cause. He set a cup of tea and saucer down before the lady and waited for the elderly lady to explain herself, but she simply took another sip of her wine. "I did not request tea," she said.

Rather than fall prey to his unspoken demand, she made the introduction to Katherine, who found the lady's forthrightness amusing. No doubt, this dour gentleman would not appreciate their laughter.

He greeted Katherine and introduced himself as William, the countess' nephew, and nothing more.

The countess scoffed.

"William is my nephew, true," she said, "He is also heir to my husband's earldom. May I present Mr. William Singer, who will one day be Lord Stratton."

Katherine felt her eyebrows raise in tandem and her mouth drop open into a small and feminine circle. "We have met," she said. "My brother made the introductions," Katherine said.

Still, it was no wonder that his countenance was familiar to her. Now that she was aware of the relation, Katherine realized that William—Mr. Singer, she corrected herself—possessed many of his Uncle Cecil's features. It was amazing that she did not notice this when Harry introduced them earlier.

"When his father passed, William was still in short pants, so my husband took him under his wing," Aunt Agnes explained. "When it became clear that we would have no children of our own, William became like a son to us." She sounded proud of his accomplishments. "It is to William that we owe the constant success of our herds. He is very diligent in the task, and although his father, rest his soul, was a great man, William has a knack for leadership that is unparalleled."

"Aunt Agnes," William spoke in a low tone that foretold the end of the conversation before turning to address Katherine. "I apologize for her speech. My aunt has not been exposed to new society for several years. I am afraid she is making up for lost time."

The countess frowned slightly at being corrected, but she did not argue. Katherine found his high-handed criticism of his aunt annoying. Was it just because she was a woman or was he this arrogant all of the time, she wondered as she pasted a smile on her face.

"Not at all." Katherine placed her hand over Agnes' but turned to William offering a small rebuke of her own. "All mothers praise their children in new company. It is clear that she thinks of you as her son, and so such hyperbole is to be expected, if indeed it is exaggeration."

"It is not," Agnes put in.

He groaned and shook his head. "Aunt Agnes," he said with exasperation and then turned as if to go, again without speaking a *by your leave*.

The countess interrupted his departure. "Do stay, William," she said. He stopped, somewhat uncomfortably. Katherine was aware that he wanted to leave them, but she did not know why. She had done nothing to upset the man, and yet he seemed to want to avoid her, or perhaps he wanted to avoid his aunt. She couldn't imagine why. The lady was a gem, and she obviously loved William. "My nephew will do the title proud when the day comes," the countess said.

Katherine could not say that she had ever met a gentleman with an aversion to praise. She felt that it must be false. Then, she remembered the loss of his father. Perhaps William did not like to be reminded of his position because it was the result of a tragedy of someone, he held dear, but didn't the countess say William was a child when his father died? The wound could not be so fresh. Katherine decided to change the topic to one that might be less painful, nonetheless.

"Are you enjoying the party, Mr. Singer?" she asked.

He nodded. "It is a pleasant group," he agreed. "Have you met my friend, Alex, the Duke of Bramblewood, and his wife Emily?"

She revealed that she had not. "My cousin Anne promised to introduce us, but I think she is distracted by her husband's presence."

"No doubt," William said dryly, tossing a look in the direction of Anne and her husband as Anne practically dragged the man onto the floor for another dance. "Alexander is a good friend and recent relative through marriage," Mr. Singer revealed. "He has done much to improve Bramblewood since he came to be in possession of the property."

"Then, I should think that the two of you would have much in common," she offered.

"We do," he agreed and offered to make the introduction, which was accepted and agreed to be completed at some later point during the course of the evening.

For several minutes, they made stilted polite conversation, but Katherine felt nervous and out of sorts, and Mr. Singer could barely keep his eyes upon her face. He kept looking over her shoulder as if he wanted to be away. Katherine soon wished for the less formal chatter of his mother when she was left to her own devices.

"I am old and tired," Lady Stratton commented with a feigned yawn. "Why do you not take Miss Katherine for a turn, William?"

Mr. Singer stiffened.

Katherine shot the Lady a reproving look from the corner of her eye. They were both aware that she had just awoken from a brief nap less than an hour before, and the next dance was a waltz, a titillating dance to be sure.

Katherine resisted the urge to run. She had never waltzed before, certainly not with so august a gentleman. She was afraid she would disgrace herself. Katherine received an innocent smile from Lady Stratton, a refusal to admit to meddling, and so there was nothing to be done.

Mr. Singer seemed uncomfortable with the suggestion, though there was no avoiding the offer now without resulting in a slight.

Mr. Singer lowered a scathing gaze at his aunt, which Katherine construed to mean that he would deal with her meddling later. "Aunt Agnes," he said. "Promise me that you will wait for me to escort you to your rooms. A fall on the stair could be disastrous at your age."

"At my age, I think I know my own mind," she retorted.

Mr. Singer closed his eyes briefly and then held out a hand to Katherine. "Shall we?"

Katherine accepted the gentleman's hand, and he led her to center of the floor, where he took her into his arms with a grace and ease that she had somehow not expected from the gentleman.

This partnered dance was much different than those which she had shared with Colonel Markey. Rather than a tentative pattern of joining and parting while moving down the collective line, she was held close with Mr. Singer's hand at the small of her back. He was firmly in control of the situation, the dance, and her.

The sensation was unsettling, to say the least. His palm was large and spanned a majority of the surface. She felt the heat of it radiate from the point of contact as if there were some energy created by his palm that could not be explained by any normal means. Katherine shook off the thought and cleared her mind, focusing instead on the music that had just begun.

She scrambled for a topic of conversation, but nothing came to mind. She felt as if she were wrapped in cotton wool in his arms; only random jolts of energy ran through the wool, completely robbing her of rational thought. She was not usually at a loss for words. She felt out of sorts. She did not like the feeling and grappled for some sort of control, but

Mr. Singer seemed to have everything so well in hand, she might have floated away. There was only the music and the warmth of his hand and the intoxicating smell of the gentleman himself. Her mind began to weave dreams.

"Have you known the colonel long?" Mr. Singer asked after a long silence.

Katherine was startled by the question. She must have somehow sunk into her own sensibilities. How did he know that she was familiar with the colonel? She soon realized that he must have noticed the dance in which she had partnered the gentleman earlier in the night. It was strange to think that he recalled her participation, and even stranger yet that he had made note of it. Had he been watching her? It made her feel excited and somewhat nervous.

"I am sorry," he continued when her expression revealed the confusion that she felt. "I met Colonel Markey years ago at school. He was a few years ahead of me. I assure you; I did not mean anything by the observation, only that you knew him."

"Yes, I have met the colonel several times now. He is acquainted with my brother Andrew," she admitted with a shaky breath. She wondered if the tremor was a response to his question or to the piercing eyes that were looking down with embarrassed apology. She did not want to consider the latter.

"Andrew is the eldest of your siblings?"

"Yes." Why, she wondered, did her voice sound so breathless? The dance was practically effortless. Mr. Singer had the steps well in hand, and she need only follow.

"And your cousin…" he continued, "is the recent Mrs. Ingram?"

She nodded. "Yes." She knew she was answering in monosyllables and yet could not seem to help herself. "Anne is," she forced herself to continue. "Her mother is my father's sister."

"Ah. And the young woman with Harry Westlake is *your* sister, too?"

"Yes," she replied, "and Harry, himself, is my brother."

"Ah, now I have the relationship sorted," he said. "You have several sisters, do you not?"

"Four in number," she said. "Lucinda, Josephine, Georgianna, and little Isadora."

He seemed surprised by this revelation, and Katherine found herself laughing at his expression.

"Yes," she responded to his unspoken thought, "it is a lot of daughters."

"Brothers? Aside from Harry and Andrew?"

"Three," she admitted. "Two elder, one younger than I, Arthur. They keep father quite busy."

He nodded, revealing a sort of half grin, as if he wanted to smile but suppressed it.

Katherine wondered if somewhere deep inside was buried the same humor that permeated his aunt's character. The thought was appealing, but she vowed not to press for it.

Her focus need to remain directed at Colonel Markey. There was no good that would come from delving into the deeper person of an unfamiliar gentleman who would one day be an earl. Such would be reaching beyond her station. Besides, he may be handsome, but he had the same bland character that Mr. Porter had. Her heart leapt in contradiction to that thought, and her hands felt warm and somewhat damp in her gloves. The weather was not yet so hot that she should feel perspiration. She demanded that she should pursue the conversation.

"Have you known the colonel long?" she asked. When he nodded, she inquired after the man's character. She might as well make use of the conversation.

"As far as I know, Jon is as steadfast as they come," he said. Then, after some consideration, he continued. His eyes narrowed as if he wished to impress a point upon her. "He does not distribute his attentions lightly."

Katherine flushed and was forced to look away. Had the gentleman meant to imply that the colonel had spoken of her? If so, what might have been said?

"I do not know what you have been told, but…" she began before he shook his head to end her speech.

"The colonel has said nothing," he revealed. "We are not so close as to confide such personal details. It is merely another observation. I have yet to see him so devoted."

"You are an observer of character, then," she guessed. "Like your aunt."

He raised one shoulder and let it drop. The act unconsciously inched Katherine closer, and she shifted to renew the space between their bodies. The movement caused her to misstep, and he pulled her even closer to keep her in the rhythm of the dance.

"Sorry," she muttered against his lapel.

"Do not give it a thought," he said magnanimously as he turned her misstep into a twirl and once again pulled her close.

She concentrated to regain her rhythm and was aware of the very maleness of the man who held her. The scent of him made her want to snuggle against him, but she dared not do so. This was exactly why ladies should not dance waltzes with gentleman they barely knew, she thought. She would not think on it. Instead, she reawakened the conversation.

"Besides," she said as she grasped for a topic, "I have only danced with the colonel three times in all of our acquaintance. That does not seem overtly attentive, in my experience."

"Perhaps not," he agreed. "But I have never seen him dance with another. Ever."

Katherine laughed in disbelief, but the gaiety sounded false. Her thoughts were not on Colonel Mackey. How could they be when she was held by this virile gentleman?

"Surely, you are mistaken," she said, clinging to the conversation at hand.

"Never," he repeated with assurance.

Katherine was shocked by the revelation. Perhaps she had been too cautious in her understanding of Colonel Markey's affections. Perhaps he cared for her more than she realized. And what would that mean? What were her true sensibilities? She bit her lip in thought as she considered Mr. Singer's words. Her mother would not be pleased with the revelation. She would not want to see Colonel Markey supplant Mr. Porter, but Katherine could not help but feel a small amount of satisfaction at the knowledge that the colonel only ever danced with her. There was something to be said about that, something flattering indeed. She let the thought blossom within her.

The music ended, and Mr. Singer bowed to her with eloquence. Katherine felt strangely bereft without his hand at the small of her back. That was ridiculous. It was only because she had been hesitant to dance, and he really was a superb dancer. Mr. Singer repeated his offer to make the introduction to the Duke of Bramblewood, and she accepted. As the pair made their way across the room, the colonel himself made an appearance.

"Miss Westlake!" He appeared in front of her so suddenly that she leapt backward and collided with Mr. Singer. A hand at her back steadied her as she regained her footing and greeted the gentleman. Then, it disappeared.

"I have been looking for you," said the Colonel.

"Mr. Singer." The colonel bowed his head to William and offered Katherine his arm.

"Actually," Katherine gestured toward the Duke and Duchess who stood several feet away, "Mr. Singer was just about to introduce me to Lord and Lady Bramblewood. Would you care to join?"

Her offer seemed to please the gentleman, who gladly joined their party.

After the deed was done, Colonel Markey was quick to spirit Katherine away for another round on the floor. They left the landowners to discuss their shared interests and the prospect of integrating certain resources that would be mutually beneficial.

As they began the dance, Katherine was notably aware that the colonel was not half the dancer that Mr. Singer was. Still, he was a kind man, and in her social circle. She found him comfortable, as Mr. Singer was not. Mr. Singer seemed to set all of her emotions on edge so that she could barely breathe. Now that he had given her space, she realized that she was in need a few deep breaths. When she had gained her equilibrium, she began a conversation with the colonel.

Katherine could not believe that he never danced with other ladies, and she asked him so outright.

"Not in a long while," he admitted with a faint blush. "Is that terribly embarrassing?"

"Not at all," she laughed. "I think it sweet and very flattering that you chose me. I am honored to partner your skill."

He seemed heartened by her words and spun her with abandon for a few steps before she was released to another partner. She smiled, and when they changed partners once again, she clung to him, certain that this was the freest that she had yet to see his behavior. Perhaps she would not have to marry Mr. Porter at all. Perhaps she would see the world with the colonel.

When the song ended, they were both sad to hear that it was the last of the night. The party began to break up and go their separate ways. Katherine said her farewells to the colonel and her new friends.

As the evening drew to a close, she was satisfied to see that all was as it should be. Josephine had met a dashing young gentleman who was visiting from London. They all had received an invite to what promised to be the most anticipated picnic of the summer at Bramblewood Park, which was to be held as soon as the weather permitted, and Katherine was now more certain than ever that she would receive her own proposal from Colonel Markey. She just had to edge the man along. If ever there had been a more fruitful evening, she could not recall.

CHAPTER 8

Two days later, Mr. Westlake received a letter that informed the family that Colonel Markey was forced to decline the invitation to dine at their residence the following evening. Katherine had been looking forward to an audience with the gentleman in a smaller group, in particular that of her family, whose opinions she valued above all.

It was a devastating blow, as the colonel could not even say if he would return in time for the picnic later in the summer; not only did it promise to be a romantic event, in any case, but it was to be the first ever picnic held at Bramblewood. The Christmas Ball at Bramblewood had been the talk of the town, and now, with a summer event, the guests need not wait much longer for another display of splendor and lively entertainment. The duchess, Katherine learned, was anxious to show off her garden.

The three remaining Westlake daughters had offered their skill at crafting décor for the event. Paper lanterns were to give the grounds an Oriental flavor, and fabric would be used to craft all manner of intricate decorations that would be hung about the garden and adjoining room. Emily, the Duchess of Bramblewood, had promised to supply the materials that would match the rest of the decor for the evening.

Anne and Jo had risen early and took horses to Bramblewood Park. Katherine had not realized they were gone until breakfast when she was dismayed to learn that she had been left behind.

"I'm sure you can ride with a groom," her mother said, but Katherine did not relish a ride, especially alone. "I could call a carriage," Aunt Agnes said. "Or if you prefer, it's not a terribly far walk, and the weather is lovely today."

The countess had been so kind, Katherine hated to be a bother. "It's just on the other side of Brackenbrush Creek," Aunt Agnes continued. "Once you are over the bridge, you turn right across the field. You can see Bramblewood the whole way, and it is all private property. No one will bother you, and you can't get lost. And if you are not finished with the decorations before dark, I'm sure Emily will provide transport home, or you can stay the night. Anne often does so."

Katherine nodded. The weather was sunny and warm, the first really warm day of spring. Katherine decided that she rather fancied a walk along the creek. It was for this reason that Katherine found herself trudging alone along the path to Bramblewood. Besides, now that the countryside was no longer plagued by sheets of rain, she was itching for an outing. She wanted to feel the sun on her shoulders and the wind in her hair.

Katherine squinted at the sky, where the sun was peeking from behind a lone cloud. There was nothing quite as invigorating as a long walk on a fine day. Even the wind had died down to a soft breeze.

She crossed the bridge that Anne had always referred to as *the thinking spot,* a place where troubles and worries could be tossed into the water below. Her fingers traced a pattern upon the rail, and she smiled as she imagined the profession of love that had taken place at this very location not so long ago. Anne said this was where Edmund had first proposed. He had been twelve. The thought made Katherine smile and think of her own life. She was more determined than ever that her mother would not marry her off to Mr. Porter.

She wanted her own offer of marriage to be just as romantic as her cousin's. She wanted love. Mr. Porter didn't have a romantic bone in his body, never mind love.

She caught the scent of lilacs growing nearby. They were just starting to bloom, and she thought what a lovely bouquet they would make to grace the table at Brambleton. She reached up and then realized that the sap from the broken branches would soil her gloves. She removed them and tucked them in the sash that encircled her waist. She broke off several branches that were within reach and filled her lungs with the sweet scent. It was the smell of spring, and the thought would have made her joyous if she didn't have to worry about Mr. Porter.

She determined that she would not think of him. She buried her face in the flowers and inhaled deeply, thinking only of love. As she walked, she pulled some of the excess leaves from the bouquet and admired the flowers. Most were barely open, so the bouquet would last for some time.

She moved on beyond the bridge with her heart swelling with thoughts of love and happily ever after. It was fortunate that the path to Bramblewood was so well trodden. Anyone sufficiently inclined could make this walk with their eyes closed, and since Katherine was so caught up in her own dreaming, she very nearly did so.

In her distracted state, she held the flowers against her chest momentarily as she removed her bonnet to brush back her hair, which was beginning to fall out of its pins in the wind. She was planning to replace the bonnet forthwith, but with the bouquet in her hands, it was awkward to retie the ribbons. Besides, the wind felt so good in her hair that she was in no hurry to put the bonnet back on her head.

As Aunt Agnes said, this was private property, and no one was likely to see her in a state. She began fussing with the ribbons of the bonnet as she walked, a habit that her mother had tried to break since childhood as it often resulted in the ruination of the bindings. Then she went back to adjusting the bouquet.

With the bonnet only laced over one finger, a single, strong, rogue gust of wind was enough to wrench it from her fingers and send the article flying into the branches of a nearby tree.

Katherine muttered an unladylike curse, thankful that there was no one around to hear her. She had also dropped several of the lilacs. She gathered them as she decided what to do about her fly-away head covering.

CHAPTER 9

The bonnet had landed on the other side of the fence that divided the properties and protected the travelers from wandering too close to the edge of the embankment that fell away at a precarious angle.

She considered abandoning the item. There really was no way to retrieve the thing. Then, she remembered that her mother had threatened that this would be the last new bonnet that her careless daughter destroyed. Katherine cringed at the thought of wearing her sister's old worn accessories, or worse, her mother's.

Plus, there would be the embarrassment of telling her mother she had lost the thing. She would have to say she was daydreaming, and her mother would once again, castigate her for her folly. Surely, she could get the thing back and no one would be the wiser.

She placed the flowers carefully on a rock and looked around for some tool to aid her in the rescue. A long, thin branch lay several yards away and was just thing to fetch the wayward bonnet from the tree. She broke off the smaller twigs until nothing remained but the center stalk, a long extension of her own arms.

If she could hook the branch under the edge of the bonnet, she might be able to haul it to safety. It was certainly worth the attempt.

For several minutes she tried to reach her prize in vain. She cursed the fence that prevented her from closing the short distance that remained. How would she explain this to her mother? What sort of lecture might she receive for the complete loss of a bonnet? At least a frayed ribbon could be replaced; this was another matter entirely.

She sighed and leaned against the fence. It was old but sturdy. Vertical posts drove deep into the ground and supported two beams whose ends were tapered to a point. These edges had been wedged into a small crevice that had been cut from the post for that purpose. It seemed much more reliable than the rickety rope connections that some farmers used near Halthaven which were always in need of mending, although she noted that the other side of the fence looked like it had been replaced recently. A pity indeed that this side had not been updated. Would the fence hold her, she wondered? She placed one foot on the lower rung and tested its strength. It seemed sturdy enough.

She looked down the lane in one direction and then the other. No help was in sight. Well, no matter. She could do this herself. In fact, it was probably a good thing no one was witness to her folly.

With a deep breath and a burst of resolve, Katherine grasped her branch once more and estimated that the extra height would be just enough to bring her within reach of the bonnet. She need only make use of the bottommost level. Surely, there was no harm in that. She could easily hold onto the top rail with her opposite hand.

With two feet balanced on the wooden brace, which creaked beneath her but held firm, she made the attempt. She released the breath that she had been holding and focused her attention once more on the task at hand. With her arms outstretched and the branch extended she tried to control the movement so that it would settle beneath the bonnet without knocking it lose and away to oblivion.

Several attempts left her arms aching but her determination steady. Besides, lifting her arms so high pulled the bodice of her dress precariously tight. She did not want to chance popping a button. She put down the branch and shifted the dress upwards to allow her a little more room in arm movement. She picked up the branch again. That was better. She was so very near to succeeding that she knew it was only a matter of time before she claimed her victory. Perhaps she should climb on the next rung, she thought. Then, she would be a foot or two taller and able to reach the blasted thing. She put her foot upon the next cross piece.

William was on his way home from Bramblewood Park when he saw the woman climbing on the fence that separated the road from the ravine. She seemed to be reaching for something. What on earth could be so important, he wondered, that someone would risk life and limb? He was a bit perturbed that anyone could be so thoughtless as to put themselves in danger, but his sense of honor said he had to help.

He kicked his horse into a gallop, and then as he realized the woman was Miss Westlake, his heart leaped in his chest. He urged his horse forward, racing towards her.

What did the foolish woman think she was doing? He was suddenly both furious and filled with fear. If she fell into the ravine, she could be seriously hurt. The thought of her hurt was like a physical pain in his own heart. *Katherine.* He could not seem to move fast enough to reach her.

"Ho!" he cried hoping she would step off of the rickety fence and face him, but she was intent upon her task. "What on God's good earth are you doing, woman?" he yelled out sternly.

She looked startled by his sudden appearance, but that didn't slow him—or her—one bit.

Just then, a loud crack filled the air, and William looked up in terror. He let out an audible gasp as he saw that Katherine had stepped upon a rotten section of the fence, and it gave way. She was moments from falling into the ravine. In an instant, he was off of his steed, and his feet moved faster than they ever had as he flew to Katherine with monumental swiftness.

A VOICE CALLED FROM THE LANE AND KATHERINE TURNED, startled. For a moment, she was relieved to see the gentleman's arrival. Perhaps he might be able to finish the deed.

"What on God's good earth are you doing, woman?" he snapped as he flung himself from his horse.

Mr. Singer. She would have been well enough without him and his rude demeanor, she thought.

"None of your concern, I'm sure," she threw over her shoulder as she reached for the branch again.

As he strode angrily forward, she leaned against the fence and stepped up onto the next rung to fetch the blasted bonnet before he arrived to castigate her, when a loud crack shook her entire body, and her eyes grew wide with fear.

The plank on which she had just shifted her weight gave way and, in an attempt to catch herself, she pitched forward over the upper rung. A hand caught the back of her dress at her waist just as she was about to plunge down the steep hillside. Mr. Singer yanked her back to safety, her shoulders colliding with both the railing of the fence and his hard chest. She allowed herself a breath of relief even as she was mortified by the rescue. The wood bit into her lower back and pressed between their two bodies as Mr. Singer braced himself to pull her over the railing and back toward safety.

Her feet scrambled on the shale that was crumbing away with every step. This act pulled the gentleman against the fence and their combined weight was thrust against it as she lost her balance.

Katherine cried out, and a deep curse rent the air as the final rung gave way, and the pair tumbled forward, leaving the bonnet waving behind them.

The path to the bottom of the hill was covered in bramble and not at all a pleasant fall. Katherine cried out in pain as her head hit a rock somewhere on the descent, and she felt a pair of strong arms wrap around her and hold her close, shielding her delicate frame from the brunt of the obstacles that shook their bodies as they tumbled, one over the other, to the bottom of the ridge.

They rolled to a stop with the weight of the gentleman driving the air from Katherine's lungs, and then he pitched to the side, and there they lay, he staring up the bright midday sky and she staring at him. Both were gasping for breath.

William suppressed the urge to run his hands over every inch of her body, with the excuse that he wanted to be sure nothing was broken. In truth, he was sure something *was broken*—his will to avoid her. He stared resolutely at the open sky.

Her eyes were wide with fear, and he wanted only to kiss away the terror in those eyes. He wanted to hold her and keep her safe. Without thinking, his grip tightened on her, and he pulled her close. She came with soft willingness, and he sucked in a breath. She smelled of the same muskiness and lilacs. The mystery flower was lilac, he thought, resisting the urge to bury his face in her dark hair, which had fallen about her shoulders in a riotous tumble. There were leaves and brambles stuck in her hair, but it was beautiful. She was beautiful.

He was keenly aware that her dress was hiked up to her knees and one leg had a long scratch from the brambles. He had the insane desire to kiss it better. To make his way from mid-calf where the scratch started to wherever the hurt ended somewhere beneath her skirts.

The ache he now felt had nothing to do with their precipitous decline and everything to do with the fact that she was sprawled across his person. Her breathless state was wreaking havoc with his control, and he told himself, just close your eyes and be still for a moment, but then she made a sound.

It could have been a groan or a moan. It was a soft whimpering sound, and his protective spirit sprung alive along with parts of his anatomy. *She was hurt. Katherine…* And he was a cad. He had not even inquired about her possible injuries.

KATHERINE GROANED, TAKING STOCK. SHE ACHED ALL over, but more than that, she was mortified. Must this man see her at the worst times?

"Miss Westlake, are you all right?" he asked. The words came in a rush, as if the speaker had not the air to say more.

Katherine coughed and nodded, which was undoubtedly a mistake. The world swam dizzily, and unable to do more than moan, she attempted to control the wave of pain and nausea that now assaulted her. Her hand went to the back of her head where a throbbing lump was forming. Thankfully, it was hidden by her hair, which was an unmitigated mess.

She waited for a lecture on her reckless behavior, or a question of what in heaven's name had she been thinking, but it did not come. Instead, she turned her head to the side and found nothing but concern in the cool grey eyes that stared back at her.

"Mr. Singer?" she breathed. Of course, her voice was breathy from the fall, not her shock at not having recognized the gentleman. Not from his close proximity. "What are you doing here?"

"Oh, this is a daily activity of mine. I like to throw myself over ledges and see if I'll survive." His kind demeanor had vanished, and in its place was a caustic tone. "A bonus if there is rescue of a silly damsel involved. So far, I am without defeat." He delivered the statement without a hint of humor, still staring up at the lone cloud, and it took Katherine a moment to recognize the jest—if it was a jest.

"I am not silly," she said, just a little perturbed.

"Are you not?"

"No," she insisted. "In fact, I was doing well enough on my own until you stepped in and broke through the fence."

"Well enough on your own?" he spat. Bright spots of color appeared on his cheeks, whether from exertion or from anger, she could not tell. "You were inches from breaking your foolish neck."

"If either of us should have broken our necks, it would have been entirely your fault."

He stared at her open mouthed for a long moment. "You are mad, woman," he said.

Something about his expression stuck her as funny, and laughter burst forth with such vigor that, had the situation been different, she might have thought that she had lost her mind. Perhaps she had abandoned it somewhere up the hill. Maybe he was right. She was mad. Certainly, the world seemed topsy turvy.

He sat up on one elbow and put her gently aside. He looked down upon her with a furrowed brow.

"I believe you are in shock," he said.

Once the laughter died down, Katherine found herself again wondering what had brought the gentleman to her aid. "Were you… following me?" she asked suspiciously.

"Of course not," he said.

"You were," she accused.

He informed her rather condescendingly that he had no reason to follow her, although it was her good fortune that he had.

She disagreed vehemently while he explained that he had just come from a meeting with the Duke of Bramblewood in which they had continued their discussion of collaboration in caring for Northwickshire and the people in the neighborhood. He noted that he had not expected to be called upon in such a precipitous manner to care for one of those people.

"No one called upon you," she snapped in defiance, and saw stars before her eyes. Perhaps this was meaning of seeing red with anger, she thought as she brought a hand to the back of her head to steady it.

"Nonetheless, my arrival was fortuitous."

Katherine was not sure she believed him, but she nodded, and the motion was a mistake. It caused her to grimace as her head spun and pulsed with pain. She squeezed her eyes shut against it and clenched her teeth, waiting for the discomfort to subside.

She felt something cool on her cheek and opened one eye to discover the gentleman brushing his fingertips over the tender bone of her cheek. She jerked away with a gasp of pain. "Don't!" The world again swam dizzyingly.

"I am afraid your skin is already turning color," he muttered and withdrew a handkerchief from his breast pocket to press against the location. Katherine was shocked to see the white fabric stained with blood. She had not been aware of the injury because every inch of her frame ached in equal fashion.

She should have taken the item from his hand and held it in place herself, but she had not the energy to do so. She hated to admit that it was nice to be taken care of. As soon as the thought crossed her mind, she chastised herself for the selfish instinct. Certainly, the gentleman was in no better condition, although he had no one but himself to blame.

She noted that the sleeve of his jacket was torn but saw no other open wounds on what little of their bodies were within view. The confounded bonnet was nowhere in sight.

She groaned and moved to take the handkerchief for herself. She was capable of mopping up her own mess. She had meant to warn him, to ask for the handkerchief and inform him that she was quite all right. Yet her hand acted of its own volition and settled over his before she could speak. Her bare hand on his. Only then did she realize that she had left her gloves in her sash, and they were, of course, lost somewhere on the hillside.

Her breath caught, and her heart began to pound in her chest. The result of the trauma, she told herself. The man didn't even like her. He thought her a silly chit who was entirely too much trouble, and what did she think of him? He was an arrogant man who showed up at the worst possible times, only to scold her worse than her own father was like to do. Whatever her heart thought of the man, it was wrong.

Mr. Singer's pupils darkened, and his eyes found hers. There they remained, locked in the moment with naught to tear them away.

Her tongue moistened her dry lips, and she tasted dirt.

"We should return you to safety." His voice was a husky whisper.

"Yes," she breathed. She might have imagined that her pain had subsisted, but in this moment, she was unaware of anything but the man beside her and the deep thrumming of her heart. A flush of heat ran through her, no doubt from the trauma of the moment.

Was he leaning toward her? Could it be that his face inching ever nearer, or was it her imagination because she willed it so? What was she thinking? This arrogant scoundrel, kiss her? Not on her life. Besides, it would be most inappropriate if he were to kiss her, and yet…

"OY!" A voice called in the distance. "I thought I heard something, and that's his lordship's horse. I'll just check it a moment."

Mr. Singer pulled away so fast that Katherine could not even be certain that the moment had happened. He scanned their prone bodies and a spot of red appeared on his cheeks. Katherine felt something move against her leg and too late realized that he had pulled down her skirts which, in the fall, had tangled themselves above her knees.

The act was too late, however, because at the same time a face appeared from the edge of a nearby field and witnessed the motion.

One long whistle revealed the man's assumption, and Katherine sat up with indignation. The motion caused her head to spin and the nausea to return with full force.

Mr. Singer called after the man, offering an explanation, but the farmer just shook his head and hurried away. William cursed and stood, but by the time William had scrambled up the bluff to chase after him, the farmer and his companion where nowhere to be found.

Katherine groaned and pressed her head to her knees, not even making the attempt to follow him up the hill.

In a moment, he was back beside her. "Let me help you," he said. When had his bossy presence become a comfort? Certainly, she did not need his aid.

"It will be all right," Mr. Singer assured her. "There is a perfectly valid explanation. I am sure it will be heard."

"You must find him," she muttered, waving him away. "I'm all right. Go! Find him!"

"I will." He placed a hand under her elbow and hauled her to her feet. "First, we must get you home. You need to be seen by a physician."

"No," Katherine cried, though her voice was weak. "You go on; I can make it on my own," she said as they stumbled up the hill.

Mr. Singer gave one short laugh to reveal that he found that hard to believe. Once they reached the path, he called her bluff. "Okay," he said. "If you can walk ten steps on your own, I shall consider it." His tone revealed that he was merely humoring her plea.

"Fine," she said and jerked her arm free. The world spun around her, but she refused to give any sign of the disturbance.

She closed her eyes and squared her shoulders. She opened them again and took one tremulous step, then another. On the third she shot a confident grin over her shoulder. The sudden head movement was a mistake. A black spot appeared on the edge of her vision, and she blinked it away.

"You do not have to follow me," she said with some venom. She had noticed that the gentleman was mirroring her steps, as if he felt the need to remain in arm's length in case she fell.

He made a noncommittal noise. "You must be the most stubborn woman in all of England," he spat.

"And you must be the most bothersome man. I told you I don't need your help."

Three more steps and Katherine was feeling more confident than ever. Her legs were shaking, and she felt as if she were about to have a reappearance of her morning meal, but she was taking steps forward. Eight. Nine. She knew that it was of the upmost importance that Mr. Singer chase after the misunderstanding witness and get him to see reason.

On the next step, the blackness widened, and she took a deep breath to will it away, but it remained. She told herself that she could rest once the annoying gentleman was gone. For her final step, she blindly stumbled forward in an attempt to complete the task.

Then, there was an abundance of colorful spots which soon turned black until there was nothing but dark and the world fell away in a sudden rush. She was vaguely aware of a strong arm around her ensuring her safety.

CHAPTER 10

Katherine woke to the light of a new day in an unfamiliar room. A vase of lilacs sat on the night stand, and their scent filled the room with cheer. She remembered picking them. Now, she had the comfort of a feather bed with her cat staring at her from the quilt folded on the foot of the bed. If it were not for the aching of her body, and the bump on her head, she might have thought that the encounter with Mr. Singer nothing more than a dream—a nightmare, more like.

She groaned, and rather than respond to her need, a servant she did not know bustled from the room and closed the door behind her.

A moment later, the door inched open, and Jo slipped inside on silent slippers.

She was chewing her lower lip, a habit that only revealed itself when she was fighting back tears, which was rarely.

"What is it?" Katherine groaned. "I am not so hurt."

"No," Jo's voice quivered. "You have a nasty bump on your head, but the physician said you will make a full recovery."

"Then, do not cry." Katherine shook her head slightly. "Where are we?"

"Aldbrick Abbey," Jo said.

Katherine understood now. They were at her Aunt Caroline and Uncle Edgar's home, but why had they left Sandstowe Hill? She asked Jo why the change of location.

"Mr. Singer thought it best, considering…" Jo added.

"Mr. Singer?" Katherine thought. What an interfering man! What did he have to do with anything? She must have bumped her head harder than she thought she did.

"He has been ever so kind," Jo said.

"Him? Kind?" Katherine scoffed. "He's a nightmare."

Her sister crept forward and sat on the edge of the bed. Her cool hands grasped Katherine's, and she felt a sinking in her stomach when she looked into her sister's eyes.

"What is it?" Katherine asked.

"The farmer," Jo said.

"The farmer?" Katherine released the words with a choking gasp.

Jo shook her head, and a tear spilled down her cheek.

"Mr. Singer brought you here, and—" Jo shook her head as if she were trying her best to process the situation. "Oh, Kat, father was furious. I've never seen him so."

"At me?" Katherine questioned.

"No, of course not. He is never mad at his little Kat." Katherine might have heard a spot of frustration in that assertion, but perhaps it was just that her head ached.

Jo continued. "They went to prove that Mr. Singer's tale was true, and they did. They found the broken fence… and your bonnet in the tree… but it was too late. The farmer had already made a report to the Vicar, and he is just an awful, rigid man. I can hardly believe he is a man of God. He doesn't know the meaning of forgiveness. He won't be reasoned with."

"What?" Katherine cried as she sat up in bed. She felt as if life itself had been driven from her body.

She could not breathe, could not think. There was only loss, such an incredible loss, and her head still ached. She brought a hand up against her scalp as if that might remedy something.

"They are trying to find a solution, but…" Jo shook her head once more. It was as if that were all she could do; the matter was too much for any other response.

"They?" Katherine said.

"Father… and Mr. Singer, but…"

"…but I'm ruined," Katherine finished for her.

Jo nodded. "We all are," she confirmed.

. . .

KATHERINE WANTED TO RUSH FROM THE ROOM AND explain herself, but Jo said she was to remain in bed. Doctor's orders. Then, she left to inform the others that her sister was awake. Katherine wondered if she was being isolated because she needed the rest, or if the shame was so much that her family did not wish to see her. She feared the latter, and the pit in her stomach grew larger with each passing moment.

Her own ruination would ensure that Jo and Georgie, and even young Dora, would never make a suitable match. No gentleman of note would make an offer to a family with a child of such ill rapport.

Katherine spent the next several hours crying herself to sleep, which made her head ache with a monstrous pain until she fell into a fitful sleep, waking with feverish nightmares and repeating the process anew. Though the servants came to check her progress, she saw nothing of her family.

When darkness began to fall outside of her window, she could stand it no longer. Katherine waited for the servant to leave and estimated that she had a quarter hour before the girl returned. She slipped from the bed and chose her lightest gown, one that would be easy to get into on her own. The task bested her, and she was gasping in pain when the servant returned and cried out in shock. Katherine had the gown draped over her body but had been unable to reach the buttons at her back, and she was so exhausted and utterly defeated that she just wanted to lie back down, but she could not. She had to see this problem through.

She asked the servant to complete the task of buttoning the dress and then ordered the girl to remain in the room while she slipped out into the hall. The last thing that she needed was her mother being alerted to her escape.

She could hear voices coming from the floor below where the parlor door was sitting ajar. Hushed tones and fervent whispers drifted into the hallway, but Katherine could not make out the words.

A deep cough behind her revealed that she was not alone, and she turned to see the ruddy face and tired eyes of her father.

Her lip trembled and tears spilled anew. She had ruined all.

He stared at her for a long while as she stood there trembling, waiting for the fury that must come. Then, he pressed his lips together and opened his arms to his beloved child.

Katherine rushed into them and buried her face in the folds of his shirt.

"Oh, papa," she sobbed. "I swear to you that nothing happened. It was only a fall… I swear it."

"Hush child." He smoothed his hand over the curls that hung down her back and murmured soothing sounds that did little to calm her agony. "I know."

"Then," she looked up at him with tear-soaked eyes, "you believe me?"

"I do," he nodded. "As does your mother. Though, our belief does little to solve this predicament."

She nodded. "The vicar…"

Her father confirmed her fears. "He is not easily persuaded. Even the physician's confirmation of the accident could not get him to see reason."

"What is to become of me?" she asked. Her sobs had drawn the others from the parlor. Her aunt, mother, and sisters, as well as Cousin Suzanna, filed into the hall.

"Oh, darling," her mother pressed a kiss to her forehead. "We do not know."

"Your cousin Anne went to speak to the Duke and Duchess of Bramblewood," Aunt Caroline said. "She hopes that the duke can make him see reason, but Edmund was full of bluster. He said this is retaliation for the fact that the Duke of Bramblewood made him look a fool. Still, a man of the cloth should not engage in grudges and the like."

"We can hope," Uncle Edgar said with a sigh. "Come, Oliver. Have a drink with me. Our girls will be the death of us yet," he predicted.

"Have you had word from Eliza?" Oliver asked, reminded of Edgar's troubles with his middle daughter.

"Not a peep," answered Edgar. "At least your girls are all accounted for," Edgar groused.

A knock at the door drew the attention of all.

Katherine looked up to her father with worried eyes as her mother shooed her away from the door and into the safety of the parlor. Her father followed the butler to greet the unexpected guest.

"Who could it be?" Jo asked.

Katherine wondered if the vicar had demanded that she be sent away. Perhaps the bailiff had been called to arrest her. What became of women who were ruined? She could barely say other than that they were never heard of in decent society again. She covered her face with her hands. Her life was over. No one of any worth would ever speak to her, or to her poor dear sisters.

HER FATHER ENTERED THE ROOM AND INSTRUCTED ALL BUT Katherine and her mother to leave. When the room was clear, he ushered Mr. Singer inside and invited him to have a seat.

The gentleman looked haggard and tired, as if he had not slept or received care since the event. His dark hair was mussed, and he hadn't shaved. Katherine noticed that he had changed into a new suit of impeccable cut and fashion, but the cloth was wrinkled and the cravat untied as if he had pulled it apart in frustration.

She stared at his shoes, unable to raise her eyes to his face even though she had no reason to fear or distrust him. He had saved her, behaved as nothing but a gentleman, and yet… she was still ruined. Oh, he might have a blemish on his reputation afterward, but his fortune and holdings would still draw in a lady of means. It was Katherine and her family who would bear the full force of the disgrace. She couldn't manage to raise her eyes to his.

She was mortified… and angry. Why hadn't he just left her alone?

She could see in the edge of her vision that Mr. Singer had rubbed his hand over his face, a motion that displayed the true level of his fatigue.

"It is settled," he sighed.

"Settled? What is settled?" Katherine asked. No one paid her a moment's attention.

"He agreed?" Mr. Westlake cried. "What changed his mind?"

"A hefty sum, I must admit," Mr. Singer scoffed. "For a man of the cloth, he places more value in coin than in truth."

"I shall repay every bit," her father began, but the gentleman waved the offer away.

"It is not necessary." Mr. Singer shook his head. "I am afraid that it is not so simple as a fee, or rather *just* a fee."

"What else?" Mr. Westlake asked with a cautious tone.

"I have also arranged for the relocation of the farmer and his family to one of Bramblewood's more remote holdings. Alex is taking care of it."

"BLESS HIM," SAID KATHERINE'S MUM.

Mr. Singer explained more of the arrangement, but Katherine was too distraught to follow the conversation. All this trouble on her behalf, and for what? There was still no ensuring that her reputation would remain intact. "He has been offered a significant income in exchange for his silence. The distance will ensure that none in the area hear more of the matter."

"Oh, bless you," Mrs. Westlake cried. Her arms were wrapped around Katherine's shoulders, and she squeezed so hard that Katherine cried out in pain. Her mother whispered an apology and pulled her daughter close so that Katherine's face was secure in her mother's embrace. She welcomed the ability to hide and allowed her mother to fret so that she might remain in the safety of the cocoon. She had never appreciated her parents enough. She wanted them to make this disaster go away, and they were doing their best to accommodate her. Was there any hope? she wondered.

"That is not all." Katherine heard her father's voice. It was not a question, but a statement.

"No," Mr. Singer confirmed.

"It is as we discussed?" The elder's voice was full of sadness.

"It is the only way."

Her father nodded and stood. "I see. Well, I'll leave you to it then. Come, my dear."

Katherine looked up to see her father standing and holding out his hand. For a moment, she thought he was offering it to her, but then her mother placed her palm over his and stood by his side. "Let us leave them. They have much to discuss."

Katherine felt suddenly bereft. She wanted to continue to hold on to her mother, but her mother was already moving towards the door with her father, leaving her alone with this stranger.

Katherine's brows drew together in confusion. Her brain was sluggish after the injury, but she knew enough to be suspicious of an unchaperoned audience with a gentleman.

The door shut behind her parents, and she turned to look at Mr. Singer, who was staring down at his clasped hands.

Realization dawned upon her like a plunge into cold water. The vicar, a highly rigid man, would only maintain his silence upon one condition… their marriage.

She shook her head, but no words came out.

No, she wanted to scream. No. This was not how this happened. This was not how it was meant to be. She swallowed deeply and still felt as if she would choke upon the words.

"No." The word came out as a squeak. She could not accept it. Would not. "No. No. No," she whispered under her breath.

She, who had such visions of love and fidelity. She, who had dreamed of this moment for as long as she could remember, was now facing the looming prospect of a forced marriage.

"Miss Westlake…" He looked at her with sadness in his eyes, a greater sadness she had never seen. Did he pity her? Or was it for his own loss that he felt regret. "Katherine…"

"Do not call me that." She snapped. "I am not, nor will I ever be Katherine to you."

He sat with his hands clasped in his lap.

The reality of the situation was that he did not have to marry her. He could leave her in ruin and go about his life with little but a whisper to his name. She did not know why, but that fact made her angry. Why should he come out of this unscathed? Not that he had any control over the markings of society.

"As you wish," he sighed. He seemed weary, and she felt sorry for him and irritated all at the same time. A wave of hot anger rushed through her.

"This is all *your* fault," she said.

"My fault?" Suddenly the passion she had seen in his eyes flared to life. "I was not the one climbing over a ravine for a bloody bonnet."

"You didn't need to do anything. If you had left me alone—"

"If I'd have left you alone, you would have broken your silly neck."

"It's my neck!" she shouted back.

"So it is," he said softly. He reached for her hand, and she shoved him away.

"Leave me alone," she snapped. "You've done quite enough already."

He took a deep breath and then went down on one knee before her. He pulled a small velvet bag from his pocket. "I am offering to marry you, Miss Westlake. Are you refusing?"

Was she? How could she when her sisters' fates were bound up in her own? The moment hung suspended.

"You are not bound to my fate," she pointed out with a scathing glare. Even though he was offering to save her, to save her sisters, she hated him for the need. He should have gone to get the farmer rather than fretting over her. Her death at the side of the road would have been better than this.

"No," he admitted. "I am not. But I offer you marriage just the same."

"How thoughtful," she snapped. "I suppose you think I should thank you." She stood and paced away leaving him kneeling on the floor. She knew that she should not be so harsh, but she wanted him to suffer as she was. That would put distance between them, and she needed distance. She could not say why, but the anger inside of her made her want to push him away, and perhaps even cause pain. From the look in his eyes, she was successful. "Do you think that marriage to you should make me happy? I am not… not happy. I don't love you. I don't want to marry you. You have ruined my life."

"You are a most ungrateful wretch," he snapped. "You are acting like a spoiled child."

"Child?" Her voice rose to a screech. She couldn't believe this horrible, arrogant man was proposing marriage. She wouldn't have him if he were the last man on earth, and she told him so.

"Someone should have taught you manners," he said, rising and taking a step towards her as if he would be the one to do the teaching.

Katherine took a step back with trepidation. She held up a hand, and he stopped, glaring at her, but he stopped. Thank heaven. She felt the fire of a blush fill her face, but this was more than manners. This was her life. It was falling apart before her eyes, and she could not stop it. Besides, he had a nerve speaking of manners when he had repeatedly left the room without a *by your leave.* He was rude and arrogant. Certainly, no gentleman.

"My manners?" she began, but he interrupted her, and she sputtered her indignation. "How dare you interrupt me!"

"You are spouting nonsense, and I will interrupt you as I please," he snapped, and then in a more level voice he continued. "The vicar has assured me that he will act with discretion." Mr. Singer spoke with a cool tone now, but Katherine was anything but cool.

He stood just inches from her. He stated the facts, nothing more. "He has even agreed to a license for this coming Sunday. There will be no need for banns, only the approval of your father, which has already been given."

Father gave permission. Her permission was superfluous. That made her blood boil. What he really meant was that the men had decided, and she had no say in the matter. She was angry but forgave her father instantly. He had no choice, much like herself.

"What else could my father do but agree," she cried, "when the fate of three of his children lies in ruin otherwise?"

The same applied to Katherine, but she did not want to face that reality. Still, what choice did she have? She must suffer alone or destroy her entire family in one fell swoop. There was no choice. She must save them, and in doing so destroy any chance she might have ever had for happiness. She covered her face with her hands and suppressed a sob. She wanted comfort, but there was no one to offer it. The wretched man before her continued in the same monotone voice, ordering her life, while she snatched at crumbs.

He took a step closer as he spoke. "There is nothing that you could want for that I am not able to provide." His voice was even, controlled, as he continued ignoring her angry diatribe. "You shall have everything you desire in addition to, eventually, a title."

He cleared his throat as if he realized that this feature was often the most appealing to a lady.

She shoved him away with indignation.

"Everything," she said the word with disgust. She shoved him again. "Everything except for love. Everything except for hope and happiness. Everything except a gentleman of my choosing." She was speaking so fast that the words began to tumble out without thought, and she did not care. "What good is a title or fine things when it is paired with a life of misery and imprisonment with a man I do not and cannot love?"

He opened his mouth to speak, perhaps to reassure her, perhaps to refute her words, but she continued on without pause.

"I shall marry you, Mr. Singer. I shall marry you because I have no choice." The tears were flowing freely, and she sniffed loudly. She needed a handkerchief, but there was none to hand. Why should she care if she was ladylike at this point? It was clear to all that she was not a lady. She was a ruined woman. She turned away from him. She could not bear to look at him.

"I shall do so for the sake of my sisters… but I want you to know, I wish I had died instead. I wish, with all my heart, that you had left me alone."

She turned on her heel and stormed from the room.

William stood for a few moments with the velvet bag in his hand. In it was his mother's ring… his mother, Kate. He had not even told Katherine that she shared his mother's name. Would that revelation also be a mistake, he wondered? He seemed to be making a bumbling mess of this. She hadn't even met his sisters, Claire and Caroline, had she? Perhaps in passing, but their opinions were important to him. What if they hated her? What if she hated them?

The only thing they had going for them was that he wanted to bed her. It wasn't enough. It bloody well wasn't enough, but it had to be. He folded the velvet around the ring and put it back in his pocket with a sigh.

Perhaps he was going about this all wrong. Perhaps he should have taken her in his arms and kissed her senseless. He was fairly certain she felt the heat too. He had hidden from its power, avoiding her. She had dealt with the attraction by lashing out—but he couldn't be sure. How could one ask a woman something like that? It might be something one could ask a mistress, but certainly not a wife. He ran a hand through his hair and over his unshaven face. He should have had a shave before he approached her.

It didn't matter. The deed would be done on Sunday, and they would have to tolerate one another long enough for him to get an heir. He wouldn't leave Uncle Cecil without an heir. She would have to understand that. Gads.

Surely, she wanted children. All women wanted children, didn't they? It was their lot in life. And then… then, if she wanted her own house, he would see to it, although the thought of letting her go cut him to the core.

He had wanted a marriage of love, like his Aunt Agnes and Uncle Cecil. It was clear that Katherine didn't love him. She could barely stand to look at him. It was clear that she didn't want to marry him, but he could not leave her and her family unprotected. He wouldn't. He could only hope she grew to care for him.

He, on the other hand, somewhere in the middle of the tumble down the hill, had come to a realization. What he felt was much more than lust. He had wanted to save her. He had wanted to cherish her. He had wanted to protect her with his body and comfort her with his spirit. In short, heaven help him, he was in love with her. And she couldn't stand the sight of him.

CHAPTER 11

Mama must have been listening at the door. "Katherine!" her mother's voice called after her, but Katherine ignored her, stomping from the room and slamming the door behind her.

Mrs. Westlake raced after her daughter and grasped her by the arm.

"Katherine, I demand that you return and apologize at once!" Mama held her arm to stop her, but Katherine wrenched it free. "Go apologize before he changes his mind and refuses to have you, you selfish, ungrateful child!"

Katherine scoffed.

"I might not know much about Mr. Singer, but I know this…" she muttered as she pushed her way into her room, "he is too honorable to abandon me now. He knows it is his fault we are in this predicament. He should have just left me alone."

"Kat…" Her mother said, using her father's nickname for her.

"Don't," Katherine warned with tears in her eyes. "If he says that he will marry me, he will, and there's nothing I can do about it. *He and Father have decided everything.*"

She threw herself onto her bed and buried her face in the pillow so that her voice was muffled. "Like it or not, our fates are sealed, and we shall be bound. Though we will both suffer for it."

"Darling," her mother brushed her hair to the side and spoke in a more soothing tone. "Do you not realize what he has offered? We owe him everything and more. You could not hope for a better match. Every eligible lady from here to London has been vying for his attention, and this issue should not prevent him from choosing any one that suits his fancy. Rather than be ruined, this union will increase your sisters' prospects tenfold. You must be grateful to him."

"Should I?" Katherine snapped. "I wish I had fallen into the gully. I wish I had perished. Now, I shall never know love."

"But you shall have a title and fortune even greater than or at least equal to Anne. How can you not be thankful?"

Katherine sighed. "I am thankful." She was, but she also felt defeated. Something died inside of her. She supposed it was hope. He left the room when she was in it. It was clear he could barely stand the sight of her. This was an unmitigated disaster. "I am thankful for what it means for my sisters, Mama, I promise. They should not suffer on my behalf. Yet… I cannot help but feel as if all the light has gone from this world. All hope of my finding love is lost. The man barely spoke to me these last weeks. He cannot even look at me. He hates me, and we shall be bound together forever. I cannot think of a worse fate. Even Mr. Porter didn't hate me."

"My darling child…" Mrs. Westlake pulled her weeping daughter into her arms as she had done when Katherine was a small child, "All hope is not lost. Sometimes we do not choose our own paths, but that does not mean that we must forsake our futures. I am sorry that this is your fate. If I could bear the burden for you, I would, but it could be worse, so much worse, and for that I shall ever be grateful, and so should you."

Katherine cried until there were no tears left to fall. Her head ached with the congestion. "I don't see how it could be worse," Katherine moaned.

"He could be fat," her mother said. "Or old, with bad teeth. Or poor."

"I don't care if he were poor or fat, as long as he loved me," Katherine said. "I wanted to have love."

Her mother drew her into a hug. "I know, dear, but there is no guarantee that he won't come to love you. That is, if you stop being such a shrew and try to cultivate some feelings for the man. He is handsome, is he not?"

Katherine would not let herself admit that she did notice his virile appearance. When they were dancing, his very presence seemed to steal away her very soul. "I'm scared, mama," she admitted in a tiny childlike voice. Her mother held her at arm's length.

"What are you afraid of?"

"I feel so unsettled around him. It's like, I lose myself," her voice was barely a whisper.

Her mother said nothing. She only held her eldest daughter tightly, and after a moment, Katherine mustered what little strength she had and returned to the parlor to make her apology. The announcement was made, and her family joined to offer their congratulations. Mr. Singer was invited to stay for dinner but refused with the claim that he had certain affairs that needed to be arranged before the wedding that would take place in two days' time. He said nothing else to her. He didn't even look at her. He rushed from the room. Katherine was glad to see him go. Once he was out of the room, she felt like she could breathe again.

The rest of the evening was spent in her room standing as if frozen while Anne's lady's maid altered Anne's own dresses to fit Katherine's frame. She cared little for the arrangements of her wedding, a day that she had once looked forward to with much joy and excitement. Whatever her mother decided would be enough. She closed her eyes and refused to listen, lost in her own thoughts. She had two more days as Katherine Westlake, and then her life as she knew it would be over.

CHAPTER 12

The day of the wedding could not have been said to have loomed in the distance. It appeared, with a flash, before Katherine could even begin to prepare herself, much like the lightning that also appeared on her wedding day, along with buckets of rain. Katherine had spent every waking moment being plied with cold compresses, balms, and tinctures so that her skin might lose some of its purplish hue. As she looked in the glass, she realized that her cheek still bore a rather greenish cast. The bump on the back of her head was still tender, but it was covered by her hair. It had been a painful process to get the nettles free of her tresses without hacking the locks short. She had told her mother to cut it, she didn't care, but Mother, Jo, and Georgiana, along Aunt Caroline's maid, took turns plying her hair with oil until the nettles could be brushed free. Katherine had no such respite. Jo had said she had managed to get nettles out of her gelding's mane and tail that were much more stuck with time and dirt. Katherine had no patience for being compared with a horse and told her so. On the day of her wedding, her mother applied a small dusting of powder in secret to remove any last sign of the accident from her face.

Her belongings had been packed and shipped ahead that morning to Winebury Court, which Mr. Singer declared reopened after it had been closed for over a year. Katherine did not know why it had been closed, or why it should be opened now, but she did not argue. No one would listen anyway. There was nothing she could do to change her fate.

The chest of items that had been collected with so much care over the years for her future household had been locked with tears. Each member of her family had added some small gift, but for Katherine, the items had lost their appeal. There was no excitement in the promise of fulfilling the duties as lady of the house.

"Mama," she sniffed, "I shall be so far away. At least Mr. Porter's property was closer." Katherine seemed to have forgotten that at the beginning of the week, she would have been happy to marry Colonel Markey. In fact, the colonel was far from her mind. Mr. Singer, even in his absence, loomed large.

"Nonsense." Mrs. Westlake smiled, for she had come to accept the fortunate union of her child as a blessing in disguise.

"I shall be alone forever," Katherine continued. "I cannot walk to visit, as I could here. You know I won't want to ride. My sisters can meet daily, and I should be lucky to visit once a year."

At this, her mother laughed and reminded her despondent child that Winebury may not be so close for a walk but was only a two day's ride by carriage. "Less with good weather, and less than an hour from your cousin Anne. You shall miss none of the important events," her mother assured her. "There is no reason that we shall not be able to visit. Even so, your sisters do not walk every day. The weather would never permit it. We should be happy that you are to live no further than this short distance. If you had lived in London, it would have been much more out of reach."

Katherine suddenly burst into tears. All of her hopes for London were gone in a puff of smoke. She sobbed miserably, reddening her eyes and making her skin splotchy with her upset.

Mrs. Westlake placed a hand under Katherine's chin and looked into her eyes with steadfast purpose as she patted her daughter's face with a handkerchief.

"Besides, I feel that I must remind you that Colonel Markey might have taken you away from us for much longer periods of time. You might have been in some wild colony for months at a time."

Katherine's heart sank whenever she thought about the colonel. All the potential that she had imagined for a great romance had been dashed in an instant.

"Mama," she whispered. "What if Colonel Markey was my true love?"

"It is best to put those thoughts aside," her mother warned. "They shall do naught but bring you sadness. You shall be a married woman now, and one of impeccable standing. It is time that you put aside your childish thoughts and fulfill your duties to your husband. You must forget the colonel. Nothing can come of it now."

"Do you think I'm childish?" she asked, thinking of Mr. Singer's diatribe.

"Of course not. You are a wonderful young lady, and you will see. This will all work out for the best." Her mother paused a moment and then said. "Try to be civil to the man. He is doing you a great honor."

"Mama—" she began, but her mother held up a finger. "Katherine, if we are to keep the rumors at bay, it is best that strangers think this is a love match."

Katherine stared at her mother, nonplussed. She had to be mad. No one who saw the two of them together could mistake this for a love match. They could barely be in the same room together without sparks flying.

Nonetheless, Katherine had resigned herself to heed her mother's advice, but she could not pretend this was a love match, when love would be forever denied to her. She felt numb. Then, when she donned the gown that was to be worn in her last moments of freedom, upon catching a glimpse of herself in the looking glass, the tears began anew and could not be contained. She had turned into quite the watering pot.

A damp cloth was pressed to her eyes to calm the puffiness that had begun to grow around them, her mother whispered soothing words to no avail, and even though the calico was placed in her arms she could not control the sobs that shook her body. She buried her face in the cat's fur and cried. Finally, her mother called for the physician. Dr. Larkin was on another call, but old Doctor Harding came, and he offered her a glass to relieve her *melancholy*.

Katherine refused the offering, claiming that alcohol would only increase her agitation.

"It is not that which I offer." The elderly gentleman pressed the liquid into her hand. "This will take away your pain," he promised, "at least momentarily. In the end, we must all face our fates."

Katherine sobbed and then looked at the old gentleman over her handkerchief. "What will I feel?" she asked. Though she no longer wanted to feel the hurt of her demise, she did not want to be forced into a false happiness either.

"Nothing," the man promised. "A haziness of nothing."

At his word, Katherine tossed back the drink and waited for its effects to take root. As promised, she felt a very shallow range of emotions. If anything, she merely would have said that she was tired. In a brief while, she found that she looked at the world through a haze of cotton wool.

"It will not last long," she heard the physician tell her mother as he passed from the room. "A few hours, at most. Enough to feel some composure through the ceremony. You don't want to spend your wedding day in tears, Miss Westlake."

CHAPTER 13

Katherine would later recall little of the vows that she made under the knowing grin of the vicar. She was thankful that she was not herself, or she might have felt the horror of the situation. Even more thankful was she that only her father and the Duke of Bramblewood were present to witness. The others would be waiting to celebrate the nuptials in a less formal setting at Sandstowe Hill.

The vicar's pocket jingled happily with coin, and he seemed all too pleased with the predicament. Katherine watched the muscle in her father's jaw twitch as he refrained from chastising the crooked man. Katherine thought if she were a man, she would have laid him out flat with a facer.

No sooner had the sacrament begun than it was over, and Katherine stood staring down upon the parish registry where she had just signed her name as Mrs. William Singer. She had nothing. Not even her own name.

The party, if the solemn group could be called such, returned to the Sandstowe Hill to share an elegant breakfast before they said their farewells to the newlyweds.

Katherine allowed herself to be handed down from the carriage but still could not meet the eye of Mr. Singer, now her husband. As they approached the door, her father and the duke stood aside allowing the couple to make their grand entrance to the small crowd within.

Katherine bore the congratulations of well-wishers.

"My aunt wishes a moment alone," Mr. Singer—her husband—said. "She is waiting."

He spoke with an even tone, but every word increased the dread that was thrumming in Katherine's chest.

She—she is waiting.

How could she face her?

The Countess, Lady Stratton. His Aunt Agnes.

In all of the chaos and upheaval, Katherine had forgotten their relation. Though she had once reveled at the thought of spending more time with the intriguing lady, she now felt quite differently. Lady Stratton had been charming and companionable at the dinner, but Katherine had also sensed that she could be quite stern and unyielding. What must she thing of this situation? What must she think of Katherine, her new niece, who was married to the man she thought of as her only son?

Katherine's stomach turned as she realized that the situation must look very much like a fortune-hungry lady doing her utmost to secure the most valuable match in the area. She wondered how much William had told his Aunt Agnes about the situation and how angry that lady must be.

"How much does she know?" she asked with a trembling voice. She could not bring herself to look up at him for fear that the severity of her punishment would be written on his features. Katherine was certain that the elderly lady only wanted the chance to speak her mind to the ill-suited pair.

"Everything," he replied. "I spared her no detail; nor my uncle."

Katherine's cheeks grew red as she recalled their shocking closeness during the tumble down the hill, and there was the near kiss. Perhaps that part had all been in her mind. It was not as if their faces had drawn close enough to cause suspicion. No, she corrected herself. It had not been a near kiss. It had only been, at best, a look of longing, and likely one that was only felt on her side, but her dress had been scandalously about her thighs. She felt embarrassment fill her face with heat.

"Well…" he continued, "perhaps, not *everything*."

Her flush redoubled, and in that instant, the thoughts of the past moment were brushed aside. His words left little doubt that he was recalling the same instance. Katherine closed her eyes and sent up a silent prayer to the heavens. May heaven help her in her hour of need.

She strengthened her resolve, as if ready to face the gallows.

"I am ready," she murmured. Her voice was quiet but strong. She was prepared for the lecture ahead, or worse, but she had hoped to be friends with the countess. Now, that seemed an impossibility.

"Katherine..." he cleared his throat. "My Lady. There is..."

He had reached a hand out toward her elbow as if to comfort her, but with a quick motion she pulled away. She did not want to hear his advice. She did not need his aid or kindness, and she felt if he touched her, she might shatter like so much glass. She was on her own now, and alone she would face this matter.

Without allowing him to continue, she straightened her spine, brushed passed the gentleman, and let herself into the room. It was warmer than she had expected, as if the fire had been stoked for hours and the lady had been waiting the entire time they were at the ceremony. She supposed that most elderly people tended to like the room warm, but the wait and the stifling heat could have done little to soften the countess' anger, Katherine worried.

The sound of the door brought Lady Stratton to her feet from the plush armchair in which she had been seated.

For a long moment, the two females stared at each other. With each passing second Katherine's trepidation grew. The countess' features were severe and difficult to read.

Then, she moved.

Lady Stratton's arms swung open, and she beckoned with wordless compassion.

Katherine hesitated, afraid that she had misread the gesture.

"Come, child," Lady Stratton called.

Katherine raced across the room and flung herself into the safety of the embrace. She had never expected a warm welcome from the woman whose erstwhile son had been likewise forced to abandon his future. Katherine burrowed into the motherly embrace, allowing her hair to be stroked and soft words to be whispered to her damaged soul.

The tears that she had been fighting fell without pause and dampened both gowns. Soon, she was gasping for breath and shuddering, not making any attempt to disguise her dismay. Like a child, she clung to the comfort, praying that it could all be made right but knowing that it could not be so.

"I know that it must feel like the end of the world." Lady Stratton wiped the tears from the sad bride's cheeks. "But sometimes Fate takes a hand for a reason. Some good may come of it yet."

Katherine snorted with disbelief. "No good can come of this. He thinks me a social climber. He won't even look at me. He hates me."

"Perhaps not," Lady Stratton agreed. "Only time will tell." A long silence passed as she allowed Katherine to cry her fill. When the sobs had subsided, she wiped Katherine's face once more, straightened the folds of her gown, and said, “I know William better than anyone, certainly better than you do.”

That was true, much to her dismay.

“He is not the kind to hold a grudge, no matter what he may think now.” She sighed and smiled at Katherine, as if she was happy with the union. “Welcome to the family, from both my husband and I,” she said. “Cecil wanted to greet with you too, but I thought it was too soon. He can be formidable, you know, and you must be feeling a bit lost.”

“A bit, yes,” Katherine replied.

“Sit down.” Katherine sat.

The countess looked at her directly.

“Doctor Harding tells me he gave you a tincture. Was the prospect of marrying my nephew so intimidating?”

A blush rising. For the first time, she felt the lady’s irritation. No wonder. No one with a mother’s love would accept a wife who had to be drugged to endure him.

Katherine flushed fully with embarrassment. “I was afraid I would cry though the whole ceremony. I—” Suddenly, all her fears broke loose and she opened up to this kind women. “It was all happening so fast, and I don’t know him.” Her voice dropped to a whisper as she said,” I’m scared. My whole future rests in his hands.”

“I understand.” The countess’ face softened. She folded her hands in her lap and looked at them for a moment. They were old hands, wrinkled and lined with blue veins and knobby knuckles. "We don't always see the world clearly when we are young. Sometimes the things that frighten us most are the very things we need. I believe you are what William needs. I thought it so when we spoke at such great length. I do not know if he is what you need, but I hope it is so. Open your heart to the possibility, please, Katherine. My husband and I have loved one another through many childless years. We have loved each other when there was nothing else. We have loved William, but we are old, and when we are gone, William only has his two young sisters. He will need you. Give him a chance to prove himself."

"I will try," Katherine promised.

"Let us go and greet our guests, then," the countess said. "You may call me Aunt Agnes."

"Thank you," Katherine said, but the name felt far too familiar for a woman she had only met.

CHAPTER 14

Katherine was shaking. Not from the cold, although the rain began again in earnest, but rather, the medicine was beginning to wear off, and she was finally beginning to realize that she was only hours away from embarking upon a monumental journey to a strange town and a strange home, with a strange man of which she knew next to nothing.

"Shall we?" Mr. Singer took a deep breath and offered his arm as he looked down at his wife.

She bristled.

Katherine wondered how she could have ever wished that he would kiss her. It was those sorts of reprehensible thoughts that had gotten her into this situation, she was sure. She didn't want to touch him. She had managed the service and the wedding breakfast in a haze, but now, she drew more and more into herself. She just wanted to be left alone. The tincture that had brought solace earlier in the evening now left a hollow feeling within her.

"All right," he conceded. "Then, you tell me how to proceed."

She bit her lip as she contemplated their course of action. His eyes followed the motion and a hint of blush on his neck revealed his thoughts. Her narrowed glare in response revealed exactly what she thought about the prospect of their first kiss.

"Let's just get through this, shall we?" With a sigh, she slipped her hand onto the bend of his elbow. He had been right. It would be best if they could at least pretend to tolerate each other. At least, that would satisfy her mother and father for the time being.

"Uh, Miss…" he hesitated. "Mrs…" He stared at her for a moment, nonplussed. "What am I to call you?"

She remembered how she had shouted at him for the familiar use of her name on the night of their engagement. Today, she realized he had been calling her *his bride.* That would not do long term.

She thought for a long while. Although he was now her husband, it seemed strange to have her Christian name upon his lips, as she had imagined it would be spoken by the man who was meant to hold her heart. She couldn't give him her name when she could not give him her heart.

"Anything but Katherine," she said with a nod.

A small part of her wanted to let her husband know that she understood that this must be very difficult for him as well, but the predominant portion of her just wanted to be left alone. Maybe in time, they could grow to be tolerant companions, but she doubted it. How could she, when this union represented everything that she had wished to avoid and denied access to all the love that she had wished to attain. "Very well, *my dear*," he said.

She cringed.

"What shall I call you?" she asked in return.

He shrugged as if he no longer cared. "Whatever you like." The words were flat and unfeeling. Then, he placed his hand upon the door and pushed it open, declaring that there was nothing more left to be said between them.

❧

KATHERINE WAS STUNNED THAT THE FEAST AND CAKE HAD been prepared with such care on so little notice. If she had not felt as if her heart had turned to stone, she might have enjoyed the party. Those that she loved most were present, the nearest and dearest of her family and friends.

When Jo embraced her sister and offered a heartfelt congratulations, Katherine was forced to fight back tears.

"I am sorry," Katherine spoke past the lump in her throat.

"I'm sure it will be all right," Jo said, as much to convince herself as her sister. "He was very attentive when you were hurt. He seems… kind."

Katherine fought back tears. She would not cry again. What was done was done. She was married now. There was no turning back.

"No," Anne shook her head. "This is an incredible injustice, and the vicar should be ashamed to force such a matter when the truth was plain as day."

"Hush," Katherine scolded. "It will do no good to speak poorly of one in his position. There is nothing to be done now. The path is set."

"I wish there were something that could be done," Anne fumed. "It is not official until the consummation." Anne's eyes grew wide with her blunder. The expression was mirrored on her younger sister's face as Katherine was reminded of the impending night ahead. "Oh, Kat, forgive me," Anne said.

"There is no escaping it," Katherine said with false confidence. Her sister saw through the act but was kind enough not to comment. She suddenly missed Lucy, who was still at home. A home that would no longer be hers.

Harry found her and squeezed her shoulder. "He's a good man, Kat. Give him time. You know, he's been forced into this too."

She nodded but could not really feel any compassion for his fate. She could feel nothing at all, but perhaps that was the tincture doing its work.

The ladies returned to the table and joined the others. Now, more than ever, Katherine avoided looking at her husband. She picked at the meal, though her favorite had been prepared with the intention of her pleasure. There was conversation and laughter, and although Katherine often retreated into her own thoughts, she now had no dreams of a beautiful wedding to sustain her. Her wedding was over, and it was awful. The marriage was to begin, and she suspected it would be just as awful.

The wedding night loomed in her mind as the party atmosphere wound down. The Duke and Duchess of Bramblewood had gone home, as had Anne and Edmund, Anne complaining of exhaustion and holding her aunt's slippers most scandalously.

"My feet are killing me," she confessed while Katherine's mother tut-tutted.

"A woman in your condition should not be dancing all night."

Only a few guests, her immediate family, and those who lived at Sandstowe Hill remained.

PART III

CHAPTER 15

When the final carriage was called and the gifts secured for the journey, Katherine felt a sudden wave of panic that she should never go home again. It was only moments before she would be torn from her parents and her sisters and the only life that she had ever known. She had only moments before she would be forced to join her husband outside. His whim would determine her fate.

The thought had her racing up the staircase for one final farewell with Patches, who would be forced to sleep alone for the first time in her short life.

The calico, who was miffed at being locked in the room during the wedding, leapt into her arms and curled herself against her. She had spent the recent days at her side without fail as if she had known that she had needed her constant presence for comfort. Katherine stroked the cat's fur and reminded her to be good, eat her food, and stay out from under the housekeeper's feet.

"Oh, my sweet girl," she muttered, and she pressed her face into her plush fur. "What shall I do without you?"

"Bring her."

Katherine was startled at the sound of the male voice behind her. She had not heard anyone follow her up the stairs, and even if she had, the face that looked down upon her was the last that she would have expected.

William leaned against the banister of the landing with a casual air that was in contrast with the tension of the day. His hair was mussed as if he had run his hands through it too many times or gotten caught in a gale-force wind.

"I—," Katherine shook her head while still clinging to the cat. "Mama said that she must remain."

It was true that her mother had told her that the cat was to stay at the Abbey. *Mr. Singer is already taking in one stray; we needn't make the situation worse by doubling the number,* she had told her daughter as her tears had dampened the poor animal's fur.

"To whom does she belong?" Mr. Singer asked, as if the matter were that simple.

"We all love her dearly," she replied.

"Then she belongs to all?"

"No," Katherine admitted. "Father gave her to m-me at Christmas two last." She stumbled over her words as she fought to hold back her tears. She would not cry in front of her new husband, not again.

"Someone had flung the poor creature into the ditch at the side of the North Road and apparently continued on their way. She was barely old enough to survive without her mother, and I fed her milk and bread. She was covered with road grime and slush. It was too cold for her in the barn, and once we washed and dried her by the fire—well, we could not turn her out again, could we?"

"I understand somewhat about rescuing damsels from roadside gullies," he said dryly. His lips quirked into a slight smile, perhaps the first she had seen, and Katherine offered a watery smile in return.

He offered a hand to help her from her seat on the floor, "If your mother allows, we shall take the beast to Winebury."

Katherine tucked the cat under one arm and allowed the gentleman to pull her to her feet.

"Why?" she asked when they were standing no more than an inch apart. He reached forward and scratched the cat between the ears. The traitor had the gall to purr.

"If you have someone familiar at Winebury, perhaps it will feel more like home."

Before she could reply, he turned and descended the staircase. Katherine was left standing there with her mouth open and a squirming cat in her arms. She placed her spare arm under its paws, and the feline settled in more comfortably.

A short while later, the trio were settled into the carriage with the cat curled in a basket between the feet of the facing couple. When they were out of sight of the manor, she claimed fatigue and pretended to sleep.

The truth was that she was exhausted, but sleep was the furthest thing from her mind. Her mind raced behind her closed lids, but she refused to open them for fear of having to make conversation with her husband. She was nervous enough without him trying to make her more comfortable with idle conversation or explanation of what to expect at Winebury.

Her mind fretted over the future. Everything from the next few hours to the next few decades was a great unknown to Katherine. In all of her daydreaming, she had never prepared herself for such a situation. Only happiness and perfection had waited in the wings of her imagination. Now, she had neither, and the prospect was enough to send her reeling.

After what seemed like days of driving, but was only hours, Mr. Singer cleared his throat to get her attention.

She looked up to see Patches contentedly in his arms. At some point, he had taken the cat from her basket, which proved to Katherine she must have fallen asleep in truth. The traitorous beast was purring as he scratched her ears.

"We have been on the grounds for nearly half an hour," he informed her. "I did not wake you because it is too dark to see much past the windows, but I did ask the servants to light the estate so that you might look upon it for yourself as we approach."

Katherine peered across the darkened carriage. The knowing half-grin on his face revealed that he had no illusions about her feigned rest. Either way, she was pleased that he had allowed the ruse.

She realized that he had already pulled open the curtains so that she might look out at the starlit night.

The reflections of the celestial lights rebounded off of the smooth waters of a wide lake. Pine trees lined the edge of the lane and the lake. Katherine imagined dipping her toes in the cool waters during the summer, and perhaps in winter there would be skating across its surface. Beyond the lake was a magnificent house.

She gasped as she realized what she was looking at. It was truly splendid. She had thought that Sandstowe Hill was beautiful, but this was perfection.

"It was my mother's estate," he said. "Her name was also Katherine. Everyone called her Kate."

"You should not call me Kate," she blurted.

"I should think not," he replied. She realized he was smiling; the shine of his teeth gleamed under the moonlight. He was quite handsome when he was not scowling at her, angry at her. He seemed utterly relaxed holding her sleeping cat, his long legs stretched out before him.

CHAPTER 16

Katherine fixed her eyes ahead at the massive building that would be her home.

On the far side of the lake sat the enormous estate. Lit candles were in every window. She had known that the grounds would be massive, she had been told to expect as much, but she had not been prepared for the sheer magnificence of the residence. It was nearly as massive as Sandstowe Hill, which she knew was the entailed house. In time, this man would own both.

The edifice stood in the distance, a beacon in the night, in some ways, even greater than Bramblewood, for that place was still recovering from years of ruin. If she had been less afraid, she would have been spellbound. Katherine shifted her position so that she might better look out at the house as they circled the lake. The nearer they drew, the more detail she was able to make out. Shimmering lights divided into individual windows. The sculpted rails of the porch, staircase, and drive were lined with flickering candles that welcomed the couple with open arms.

Katherine wished she were not arriving under such circumstances. She felt undeserving of such a regal welcome.

"It's beautiful," she whispered. "Even if I tried, I could not deny that."

"Yes," he replied, but the word was halfhearted, as if he were not at all thrilled to be home. Or, she thought, perhaps it was that he was not at all thrilled about the company.

She could not help but think that, under different circumstances of course, the scene would be romantic. The thought caused her to blush, and she was grateful for the cover of darkness. The last thing that she wanted to think about when it came to Mr. Singer was romance. In fact, the fast-approaching threat of the wedding night brought Katherine nothing but anxiety and apprehension. She did not know this man, and yet she would have to give him license to her body. The thought brought a trembling to her lip. In fact, she thought, her whole body was shaking. Perhaps it was the tincture wearing off. She could not imagine what else would make her tremble so.

What little happiness she had gleaned from the view dissipated with each minute that brought them nearer to their destination. By the time that the carriage stopped at the base of the elegant, curved staircase which led up to the main entrance, she was beside herself with anxiety.

Mr. Singer made certain that the sleeping cat was secure in the basket before he preceded her from the carriage. He had tucked the basket under one arm and then offered the opposing hand to steady her descent. She stared at his hand for a long while, wondering if she could decline the service without causing an affront, or worse, falling on her face as she tried to find the step out of the carriage unassisted. The step was unaccountably small, and it was nearly dark. She could not see it beneath her skirt. With a sigh, she gave in to propriety and allowed him to help her to the ground.

Katherine distanced herself as soon as both feet were secure upon the ground. She held her hands out for the basket, but William shook his head and swung one arm wide to gesture that she should walk before him. A lump formed in her throat, and she had the foreboding thought that she was about to walk into a trap.

The house was silent despite the fact that the flicker of flame from lamps and candles gleamed from every available surface. Katherine could see their dancing forms in the edges of her vision, but she kept her eyes solely focused on the intricate tile pattern of the entrance hall. They deposited their cloaks in a tall cabinet that was hidden beside the door. Though the air was warm, she continued to shiver. She wondered why no servants greeted them.

She followed Mr. Singer down the passage until he paused in front of a double set of doors. He turned to face her and gave her Patches' basket. He put his hand on the knob but did not enter.

"There is some cold venison. Cheese and bread. I brought it from Sandstowe. Are you hungry?"

She shook her head.

"I noticed you did not eat much," he said, "after the… ceremony."

How could she eat? She wondered. She would be likely to lose the contents of her stomach. Even now, it was roiling with anxiety. She gripped Patches' basket with both hands. "I'm not hungry," she blurted.

"Then, come," he said.

She froze.

Mr. Singer held the door open so that she might pass into the hallway, then led her up the winding staircase to the second level. He carried himself with confidence, a firm and sure nature that Katherine had found to be constant. She wondered how he could be calm at such a moment and attempted to school her features and movements to mirror those of her husband.

Husband.

The word felt foreign and hollow, decayed, as it rolled around in her gut. Never, in all her romantic musings, had she imagined her wedding day and night thus. It was true that she might have pictured a gentleman who may have resembled Mr. Singer, a tall, handsome fellow with impeccable breeding, roguish good looks, and a character above reproach. Those details brought her no joy now. Instead, his perfection irritated her. While many women would swoon at the sight of him, yearn to hear him call her *My Lady*, Katherine was determined to hate him.

Not the man personally—he had shown her nothing but kindness—but the situation. The rage and frustration that burned inside of her from that wrong was beyond repair, and she couldn't seem to squelch it. Instead, she fed that anger.

Anger was better than the alternative, stark terror. She would never look at her life, at the promise of love, the same again. Perhaps her reputation had been repaired, but her heart had not. That organ would remain as it were… ruined forever.

Mr. Singer came to a halt in front of a wide door that was carved with an intricate woodland scene. It was beautiful craftsmanship, and she wondered if all of the doors on this level had been made with such care.

He turned to face her but did not enter. If her heart beat any louder, she would need to worry that he could hear its rhythm outside of her body.

Both of them stood uncertainly on the threshold. Wasn't he supposed to carry her over it as a sign of good luck? Oh please, in heaven's name, she thought. Don't.

"I just want to go to bed," she blurted, and turned a hot shade of scarlet as she put her hand over her mouth. Patches in the basket was upended with her sudden movement and dropped to the floor with typical catlike grace.

Katherine had no grace. She turned and yanked on the door, but it was heavier than she thought it was. She only managed to open it a crack. Patches slipped through with ease. Then, she realized that she would never be able to undo the buttons that spanned the length of her spine. She suppressed a sob.

Perhaps she should have accepted the offer of food just to prolong the inevitable. Now, there was nothing to be done but resign herself to her fate. Of all her suffering, this would be the worst.

He put his hand on the door, pushing it closed momentarily. When he opened it again, he gave her pause. "These will be your chambers," he informed her. "I shall call Mrs. Davenport to help you to…" Mr. Singer's ears flushed and then he turned and left her standing in the frigid wave of her renewed panic. This was the worst punishment by far.

"Wait!"

He paused at her word but did not turn around.

"I have given the entire staff the evening off except for Mrs. Davenport. She was my mother's maid," he said. "She can help you. I will send her to you."

Katherine was glad for the shadows of the hall that disguised her blush. Had he hoped that this gesture of magnanimity would ease her fears? Certainly, there was nothing that could be done to alleviate that burden.

Except…

"I shall leave you here, at your chamber door." Mr. Singer gave a shallow bow and moved to leave her, but she called him back.

"I do not understand." She spoke the words slowly as if the answer might find itself. "These are MY chambers? Alone?"

He released a deep breath.

"I thought you would prefer it this way." He nodded. "I have emptied the estate of watchful eyes for the night so that there can be no rumors as to the validity of the union. Furthermore, my staff is well-trained in the art of discretion. They will not question our separate rooms. Most of our station have their privacy. There is a private door which separates the bedrooms, of course, and I will not put a lock on that door, but I assure you, I will not accost you. You have my word."

Katherine could not believe what he was saying..

"I…" She shook her head in shock. "I do not know how to thank you, Mr. Singer."

He reached one hand behind his head and rubbed the back of his neck.

"You could start by calling me William," he offered.

Katherine pursed her lips. It went against the grain. It would be much easier for her to keep the gentleman at a distance if she could avoid any informality between them. She started to shake her head.

"Hear me out." He spread his hands open. "We can live our separate lives in private if that is what you desire, but it cannot be done when others are present."

She did not understand and said so.

"Only a handful of people know the truth outside of our immediate families," he continued. "Everyone else will assume that we married because we were madly in love. If we truly want to avoid rumors, it would be best to encourage that perception. This means that there will be times that you will have to pretend to do more than loathe this arrangement. You will have to pretend to be happy. Tomorrow will be one of those days."

Katherine chewed her lower lip as she considered the truth of his words. He was right in the assumption that if she revealed overt distaste for her husband and marriage, others would begin to search for answers.

"I see," she muttered.

He handed her the cat's empty basket and began to walk away, leaving her to consider his words for the evening.

"William," she called after him when he stopped at a door at the far end of the hall.

He turned but did not speak.

"You may call me Katherine," she added, "but only when necessary."

Her point was clear. She would play along, but it would not soften her icy demeanor.

He nodded and entered his rooms which were, troublingly, right next door. Katherine did the same, searching for the one creature in this godforsaken place that could comfort her. The cat had climbed on the bed and chirped at the sight of her. Katherine's posture softened.

"It is just us now, my dear Patches," she said as she scratched the animal behind the ears.

With a grimace, Katherine noted that Patches seemed quite at leisure in her new home.

"Traitor," she whispered as set about getting herself ready for bed. She began pulling pins from her hair.

There was a tap on the door, and for a moment she froze, brush in hand. "Who is it?" she asked after a moment.

"Mrs. Davenport," came the reply, and she remembered that Mr. Singer had said that he would send a maid to help her. She felt slightly less animosity towards the man as the woman entered and curtseyed. She had a bottle of wine in her hands.

"A gift from your cousin, Anne," she said. "The young master said I should bring it here."

"Thank you," Katherine said softly.

The woman was elderly, but there was a softness about her that gave her an approachable appearance. "Let's get you ready for bed, shall we?" she asked, sitting the open wine bottle and two glasses on the nightstand. Two glasses, Katherine thought, but he had given her his word. She would have her peace, at least for tonight. Nonetheless, her eyes strayed to the door, beyond which slept her husband.

Katherine turned to let the maid unbutton the dress. She had a reprieve, but eventually, she realized, it would be her husband's hands on her buttons.

CHAPTER 17

The new day dawned like a phoenix rising from the embers of the tragedy that was her wedding day. The sun was well high in the sky before Katherine dragged herself from her sleep. She had tossed and turned most of the night, only falling asleep at dawn. Now with the morning, she was uncertain what to do in this new and strange house. Worse, she didn't want to bump into Mr. Singer, or any of the servants for that matter. Surely, they would be returned by now. A house this size needed servants to run it.

However, Katherine did at last ring the bell. She became more acquainted with her new maid and liked her more than she did the night before. Ruby Davenport was a pleasant older woman with a gentle touch and clear love for animals. They got on at once.

She chatted on about her previous lady, Kate, who Katherine knew was Mr. Singer's mother. At first, Katherine thought the running commentary would bother

her, but then she realized she wanted to know something about the man to whom she was now tied and asking him seemed out of the question. The insight the old abigail had was helpful indeed.

By the time Katherine had donned the lavender gown with a clean white inlay and three-quarter length sleeves, she was famished. Mr. Singer was right. She had barely eaten at the wedding feast, and it was probably midday at this point.

She was about to leave the maid to attend to the cat. Patches had accepted the bowl of cream as a peace offering and was now curled in comfort at the maid's feet as she stitched a frayed edge on one of Katherine's dresses.

"Although," the maid reflected, "Mr. Singer will likely buy new when you go to London.

"London?" Katherine said. She turned to look at the maid.

"Why yes, when the two young misses come out, likely next year, although Claire loves her horses so much, I don't think she will mind waiting until Caroline is older, if that is what the young master decides."

Yes, Katherine thought. Her husband would decide. Still… London.

"How old are the girls?" Katherine asked. She had met them briefly at the wedding breakfast, but in all truth, she had not given them a thought. She was so distraught that she had not thought of much of anything yesterday.

"Clare is fifteen, and Caroline will soon be thirteen, so there is certainly time to plan a Season."

She realized she should have been more attentive to the girls. There was no repeating a first meeting or making a better first impression, but she would be more cordial from this point forward. With that thought, she asked the maid for directions and headed downstairs to break her fast.

THE HALL WAS BRIGHTENED BY TWO ENORMOUS WINDOWS at either end that let the sunlight flow throughout. It was clear that it was well past morning. Katherine realized that she had hardly taken in any detail of the place upon her arrival, too focused had her attention been inward to be observant of the finery. They were located in one of two wings that flanked the main portion of the estate. If the second floor of the other wing was identical, which she assumed it to be, then it was very like that Winebury could house dozens of guests without causing any intrusion on the family quarters. She imagined that at one time this entire floor might have been filled with relatives of the presiding Lord of estate. Now, it seemed empty. She wasn't even sure if any of the servants were available. Mr. Singer had said he gave most of them the night off, but she assumed someone was about now.

At the base of the stairs, she was met by a manservant who ushered her to an elegant breakfast hall that was almost unbearably bright. She wasn't sure if he was a footman or the butler. She had so much to learn. Light entered the room from two full walls of windows, and the sunlight was only tempered by a sheer set of curtains that flowed from the ceiling and pooled on the floor. Katherine thought marginally that she hoped Patches would not decide to climb the things.

"Good afternoon," Lady Stratton's perky voice greeted her.

"Lady Stratton," she said. "I did not know you were here."

"My husband and I came earlier this morning to help with the reception this afternoon. Come, break your fast, although it is nearly time for an early tea, but I suppose that is to be expected on the day after one's wedding."

Katherine blushed with the insinuation.

"You shall soon learn that we have the best cooks in the county," Lady Stratton continued. "They have been laboring all morning."

"Is your husband here too?" Katherine asked, looking around for the earl. It felt strange to be so out of sorts in what should be her own home, but in some respect, she was relieved to find Lady Stratton here. She was equally relieved that Mr. Singer was not.

"Oh, Cecil is off with William, who had some business to attend this morning," the woman informed her without prompt. "As you know, my nephew was away for longer than he had intended, and he had not had the opportunity to leave instruction for such a departure."

Katherine took her seat to the lady's left and chose a selection of fruits, cheese, and meats to sustain her. The plate was well stocked considering that the house was closed just days ago. The servants must have been working around the clock before the wedding.

"Is there anything else that you would care for, My Lady?" A servant bowed so low that his face nearly touched the tray that was balanced with ease on his hand.

Katherine was busy placing cheese beside a small cracker when she heard a cough that gained her attention.

"I am sorry, Mrs. Singer," the man continued, "but is there anything else you would have from the kitchens?"

Her hand flew to her breast as she realized that he was addressing her.

"OH, I did not mean to be rude." She grimaced. "Forgive me. Please, call me Katherine."

"As you wish, Mrs. Singer," he replied with perfect ease. "Would you care for an egg? Our hens lay every morning."

Lady Stratton's mouth was pinched as if she were holding back laughter. She was amused at Katherine's blunder and the servant's smooth etiquette. Katherine accepted a boiled egg just so that she would have a moment to recover before the man returned.

"Oh dear," she sighed when she was alone with the Lady Stratton. At that, the woman chuckled.

"You are the very opposite of everything that I had expected in a lady for William," she chortled, "and I am beside myself with pleasure!"

Katherine knew that the Lady had meant to offer a compliment, but she wondered how she was so unlike a lady that Mr. Singer would be expected to wed. She was not ill-bred nor poor. She was learned, accomplished, and charitable.

"What had you expected?" she asked when she could not see why she was so devoid of the projected characteristics of a lady.

Lady Stratton waved one hand as she broke a piece from a fruit which must have been very expensive to acquire at this time of the year since most of the local fruits wouldn't come to harvest for several months yet. Katherine wasn't sure what it was. It was too small to be an orange, surely, yet it smelled like an orange.

"I had prepared myself for a stuffy ingrate with no sense of humor and a call only for the title," the Lady explained. "A woman whose sole desire was to marry well, without a care for William's sensibilities." Lady Statton popped a segment of the fruit into her mouth.

Katherine cleared her throat.

"My arrival is not so different," she argued with a gentle tone. "Mr. Singer is still set in a marriage in which function is set well over emotion." She made sure that there were no ears in the room to overhear. "We do not love each other."

"Oh, I know. So, you said." Lady Stratton sighed as if it were no matter. "I am sorry for your loss. I know that you were attached to that colonel."

"Not formally," Katherine shook her head. "It is no matter now. I must try to make the best of things."

"Well," Lady Stratton covered Katherine's hand with her own, "I think that is a wise choice, and I am glad to have you. Are we allowed to celebrate that?"

Katherine could not refuse a slight smile. She nodded. This small blessing was more than she might have hoped for. She did enjoy the elder Lady's company. That could not be denied.

The Ladies passed the hour in conversation. Katherine was almost able to forget that she was anything other than a visitor until Mr. Singer and Lord Stratton made their appearance.

Their greetings could not have been more different. Lord Stratton went straight to the countess and kissed her cheek, but the greeting was warm, and Katherine felt that if she had not been there, the kiss would have landed on the lady's lips. Indeed, regardless to their presence, the earl may have kissed his wife's lips, but she turned her head with propriety, even as her eyes sparkled. This somehow seemed like a game they played. He trying to steal a kiss, and she being coy.

Mr. Singer offered her no such greeting, and she told herself that was surely for the best. Any physical contact with the man seemed to make her fall completely out of sorts.

"We must adjourn to the East Hall," Mr. Singer said by way of greeting. He gave her a small and proper bow. "The guests shall begin arriving soon."

"Guests?" said Katherine. Her eyes widened with fear.

"Do not worry, my dear." Lady Stratton patted Katherine's arm and tweaked her cheek. "It is only a small reception of thirty or so. It will be easy to lose yourself in the distraction of introductions. The time shall pass before you know it, and I am here to help you with the hostess duties."

Lady Stratton winked and then hurried away to refresh herself before the arrivals. Her husband went with her. Katherine was left standing beside her own husband, a stranger, and his piercing grey eyes. She wanted to shift under his gaze but refused to reveal that he made her uncomfortable. It was as if he could see her very thoughts, and that was unnerving.

"Shall we practice?" He offered an arm, and she cursed the blush that rose to her cheeks.

She placed her hand at his elbow and stood beside him with her face turned away from his gaze.

"Excellent," he laughed. "A shy, blushing bride will be just what everyone will be expecting."

Her head snapped to face him, and her eyes drew together in confusion. She wanted to pull away in anger. He laid a hand atop hers, causing her to stay.

How dare he call her discomfort into focus! Then, she realized that most brides are bashful following the fateful night of their wedding. Her reserve and discomfort would suit the act well, for the time being.

She released a slow breath to remind herself that they were in this together. Neither she nor William had to enjoy the situation, but they were too deep into the act to allow the dishonor to be made public now. She allowed herself to be led to the East Hall, a wide room that was set to accommodate the informal meeting. One half of the room was arranged into clusters of sofas and chairs, while the other offered tables of food and drink so that the guests could eat at their leisure.

"Aunt Agnes thought this would be best," he explained. "But there is still time to change things if you do not like it. We shall not have to be interrogated at a long table, rather we can mingle throughout the group and devote only a brief amount of time to each guest."

Katherine nodded as she took in the elegant furniture and plush rugs. This residence was grander than any place she had ever set foot in, outside of London's High-Society at the height of the Season.

"This will do nicely," she agreed.

"Then, I will allow you to dress for dinner," he said. "Shall I escort you to your room?"

"Yes, please," she answered. She was not certain she could find it again in the twists and turns of the estate, but she was determined that she would learn her way around the house."

He left her at her door with a bow. Mrs. Davenport was no where in sight, nor was Patches, but a ring of the bell brought them both.

CHAPTER 18

Later that evening, Katherine and Mr. Singer settled themselves at the far end of the room near the hearth so that they might appear from afar like two young lovers enraptured with their private conversation. In truth, they were discussing the business that William had attended to that morn. She asked him about the business because she felt incapable of holding a conversation, she was so muddled. By asking him to explain, he could speak, and she could retreat into her thoughts.

Her palms were sweating in her gloves, and she had the inclination to wipe them on her dress, but of course, that was silly. She attended the conversation more than usual. Although she was not at all versed in farming techniques and even less in shepherding husbandry. She did, however, care for the people of Northwick. Mr. Singer informed her that all was well with the farmers, but the stable boy had discovered a crack in the hoof of one horse that would leave the animal unable to pull the carriages for some time.

Guests began to spill into the room, followed in prompt fashion by Lady Stratton, until the sound of voices greeting one another was too much for Katherine to process.

She did her best to tie faces to names but was certain that she would not remember more than a handful of guests by the end of the day.

"Take a breath." Mr. Singer pulled her close and spoke into her ear under the guise of a romantic whisper. "You are as rigid as a maypole, and you are trembling."

"Perhaps if you would stop making our first meeting sound so romantic, I would not have to make such an act," she replied with a forced smile.

"How else would you explain the need for a license, other than our unbearable love and determination?" He wrapped one dark curl around his finger, pulled it straight, and then released it to spring back into form. "Besides, a waltz at your newly married cousin's home sounds just the place to find romance and adventure."

She rolled her eyes in a most unladylike fashion but covered the act with a hearty laugh.

"Oh, William," she giggled. "You are too comical." He pulled her close and kept her at his side for most of the event, but a short while later, she found herself separated from the protection of her husband. For, she realized, his presence had been a shelter against the circling vultures of the room. While most of the guests seemed overcome with joy at the surprise union, some were disappointed that a young bachelor was no longer free.

There was one who it was clear felt more than a slight dismay.

Lady Isobel DeGent, daughter of a local baron, had waited to catch Katherine alone at the punch before she dove in for the kill.

"Well…" The willowy creature with strawberry blonde tresses looked down her perfectly shaped nose and smiled at Katherine. "Aren't you a breath of fresh air?" The words were laden with malice.

"I'm sorry?" Katherine replied with as even a tone as possible. Lady DeGent had been shooting covert glares her way all afternoon, only disguising her hatred when others might fall witness. Then, she would transform into a dainty creature of smiles and compliments, fawning over the gentleman as if Katherine were not nearby. Katherine was not jealous but annoyed at the woman's overt behavior against a stranger.

"It is only that it is clear that you are not from the neighborhood," said Lady DeGent. "We were quite settled in our ways before you arrived. What a relief that you have managed to secure Lord William's heart and… shake things up." The sarcasm was thick.

"Mr. Singer?" Katherine said. "He is not a lord."

"Not yet perhaps, but I venture you knew that." Although her tone was honeyed, and her delivery executed so as to be above reproach, her eyes told another tale.

Katherine wondered who this woman was to Mr. Singer. Green eyes flashed at Katherine, and the words, although delivered under the guise of kindness, revealed the spiteful intent within.

Katherine raised a finger to her lips and hummed as if she were thinking.

"I am afraid that my dear William has never mentioned you." Her opponent turned rigid at the rebuttal. "Pray, remind me? How is that you are related to *our family*?"

Katherine's choice of words did not go unnoticed, and Lady Isobel clenched her fists and teeth as if very near a tantrum.

"Listen here, you little minx." Lady DeGent leaned in close so that there could be no mistaking her words. "I was meant to be his wife and the next countess, not some raven-haired temptress without even a title. Long before you were ever a thought, I was there. When his mother took ill, I was there for William."

"William?" Katherine repeated. "You are vulgarly forward."

"I will not be thrust aside." Her voice was low, and Katherine knew that the Lady was skilled enough to deny all recollection of this conversation. Her sweet demeanor had blinded all to her lethal intent.

"I am sorry," Katherine said with the same honeyed tone, "but William and I are married." The taste of William's given name felt strangely good on her tongue. "You have already been thrust aside."

"I do not know what you did to ensnare Lord William, but I will get to the bottom of it. Do not get comfortable in your new position. You are not the one that belongs."

She stormed away before Katherine could reply.

Katherine was still standing there, stirring the punch with indignant bursts, when Lady Stratton appeared at her side.

"She is precious. Is she not?"

Katherine did not want to speak poorly of an honored guest. Isobel had said she was there when William's mother passed on. She must have long ago ingratiated herself with the family.

"She was very welcoming," Katherine lied.

Lady Stratton released a burst of laughter. "Oh, I doubt that," she said. One look told Katherine that the lady was not fooled by Lady DeGent's pleasantries. "She has been trying to get her hands on my nephew for years. I think she might have succeeded just after Kate died, but the foursome took her in hand."

"The foursome?" Katherine repeated.

"Anne and Edmund and Emily and Alex."

Anne and Edmund, she knew, of course. Yes, Anne would have gone toe to toe with the woman, she was sure, but Emily and Alex? "Emily and Alex," she said. "I don't believe I know them."

"Oh, you do. William said he introduced you. The Duke and Duchess of Bramblewood. I have known them both since they were in their nappies. I can't think of Alex as a duke, although he does deserve my respect in every way. His mother was my dearest friend, and I think of them all as my nieces and nephews, or perhaps my own children. Anyway, you would do well to steer clear of DeGent. She is a snake and used Kate's death to try to wheedle her way into William's affections. I find it abominable."

"What does Mr. Singer think of this?" Katherine asked. "Or rather, of her?"

Lady Stratton huffed. "He knows of her fraudulence."

"Did you warn him?" Katherine asked.

"William is my husband's heir. He will be the Earl of Stratton one day. He must be trusted to make his own decisions."

Katherine took the hint that she should be cautious in telling William what to do, but being true to herself was such a huge part of her make up, she was not sure she could suppress the urge.

Lady Stratton shrugged. "I do my best to stay out of William's ear unless he requests my counsel."

Katherine grimaced.

Lady Stratton picked up her wine glass and gave Katherine a small toast. "It is no matter now. You are here, and Lady Isobel must stand aside."

"She seems determined to do otherwise," Katherine revealed.

"Will you allow it?" Lady Stratton turned upon her new niece with eyes wise from years of societal mêlée. "I am aware that you have no desire to be Countess of Stratton, but one day the title will be yours, and I think you will do the title proud.

"You have a naivete about you. It is a quality that I both admire and wish to see fade over time. You might have no vested interest in fighting for the affections of my nephew. I am well aware that your heart lies elsewhere. However, you might wish to consider a defense of your future. Lady Isobel, left unchecked, is a grave threat to your position. She will stop at nothing to see you upended—in reputation if not in truth—and at what cost to you or your sisters?"

Katherine had never considered that she might need to defend her future title and her marriage, against one so devious as the Lady Isobel DeGent. It seemed as if this life of hers was destined to become more and more complicated by the day. Would she ever be able to find solitude in her misery? Or would she always need to guard against the ruination that seemed determined to dog her every move? Lady Isobel was an unforeseen complication. One that, to Katherine's surprise, made her want to prove that she could be the lady this title deserved, the lady her husband deserved.

With the thought of Lady Isobel in the back of her mind, she located her husband and wound her way through the crowd to stand at his side. He greeted her with a grin and opened his arm so that she might fold herself against him. The motion looked natural, though it felt anything but. Her heart raced as she pressed her cheek to his chest and used her hand to cover a feigned a yawn.

"I am tired, My Love," she murmured. William' eyes grew wide in surprise at her words, but he covered his shock with skill. "Perhaps we might postpone that stroll you promised me until tomorrow. I am afraid that I am in need of rest." She lowered the tone of her voice, but not the volume. "I hardly slept a wink last night."

A hiss over her shoulder was all that she needed to confirm that Lady Isobel was spying.

She looked up with heavy-lidded eyes and did her best not to laugh at the color rising in her husband's cheeks. She had no experience in the ways of men and would never have guessed that it would be so much fun to tease him. She wondered how much more thrilling the art would be if she harbored true feelings for the gentleman.

"Well, then," he replied in a thick voice. "I believe that can be arranged. We have many tomorrows, as you well know."

A rustle of skirts pushed past her, and Katherine knew that she had won this round. Lady Isobel stormed off to the far side of the room where she remained until the end of the dinner party an hour later.

It was true that Katherine was exhausted. She had experienced so much stimulation in recent days that she was emotionally spent. When she returned to her rooms, she found Patches with a wide selection of toys and a plush pillow on which to curl by the fire.

"Oh dear," she laughed. "You shall become spoiled after all."

The cat cried out for her attention, which she supplied with pleasure. After a hearty rub of her belly, she scooped her up and deposited her on the bed. She did not bother to change or even pull back the coverlet. Instead, Katherine fell onto the pillows and drifted to sleep without a moment's pause. Being married, and to a peer, was going to be much more difficult than she had ever imagined.

CHAPTER 19

The next day, Mr. Singer mentioned that he wanted to go back to Sandstowe to collect his sisters, and Katherine made no objection. In fact, she wanted to make friends with them and try to remedy the slight that she had inadvertently delivered when she was introduced.

Mr. Singer did not appear again until dinnertime. She had hoped to meet his sisters, but they chose to dine in their room with their governess, who Lady Stratton reveled was much more of a companion than a governess at this point. After all, they would be coming out soon.

Dinner was a quiet affair with only family. Lady Stratton seemed tired following the events of the afternoon and, though she and her husband attempted to keep the conversation going with witty jokes and observations, they soon joined her companions in silence.

At the conclusion of the meal, a servant entered with a small paper folded upon a silver tray.

"A letter arrived in your name, Mrs. Singer." He offered the correspondence with a bow. "You were sleeping, and I did not wish to wake you."

She thanked him for the thoughtful gesture and accepted the letter. Two pairs of eyes turned toward her with surprise, and one pair of masculine eyebrows raised ever so slightly.

"What is it child?" Lady Stratton asked. "Another note from your family?"

Katherine had been blessed to receive a message from her sisters, meant to bolster her confidence, earlier in the day. This paper did not have the artful folds or the smell of rosewater that indicated her sisters' doing.

She shook her head.

With trembling fingers, she opened the letter. A keen awareness of her audience ensured that she schooled her features to a passive state before reading the text within. Lord William had returned his attention to his plate, though there was hardly enough food left to pick at.

The letter was addressed to *Mrs. Singer. It felt like a stranger's name.*

My dear Madam,

I write to you with the sincerest of congratulations upon your recent nuptials to the most honorable, Mr. Singer.

Such a fine match is well deserved for a Lady of your beauty and stature. I wish you all the happiness and beg that you dwell naught upon my position of dismay. I will do my utmost to move forward, in time, and mend the pieces of my heart and wish only to impress that I hold you without fault for my own affections and delayed course of action.

I shall always look upon you as a dear and valued friend. I hope that you will grant me the same courtesy in the future.

With all my lowly heart,

Colonel Markey

Katherine felt the air rush from her lungs as she stared at the paper in her hand. With slow, practiced movements, she folded the paper and set it beside her plate so that it would appear as if nothing were amiss. In truth, she could think of nothing but the desire to race to her room and read the words a thousand times over before burning the evidence in the flames of her hearth.

Colonel Markey had loved her, and despite the depth of his love, he had shown her the courtesy of a congratulations for what he thought to be her preference of choice. Never would he know that Katherine had not married Mr. Singer of her own will.

"Has there been trouble?" Lady Stratton asked with a worried frown. "You have lost your color."

"Not at all." Katherine laughed away the comment. "It was merely a word of congratulation from an old friend. I was only surprised that news had traveled so fast."

Lady Stratton nodded, but Katherine suspected that she had not been fooled. It was with relief that she noticed her husband whispering to the servant about a different matter that had been brought to his attention. The entire exchange had gone unnoticed.

Katherine excused herself from the table and took her letter to peruse with more privacy.

Mr. Singer and the earl stood at her departure, but she could not take note. Her heart longed for the future that had been dashed in an instant. The ability to choose had been taken from her, and even if the colonel had not been the man for her, she would never know now. She would never have the chance to find out what might have been.

She realized having such a letter in her possession could be misconstrued. She took a candle with her to the fireplace and stooped down to touch the letter to the flame until it lit. She then dropped it into the fireplace, and it immediately caught, curling into a single sheet of paper, flame and ash in the well swept grate. As she watched the flames lick at the parchment, she realized the paper was conspicuous. She used the dust brush to disperse the small amount of ash.

She wondered how long it would be that she resented her loss of choice. A deep pit in her heart that had grown darker with each passing day told her that she might never recover from the loss.

. . .

The next day, Katherine decided there was only one way to brighten her mood. She would go and find Mr. Singer's young sisters and try to make amends with them.

With her feline shadow at her heels, Katherine made her way to the drawing room, which overlooked the stone porch. It was still cool outside, but the sun was perfect this fine spring day.

Both of Mr. Singer's sisters, Claire and Caroline, were painting, and paused to curtsey when she entered, but the movement was for good manners, not for esteem.

Katherine was sorry she had not made more effort to befriend them earlier, but it seemed time had run away with her. Now, the young girls were her sisters too, and she wanted to get to know them.

She complimented both girls on their watercolors now, but Claire scowled. "I'm rubbish at painting," she said, "but Mrs. Catchpole says it is a lady's gift."

Mrs. Catchpole, Katherine assumed, was the girls' nanny and companion.

"Claire is lucky if she finishes without working a hole into the parchment," Caroline commented. "Would you like to join us?"

Claire scowled, but Katherine was not sure if that frown was for her or the painting.

"I would," Katherine said, smiling at Caroline and trying to woo the girl into conversation. "I like to paint but have not done much lately."

"You can have my spot," said Claire as she pulled her easel closer to the window where the sun was better and gestured Katherine forward.

The curtains had already been thrown wide, and the paints were spread upon a small table.

"Oh, is this your cat?" Claire asked as she flopped on the floor in a most unladylike way and pulled the feline onto her lap. Patches most accommodatingly shoved her head beneath Claire's hand, angling for a good pat.

"That is Patches," Katherine said. "My most loyal companion."

"I wanted to get a cat or a dog," Claire said as she petted Patches. "Did you know that the Duke and Duchess of Bramblewood have puppies?"

"I am quite sure it is their dog that has puppies," Caroline said knowingly, "not the duke or the duchess."

Claire chuckled. "You knew what I meant."

Katherine smiled at the banter and took a seat beside Caroline, who handed her a paintbrush.

"What shall we paint?" Katherine asked, looking at the blank parchment in front of her.

"Anything you like," Caroline replied. "We were just experimenting with different colors and brush strokes."

Katherine dipped her brush into the water and then the green paint on the glass palate. She began to create a small landscape. Claire had been working on a portrait of a vase of flowers, which was left undone, while Caroline was creating a bird on a branch with obvious skill.

"Do you both enjoy painting?" Katherine asked, trying to make up for her previous indifference towards them.

"Yes, we do," Caroline said. "It's a nice way to pass the time."

"And it's fun to see what we can create," Claire added. "Mrs. Catchpole says I scrub the paper too much. I must think before I put brush to canvas." She continued petting the cat, the canvas neglected.

Katherine nodded in agreement, enjoying the peacefulness of the moment. They continued to paint in silence for a while, each lost in their own thoughts and creations.

As Katherine finished her landscape, she looked over at the Caroline's painting and was impressed by her talent. She had not expected her to be so skilled at such a young age.

"That is lovely," Katherine said, admiring the work.

"Thank you," Caroline replied with a smile. "We have been painting for as long as we can remember."

"Caroline has even had some of her paintings displayed at the local art gallery," Claire added, grinning at her sister.

Caroline blushed.

Katherine was impressed. “That is quite an achievement. You both have a real talent. I’m sure your brother is very proud of you.”

“I’m not sure he’s ever noticed,” Caroline said softly.

“Well, I’m glad he’s not noticed mine.” She wrinkled her nose delicately.

“Don’t worry, Claire. It just takes practice. I’m sure you will get better in time. Otherwise, I’m sure you have other talents.” Katherine didn’t mention it, but she noticed that William must have been cool to his sisters too, although she was sure he cared for them.

“Thank you,” they both said dutifully.

Claire put Patches aside and went back to the flowers she had been painting. Katherine offered some suggestions to the girl.

As they worked, Katherine felt grateful for the chance to spend time with the girls.

She hoped they could get past their rocky beginning and be friends. "Are you excited for your Season next year?" she asked Caroline.

Caroline blushed and looked down at her painting. "Yes, I am," she said softly. "But I am also a little nervous. I have heard that it can be quite overwhelming."

Katherine smiled sympathetically, but she had no real advice to offer, only comfort. "I’m sure can be, but it can also be a wonderful experience. You will meet many new people and have the opportunity to attend some amazing events."

Clare nodded in agreement. "And you will have plenty of suitors vying for your attention," she said with a mischievous grin.

Caroline's blush deepened, and Katherine couldn't help but chuckle. "Don't worry, Caroline. You will have plenty of time to decide which gentleman catches your eye." Unlike herself, Katherine thought, who had their brother thrust upon her, quite literally.

As they continued to talk, Katherine found herself enjoying the girls' company more and more. She admired their intelligence and their passion for art, and she found herself wishing she had been kinder to them in the past few weeks. She hoped she could make up for the lack. Perhaps, Katherine thought, this could be the start of a new friendship.

They fell into a comfortable silence as they each continued to work on their paintings. Katherine found it calming to focus on the brushstrokes and blending the colors. She could feel the warmth of the sun on her back and the faint smell of the flowers wafting in through an open window. It was a peaceful moment, and she was grateful for the chance to spend it with the girls.

Katherine had been so preoccupied with her own problems that she had forgotten the joy of simple pleasures like painting and spending time with new friends.

She made a mental note to spend more time with Caroline and Claire in the future. The fact that they noted how busy

William was all of the time meant that they were hungry for adult company, and she had no friends here. She hoped she could help them. She hoped they could help each other. Perhaps they could go for walks or read together in the library. She had cried thinking how much she would miss her own sisters, but she realized she could have two new sisters too.

After a while, Caroline spoke up. "Do you think William will let us have a picnic in the garden this weekend?"

Claire rolled her eyes. "You know he won't. He's always too busy with his work."

"He might surprise us," Katherine said optimistically.

"I doubt it," Claire muttered, but a small smile tugged at the corner of her mouth. "Will you ask him, Katherine?" asked Claire.

"Me?" Katherine said, thinking that she would be the last person William would be inclined to listen to.

Both girls stood anxiously nodding their heads.

Katherine was nonplussed.

. . .

Just then, the door opened, and Mr. Singer entered the room. He looked surprised to see Katherine there with the girls but quickly composed himself.

"Good day, my dear," he said, nodding his head in greeting. "I didn't expect to find you here."

"It calms me," she murmured, never taking her eyes from the canvas.

After greeting her and his sisters, he asked, "What did you want to ask me?"

"You heard us," Claire accused, blushing.

"I did," he said.

"Has no one told you it is exceedingly bad manners to eavesdrop?" Caroline said.

"I am now apprised of the matter," he said seriously, as he looked at the three ladies' paintings.

Katherine had painted the scene from the window. A trio of flowers had broken through the dirt to stand against the passing cold. "See how they turn their heads to the light?" she asked. "The light must be captured perfectly."

Why was she sharing her thoughts with him? Her visions and her paintings had always been a very personal part of her that was shared only with her immediate family. She had even refused to allow her mother to sell the art for fear that others might learn that she had created the masterpiece. Somewhere, in the attic of her old home, were dozens of paintings that she had completed over the years.

She was sure that they had kept the moths and mice well fed.

"I'm sorry," she murmured sitting her brush aside.

"Not at all." His voice held a tone of wonder that she had never witnessed before, as if he were looking upon her as a different person than he had expected. She bristled and reminded herself that he did not know her, would never know her, in the way that a husband should.

"Yes, well…" She closed her paints away and began tidying the space. "I am finished for the moment." She had suddenly lost her desire to paint. The calm that had embraced her with the girls had deserted her now.

"Excuse me," she said, "you must have much to discuss with your sisters."

She fled the room with no real reason except that being close to him upset all of her sensibilities. She could not seem to speak properly or even think. It was a bother. She no longer felt wretched, but she still felt uneasy in his company. The only man she had ever been close to was her own father, and occasionally Harry, but they were both so jovial. They were so different than this brooding man.

She had reached the corridor when she realized he had followed her.

"I wanted…" He reached out to stop her when she moved to brush by him but withdrew his hand before contact was made. "I wanted to be sure that there was nothing that you lacked while you are here."

"Am I a guest?" she asked. She had not meant to sound harsh, but his comment sounded like something one would offer to a person of temporary attendance, not a wife who had been banished to this location for all eternity.

He grimaced, and Katherine realized he had not meant to imply that this was not her home. Yet the truth was that it did not feel so to Katherine. She did feel like a temporary figure in the household. Perhaps Lady DeGent had not been so far from the mark.

"Of course, that is not what I meant," he replied. "I only meant to inquire if there was anything else that would increase your comfort. Something that would make you feel more at home?"

"There is nothing that can make this place home," she replied with a voice devoid of emotion. "I shall live here. I shall do my—my duties, but it will never feel like my own."

"I am truly sorry for that. I never intended for my life to be forced upon you." He took a step closer, spread his hands, and implored Katherine to understand that he was a victim of the same circumstances. Though deep down she knew that he was right, she was unable to see beyond her own hurt. "If I could make it better, I would."

He sounded at such a loss to please her, but the truth was that Katherine did not want to be pleased. She wanted to wallow in the injustice, steep herself in the anger of such a terrible fate. If she could not have the life and the love that she had once imagined, she wanted nothing at all. It was a selfish mentality, she knew that, but the anger was the only thing that made her feel alive anymore. She was afraid if she didn't embrace the anger, she would fall onto her bed and cry herself literally to death.

"But you cannot!" she shouted and shoved him away with two open palms. "We are both sentenced to this fate, this misery, and I hate every moment of it." She had never laid her hands upon a man before, upon anyone for that matter.

He did not seem surprised by her reaction. Instead, he took a patient breath which only infuriated her all the more.

"Why could you not just have left me there to my own devices?" She shoved him again, this time forcing him to take a step back. "Why did you have to play at nobility when I needed none of it?"

William clenched his jaw and tilted his head like an adult on the verge of chastising a child. Yet he remained silent. Why was he not as angry as Katherine, she wondered? How was he so calm all of the time? She wanted him to be furious too. She did not know why, but she wanted to see him break, to witness that she was not the only one suffering.

"This is all your fault!" She placed her hands upon his chest a third time, but her wrists were captured before she could deliver another blow. The action threw her body against his, and for the first time, Katherine realized that he was standing as rigid as a board. Despite his outward appearance of calm, she had upset him.

He pulled her close, effortlessly, making her realize how utterly in his control she really was. The feeling was daunting.

"Let us not play at blame." He spoke in a low, lethal tone. "Nor shall I have this argument in the corridor where the servants and my sisters can hear."

She was immediately ashamed. "I'm sorry," she said.

He continued. "I am not going to inventory what could have or what should have happened. What is done is done. There is no altering our fates now. You can be cross until the moon turns blue, or you can get on with it, as I intend to do."

Katherine deflated. What fight she had washed away in the censure of his words. With their hands still clasped between them, she leaned her forehead to his chest in shame. There was no crying left in her. She took several deep breaths, using the closeness of their bodies to shield her from the external world. He smelled of sandalwood and the outdoors. It was a pleasant scent. She inhaled and leaned in to him.

She dared not look up at him and see the disappointment in his eyes. What a poor cause for a wife she had provided.

He released her wrists, and to her everlasting surprise, she felt the warmth of his arms wrapped around her. Rather than the contempt that she deserved, he provided her the strength and comfort that she had not known she had needed. She allowed herself to be held, settling close and matching her shaky breaths to his steady ones.

Though she wanted to do so, she could not remain forever and hide from her wrongdoing. She leaned back and lifted her sorrowful eyes to his. He did not appear angry any longer, merely tired.

"I was out of line," she breathed. "I am sorry."

He neither confirmed nor denied her statement, for which she was grateful.

"I assure you; it will not happen again." She spread her hands against his chest, smoothing the wrinkles from what had once been a crisp shirt. "Thank you," she raised one shoulder with the embarrassed admission, "for this."

She had meant her words as an expression of gratitude for the profound understanding and patience that he had exhibited but soon realized that her words sounded more as if she were enjoying being held. Even if she was, she would never admit such a thing.

She drew her lip between her teeth. His eyes followed the motion, and Katherine felt a sudden flooding of heat to her entire body. Her steady breath shook once more, and she found that she could not tear her gaze away from the penetrating focus of his eyes. Her fingers curled into the fabric that she had smoothed a moment earlier, and she clutched the fabric of his shirt as if afraid that her trembling legs might give way. The space between them seemed an illusion.

In her mind's eye, she imagined him kissing her with full abandon. His full lips and warm breath would melt over her like the hot sun of a summer day. She would lean into him like the lovers she had glimpsed at parties, lost in their newfound love and marital bliss. Her imaginings had never gone past that sweet first kiss. Could it be so romantic for Katherine and William?

She blew out another shaky breath, more vocal than she would have liked, almost like a sigh.

He kissed her, and the reality was, perhaps, more devastating than her imagination. Right there in the corridor, he kissed her. Of course, it was his corridor.

His lips brushed against hers, the barest of touches sending a torrent of sensations from her lips, down through her stomach, and swirling through her middle to her toes. Her eyes drifted closed, and she leaned against him, permitting a repetition of the act. The second round, he lingered a moment longer, allowing for the briefest of tasting before the contact was broken.

When their lips brushed a third time, Katherine leaned against him, stood on her toes, and increased the pressure, giving herself over to the miracle that was her first-ever kiss. His arms tightened around her waist, pulling her closer yet, lifting her slightly against his body. His was all hard angles and hers soft curves, and yet they fit together perfectly.

They had not been required to complete the act for the ceremony, and a small part of her questioned why she had waited so long to experience this wonder. She reveled in it, allowed his movements to be her guide while taking liberties of her own that she would never have expected of herself. Her teeth caught his lip and gave a playful tug, eliciting a groan in response.

"Katherine," he murmured against her.

Her name was like a cool bucket of water that had been released over her head. She leaned away, but his arms remained fastened about her waist.

"No," she cried. "We cannot."

"Why not?" He laughed, pleasure and surprise still written upon his features. "We are married, you know. There is no wrong in it."

"But it is wrong," she argued. "It is all wrong. Let me go."

He released her, and Katherine stepped away to smooth her hands down the crumpled folds of her skirts. The act was more a distraction than anything, an excuse not to look at him.

"Katherine," he whispered, reaching out one hand to soothe her, but she jerked away.

"No," she repeated. "It cannot be so. Husband or no, I do not know you."

"That can be remedied," he said, as if the solution were obvious. The intensity of Katherine's reaction told her otherwise. William Singer needed to be kept at a distance. Whatever it was that had flared between them needed to be put out at once. It was not the calm sweet romance she had imagined in her mind. It was something raw and wild and uncontrollable, and she could not trust it. She could not trust him. She could not trust herself.

The image of Colonel Markey flashed in her mind, and she covered her face with her hands and groaned. Perhaps if this were to be the mark of her behavior, she had deserved disgrace.

"I am sorry," she muttered and turned on her heel to leave the room. "Please, just leave me be."

William might have called after her, but she did not wait to listen. Instead, she shut herself in her room for the remainder of the night, wishing that she had not burned the letter from Colonel Markey. She had been afraid that someone might discover it and guess the truth of the situation, but now, with the raging emotions and confusion that swirled inside of her, she wished that she had a small reminder of the man with whom her love had been thwarted.

CHAPTER 20

The next day, as was often the case, William left Katherine to break her fast with his aunt while he settled whatever dealings were necessary for the running of the estate. This morning, the two girls were with their Aunt Agnes.

Katherine wanted to ask Lady Stratton what she knew about the circumstances of the previous night but found herself unable to do so with William's sisters present. She thought of her own relationship with Harry and tried to be civil. The girls had no part in her misery.

A letter arrived halfway through the meal that took both Ladies by surprise. The Duchess of Bramblewood had written to share the greatest of news. The ball that had meant to be hosted in honor on the day of the Equinox was cancelled.

Katherine revealed her devastation at the loss of such an event. The duchess explained that she had made all preparations, but the large feature window of the main dance hall, made up of many small panes of colored glass, had been broken in a recent storm and would not be repaired until the weather improved.

"Oh, that window," Lady Stratton exclaimed. "It has been broken more times than I can tell. I think Alex and Emily should board the thing up and replace it with book shelves."

I guess that means Bramblewood will not be hosting any parties until later in the summer, at least, she thought mournfully. "What other losses shall I suffer at the hands of this new year?" she grumbled into her eggs.

Lady Stratton laughed. "Such a dismal outlook for one so young."

"I am sorry," Katherine replied. It seemed as if she had spent the past month doing nothing but apologizing. "It is only that I was so looking forward to the ball.

"Me too," Caroline chirped. "I know I am not out yet, but William promised me one dance."

Katherine's mind jumped the last time she had danced with Mr. Singer, and her hands felt damp on her silverware. She dropped them to her lap and wiped them on her napkin. She had hoped the festivities would help her to forget her misery. "I was ever so excited for the party."

"And I might venture a guess that this was to be your first year with a true gentleman at your side," Lady Stratton provided.

Katherine's blush was enough to confirm the truth.

"Not that it matters now," Katherine admitted, "but I would have liked to attend the ball. Though, love does not work the way I once thought. My fate has taught me as much." She had never expected to be able to speak so freely with Lady Stratton about her lost love, but the elderly woman made no bones about the fact that she was aware of Katherine's feelings. So long as her new daughter did not act upon them and bring shame to the family, a fact was nothing more than that.

"Oh, I do not think we should let the equinox go to waste," Lady Stratton said. "And you know, Cecil is one for theatrics." She leaned in a whispered. "We met at a midsummer ball."

Katherine giggled and could not imagine the wrinkled old Lady meeting her earl, although it was clear to all that they were both besotted in love even at this late date.

Perhaps William's father had been stern, Katherine mused. Perhaps she had only assumed so because his son seemed so steadfast and rigid. Although her husband was, without a doubt, a good man, she did not see the same frivolity in him that she oft witnessed in his aunt and even in his uncle. She had assumed that he must have learned these characteristics from his father. Everything Mrs. Davenport conveyed suggested that his mother had been sweet and gay.

Katherine filed away the information away in her mind under the enigma that was her husband.

"Now," Lady Stratton leaned forward with a conspiratorial wink. "We shall have to see what can be done about this ball."

"Nothing can be done!" Katherine laughed. "The window was broken and has been boarded. It must wait to be repaired. A duchess would never consider hosting guests with such an abomination in her household."

"Well certainly not at Bramblewood, no," Lady Stratton agreed. "But we have two fine ballrooms here that have not been used in years. Have you seen them yet?"

"Oh, Aunt Agnes, could we?" asked Caroline, eyes shining.

Katherine admitted that she had not considered that. Lady Stratton vaulted from the table without waiting for her companion to finish her meal and the two girls came after her with likewise excitement. With a wave of her hand, the countess implored Katherine to follow her and proceeded to show Katherine some of the finer features of her new home.

Katherine was in awe with all that had been revealed as the girls chattered about this relative and that, all of who were memorialized in portraits.

Katherine paused before one of them.

"William's mother," Aunt Agnes said of the woman who held a young boy in his Christening gown on her lap. "He was born just under a year after she and my husband's brother were married, and then both he and Cecil went to war, and the girls did not arrive until years later."

"She was beautiful," Katherine said.

"I see her in William," the countess said, and Katherine had to agree.

"So, you agree my nephew is handsome," the countess teased.

"I never said he was not," Katherine retorted and then she hastened to change the subject back to the topic of the ball. "I think this will be a wonderful venue for the ball, but I must tell you, my lady, I know next to nothing about planning such an event."

"Are you up to being the hostess?" Lady Stratton asked, but it was clear she was not taking no for an answer. "Of course, I will help you," she said.

"Thank you." Katherine was suddenly excited.

The girls held hands and danced in a ring.

Never was there a finer location to host such an event. Two large ballrooms could accommodate no less than two hundred guests with ease. It promised to be the largest event that Katherine had attended, and it was in her new home.

Once the countess had been put into motion, there was no stopping her. She soon had an army of servants at her fingertips as she delegated all of the preparations that must be completed in the next fourteen days. Invitations were to be sent out the following afternoon, for which the Lady Stratton set two servants to the task within minutes of her decision.

"Invite every reasonable household in three counties," she heralded. "Ensure that the Duke and Duchess of Bramble-wood are made to be guests of honor for the inconvenience that they have suffered. Send word to the duchess for any guests that might be overlooked. Prepare all of the guest quarters."

"ALL of them?" the housekeeper asked with wide-eyed fear.

"Yes, all," Lady Stratton confirmed. "Set Katherine's father, mother, and sisters in our private hall. I want no comfort spared for our new relatives."

So it went, with the countess barking orders with a skill that bespoke of someone who threw balls at regular inter-vals. Katherine wondered how often this quiet home, or Sandstowe, must have been filled with guests. The building came to life before her very eyes. Katherine had not realized how many servants were employed within the main house. She rarely had occasion to see them, and their invisible nature only attested their skill.

Mr. Singer soon caught wind of the activity and came to confront his aunt.

"What is the meaning of this?" he demanded.

The countess explained the circumstances and her desire to remedy them.

William's eyes turned to Katherine and narrowed as if he wondered how she had convinced his aunt of such a scheme.

"It was my idea," Aunt Agnes professed.

"Yours?" he said in an incredulous tone. "You and Uncle Cecil always say you like a quiet life."

"I do," Lady Stratton agreed. "But why can't I enjoy a party to celebrate my nephew and his bride?"

"No reason, I'm sure, but to what do I owe this change of heart?" He spoke as if he were suspicious of her motives. It was clear that he was well aware of his aunt's capricious ways.

"What better way to welcome my new niece, or rather for her to welcome the neighborhood, than for you and she to host a ball? It will flush all the gossips into the open."

"Yes, but…" He took his aunt's arm and turned her away so that they might whisper. Katherine pretended not to hear, though their words were clear. "Are you certain you are willing to do this? It is a lot of work for you."

"What? At my age?"

His ears reddened at her words.

"I'm not in the grave yet, William," she said. "You need not worry over me, my dear." She reached up and placed on wrinkled hand on her nephew's cheek. "Your mother has been gone over a year, but I am not going anywhere. There is no reason we cannot celebrate, and I'm sure Kate would want you to do so. Your mum always loved a party."

"All right." He nodded and pressed a kiss to his aunt's forehead. "I remember many parties when I was young."

"Good. You would do well to remember," she replied.

"I shall try," he promised. Then, without a word to his wife, he left.

Katherine looked after him for a long while, wondering at the man she had married. However, she was unable to be lost in thought long, for Lady Stratton soon called her back to the task at hand.

PART IV

CHAPTER 21

That evening Katherine padded her way to her bedroom on tired limbs. Never had she completed so much work and so little time. There was much to be done in preparation for the ball, and with holdings as large as Winebury, the tasks had increased tenfold.

Anne had arrived via carriage but begged off, saying she was riddled with exhaustion, and her feet had swollen so they did not fit in her riding boots.

"Just as well," she said with a grimace. "I do not feel I have my usual balance on horseback. I suppose I should follow everyone's advice and remand myself to the carriage. Speaking of," she continued. "I should go home. It looks like rain." She called her groom to ready the carriage so she would be home in time for tea.

The rain started again, and the inclement weather did not help, for the acquisition of supplies to make the themed decorations had been delayed by a rain storm that had moved in from the south. All was well, however, when the return letter from the Duchess of Bramblewood arrived and expressed her elation for the turn of events. Emily had also offered to send over all of the trinkets and the core that she and Anne had spent the last few weeks preparing.

Katherine's tired eyes almost missed the envelope tied to her door handle, and if it had not been for the sound of it slapping against the wood, she might have gone to bed without another thought.

Inside the envelope was a small, handmade card. Its simplicity intrigued her. With trepidation she opened the letter and read its contents.

My lady wife,

I have considered at great length the type of gift that one might give one's new wife upon this celebration. Perhaps some jewelry that you might wear for the occasion, and yet, I do not know what you like.

You were right when you said that there could be nothing between us when we do not know each other. Though I do believe that I am developing an understanding of your character, there is still much left to discover. I believe that the same applies from your perspective. Our union does not alleviate that truth. As such, I am afraid a romantic gesture or valuable gift would only serve to deepen the rift between us. Such action, without affection, can mean little to the recipient.

I realize that my offering is anything but conventional. However, I hope that you might find some way of appreciating it in time.

I offer you no verses, no treasures or treats, and no expressions of love where I believe they are not wanted. Instead, I offer you only the barest truths of my being that you might find it in your heart to know me a little more. What might come from this, I cannot say. My only hope is that we might not be strangers in this long path of life that lay before us.

And so for today, I leave you this; make of it what you will. I had a friend. Perhaps, I use that term loosely. I thought he was my friend.

I had known him for many years and felt that I had gained a good estimation of his character. But the honorable truths that one might profess mean nothing to one's character and are mere fodder if not sustained by one's actions. I believe this to the depths of my soul.

This man spoke of honor and duty, but some years ago, he got a seamstress in one of the port towns with child and had no desire to marry her since she was without income or status. He and I had a falling out.

He declared that he would marry her if I were to provide a significant income or an affluent position in my employ. Of course, I declined, for he was undeserving of such a benefit. He abandoned the girl, as did her family, to a life of destitution and shame. He, who had spoken of honor and duty, had failed abominably on both of those counts.

We parted ways. I have no idea where he is now. Last I heard he was driving a Hackney in London, but that was several years ago now.

I vowed from that moment that I would do right by my words as well as my actions, and I have done so to the best of my abilities. Though I declined a life of leisure to my 'friend,' through the help of a man who was maligned due to his father's actions, I was able to search out the mother of his child and offer her what could not be given to him. She now resides within my employ, her son provided for with every opportunity for a promising future. I cannot keep harm from coming to those in this world, but I can do my best to do what is in my power to make good of it.

I am not certain if this story tells the good or bad of my character. I may have been a good man to the seamstress, but I know my acquaintance considers me a horrible friend. I only know that I feel strongly that words are easy. Actions are what count in this world. I will leave it to you to decide.

Yours,

W. Singer

Katherine read the letter with fascination. The story revealed to her much about the character of her husband. He could be both merciful and unforgiving. She realized that it was this vow that had caused him to marry her without hesitation. He had viewed her as faultless in the situation. She thanked the heavens for that. As such, he had done what was necessary to repair her reputation and ensure that no harm came of the blunder.

There was some relief to learn that her husband was bound by a strict code of honor. She also felt a small amount of trepidation at what wrath might descend upon those that wronged him, herself included.

THE DAYS LEADING UP TO THE BALL WERE FILLED WITH activity from morning until night. Katherine spent much of the time with Caroline and Claire and Aunt Agnes making preparations. She had little opportunity to encounter her husband or speak with him about the letters that appeared nightly at her door. She did not mention the notes to anyone. After a long day of hostess duties, she found herself looking forward to his words and all that they revealed. Sometimes, they shared his deepest secrets. Others were silly and whimsical and made her laugh. Though they rarely crossed paths and spoke no more than ten words to each other each day she found that she was getting to know her husband, little by little. To what end, she could not say.

DAY 2:

My lady wife;

My favorite pastime is riding. There is little that can compete with the thrill of racing across the countryside on a beast bred to perfection. Our land is known for its cattle and sheep, but what horses we have are sublime. I am thinking of my favorite mare. A thoroughbred, she is gentle but spirited in her own way. She reminds me of you, and if you ever chose to ride, I would put you to her in an instant. She is trained for sidesaddle since I thought to make a gift of her to Caroline, but Caroline chose another.

I do not even know if you enjoy the activity. For all I know, you have a great fear of the beasts. Though, my suspicion, forgive me if I am wrong, from your bond with that feline, is that you have a great capacity to care for animals.

Yours,

W. Singer

Day 3:

My lady wife;

My least favorite activity is shearing. I am glad to say that we have a skilled group of men that perform the task. As the owner of sheep, it might seem strange that I loathe the task so. Wool is not at all softened before the washing. It bristles, sticks to you, and makes you itch all over. I am very glad that I am the lord of the manor and can give orders from afar. Do not think harshly of me for it.

Yours,

W. Singer

Katherine chuckled at the thought of him involved in the shearing. Most aristocrats would not even think of such a thing. She was sure that he could do it if the need arose, but as he said, he was the owner of the sheep, and he had servants for those things. How many servants, she could not fathom. She was lost trying to remember everyone's names.

DAY 4:

Dear lady wife;

Mother used to tell me that I raced through life with my head in the clouds. I was forever lost in my own thoughts and imaginings. I do not recall the exact moment when I stopped dreaming so, but at some point, I was forced to put such things aside as childish or perhaps unmanly.

Sometimes I miss it. I was reminded of it when I watched you paint. Correct me if I'm wrong, but I think you know how to dream. Shall I tell you of my dreams? Will you tell me yours?

Yours,

W. Singer

THE THOUGHT OF THE STOGY MAN SHE KNEW DREAMING shook her. How little she knew of her husband. Of what did he dream? Now, she was curious.

DAY 5:

. . .

Dearest Wife;

I have observed that you are close with your sisters. I am also close with my sisters although in a different way. I think a brother must always be a little distant from younger sisters, especially as their father died while they were just out of the cradle. I feel an almost fatherly affection for them.

I hope that you and they will make…

The line was crossed out and Katherine wondered what he had been going to write. Instead, the letter changed track entirely.

One day, I will become the Earl of Stratton and you will become the countess. The honor of taking that title comes at a great loss. I love my aunt and uncle dearly. You are the first kindred spirit that I think might understand what it feels like to be granted such an honor when you do not wish it. Perhaps, one day, we might both grow to accept the gift with pleasure. I, at least, have yet to do so, because my being the earl means that my dearest friend and mentor will be gone from this world.

The thought of taking a wife who was anxious to become a countess with the loss of my aunt and uncle was abhorrent to me. I am glad to see that you and my Aunt Agnes are becoming friends.

W. Singer

Katherine considered. Yes, the way of their courtship was in no way what either desired, but she could see how hurtful it would be if his wife wanted the title at the expense of his dear aunt and uncle, although Uncle Cecil still scared her a little, truth be told. She was never quite sure when he was joking and when he was serious. It was understandable that he was William's mentor. William was his heir. Now that she thought about it, she sometimes saw bits of his Uncle Cecil's personality reflected in William, but his Uncle Cecil loved Aunt Agnes deeply. Did both Cecil and William have the capacity for such a deep love?

Day 6:

Dearest Wife;

You should have no fear that I might lose my fortune at the tables. I do not tell you this to brag about my moral superiority or my skill for hands. Rather, I am forced to admit that I am, quite possibly, the worst card player in existence. I have no talent in the bluff. Having discovered this about myself quite early, I never play what I do not expect to lose. Though you shall never find yourself in want of coin, I can promise you this: if you were, challenge me to a game and it shall be yours in an instant.

W. Singer

Day 7:

Dearest Wife;

I tried very hard to be close friends with Alex and Edmund when I was a child, but I always fell short of their adventures. Instead, my foremost childhood friend was a lowly stable hand by the name of George Gregory, who took pity on me. Though he is no longer at Winebury, it is because he is in Yorkshire with his wife and seven children. They live a happy life surrounded by her relatives, and I send for their visit at least twice each year. Their oldest son, Gabe, may come to apprentice at our stables when he comes of age. He has an excellent hand for horses, as did his father before him. You must tell me if you like horses.

W. Singer

Day 8:

Dearest Wife;

You should know the tale as to the scar on my brow is neither exciting nor heroic. In fact, it is second-rate when compared to what most would conjecture for such a remarkable feature.

When I was eight years of age, I fell from the roof of the bale house. I had climbed it for no better reason than to see if it could be done, as boys of that age are wont to do. Actually, Edmund may have told me that it could not be done, or at least it could not be done by me. In fact, I soon discovered that he was correct.

I sustained no greater injury than the bleeder, which was sewn and then resulted in the scar.

The only good to come of it was hearing the fantastical stories that were told as to its acquisition. I assure you that the mark had bolstered my reputation on more than one occasion, and I took great pleasure in hearing the many tales of misdeeds that I was said to have endured. This may have been due to the mendacities told by both Alexander and Edmund when recounting that day.

The following summer, Anne climbed the same route without incident, except that when her nanny discovered the event, Anne was severely chastised for being unladylike. I think I had the lighter punishment.

W. Singer

Day 9:

Dearest Wife;

Having discussed my injury in the previous card, I feel inclined to inform you that my father was missing the smallest toe on his left foot. He lost it in a carting accident before I was born, and almost none know of the strange fact as the offending limb was always covered by his boot. I am not sure how this information will help you, only that it is an interesting detail of which to be aware, except perhaps that my dear friend Alex was also in a carting accident and very nearly lost his life.

I can confirm, if you were wondering, that I am currently in possession of all ten of my own toes.

W. Singer

Day 10:

Dearest Wife;

I often find myself mulling over incidents in the past and rewriting them in my mind, as if by my very concentration, I could change the outcome.

If I were to have the chance to do things in an alternate manner, on that fateful day that we took our tumble down the ridge, I can say with pure honesty that there is little that I would change. If you recall, I am inept at the art of falsehoods, even in writing. My instinct was to aid you, and if the situation were to repeat itself, I would do the same again and again, even knowing the consequence. The prospect of you having come to greater harm, permanent injury, or death is a thought I cannot bear, moreso now than ever.

My only regret, on your behalf, is that I was too dazed and upended to have recovered before we were happened upon, though I have sincere doubts that it would have made a difference in the farmer's observations. Only, he might have thought that I had abducted you if I had carried you off sooner. I do believe that here we would be, no matter the course. I believe we have a destiny.

I cannot say whether this might provide you some form of consolation. I am well aware that you wish otherwise, but I find it necessary to express my view, that you might better understand my thoughts on the matter.

W. Singer

THE ELEVENTH DAY WAS NO LESS THAN SEVEN PAGES THAT detailed his plans and hopes for the future of Winebury's extensive holdings. Though the information was dry and displayed little of what she had come to know as his playful tone, she was grateful for the opportunity to be enlightened.

What man gave such information into the hands of his lady? It was as dry as dirt. It was a marvel.

Furthermore, he concluded the letter with an open request for her counsel.

Katherine had never expected to have her opinion valued in a matter of business or holdings by any husband, let alone one that she had been forced upon. The gesture warmed her heart, and she spent the following day with a happy grin on her face.

Perhaps she could have some influence here. Perhaps she could make her mark upon this land and those whom it supported. Her role as his wife had never been more appealing. Her husband did not expect her to be some mere charm that decorated his accomplishments. No, he offered the future to her as well, that she might have her opinions and wishes heard and respected. It was a bigger gift than she deserved, and she wondered if he was aware of its value.

. . .

Day 12:

Now that you have had some small chance to know me, I must reveal what I have learned of my wife through observation and of course the gossiping of the staff. You have not gone unnoticed in the weeks since you have joined us, and since our paths have had rare chance to cross since the planning of the ball, I shall share with you what has become my method of knowing your character.

Mrs. Davenport speaks nothing but praise for your person, as a loyal servant should, but Ruby's affection is deeper than that required by her position. You must remember she was my mother's maid from a date before my own birth. She is more than a servant. On your first morning, she informed me that you were both friendly and kind. This is no small matter considering the circumstances upon which you came to be at Winebury.

The way that you treat those beneath you, particularly in times of melancholy and trial, is by far the greatest test of one's character. She goes on to share tales of you 'taking up her tasks,' which she finds amusing—and shocking—for a Lady of your position. Perhaps you had a smaller staff. I am beginning to realize how little I know of you.

Or perhaps it is a result of your collaboration with your sisters. I cannot say. Though, I do wish to learn the truth someday. I can only inform you that your 'helping' Mrs. Davenport in her duties has left a mark upon her estimation of you, a mark of respect and friendship. Mrs. Davenport is well aware that her service to my Lady might have been very different depending upon the Lady of choice.

For this reason, I gave her the option of retirement which after just one day with you, she refused. It behooves me to say that she has grown quite the attachment to you. I had expected her to remain in retirement after her many years' service to my mother, but she has expressed the wish to be of some use. Of course, if you wish another younger maid to attend you, the choice is yours.

Our footmen and butlers speak in a similar fashion. Amused they are with your inability to recognize your status. Your offer that they address you in an informal fashion means more to them than I think you realize, even as it scandalizes them. In addition, your requests after their families and ability to recall the names of their spouse or children brings them great joy. I would estimate you know the names now of perhaps half of the servants, which causes me to marvel.

I wonder if it is because I had only ever been expected to wed a Lady of title, a lady of the Ton, that your behavior seems so out of sorts. I mean this only as a compliment, I assure you. Most Ladies of my acquaintance make a concerted effort to ensure that their position and title is held before them like some beacon that others must revere. You do no such thing, and perhaps that is the greatest sign of a Lady. Deference is given out of respect, not because it is demanded. It is refreshing, and the entire estate has made note.

Though you have never spared the opportunity to express your displeasure in my presence, I am glad to bear the burden if it means that you make no other suffering for our fate than I. These individuals are not to blame for your misery, and I am honored that you have displayed such grace and integrity.

Lastly, I must comment upon that beast that you have brought along. I am not sure that you are aware, but she has taken to dogging, excuse the term, my steps whenever I am about the stables. She is a constant reminder of your presence at Winebury and seems to have made herself a home of it. What few children live on site spend much of their time petting and feeding her.

In addition, I think cooks and groomsmen are in a competition to see which bowl of cream she chooses. If the cat has appeared to have increased in size, then it is that which is to blame. She has been an ambassador to your nature, along with the praise that they overhear from their elders, and has served you well in that respect.

W. Singer

CHAPTER 22

The day of the ball opened with beautiful sunshine. Guests began arriving as early as noon to settle into their rooms. The bulk of the party who lived within driving distance would make their appearance for dinner at eight, after an early tea, so that the dancing might run for the duration of the evening. A cold supper would be had at midnight.

Katherine embraced her family and showed them to their rooms personally. Their eyes grew wide, and they gasped at the life to which their daughter and sister had been left. None had realized the true extent of the Winebury holdings, as it was always thought to be too far to have been a regular addition to their social circle. All that would change now that Katherine had taken up residence.

She left her sisters to settle into their rooms and explore the enormous house while she searched for the Lady Stratton to complete the final preparations for the evening's festivities. Not long after, she had located the Lady, but the four Westlake women appeared with their sleeves pushed back and ready to be of service.

"My, but you have an army at your disposal!" The countess laughed.

"We must stay in your good graces," Josephine teased with a wink, "for we have not forgotten the picnic that was promised."

"I am afraid that I am unable to fulfill such a promise," she offered with a frown. Katherine now knew the Lady well enough to see that she was resisting a smile, but her sisters had yet to see past her mask of severity. They believed her.

"Oh," Jo breathed. Her eyes flew to her sister as if wondering if the loss was a punishment for her marriage. "I understand."

Lady Stratton threw her head back and chortled. Jo had stepped neatly into her trap and not even realized it.

"I only meant that *I* can no longer provide such permissions," the countess continued in an exaggerated tone. "Not in this house. You must make your request to the *new* Lady of the house. Heaven forbid we cannot have two Ladies steering the ship. Only disaster would come of it, and it is long past time that I gave up the wheel."

"Well, Katherine?" Jo laughed and turned to her sister with crossed arms and raised eyebrows.

Susanna giggled and placed an elbow in Jo's ribs.

"Bless my soul, you girls are trouble," Mrs. Westlake chimed in. She turned a pointed glare from Susanna first, then to Jo. "Stop being a pest and see what you can do to help."

"Yes," Katherine intoned with mock sternness. "Jo and Georgianna, do stop pestering the Lady Stratton and ask where you can be put to service."

With a giggle, the girls did as commanded and were sent away to hang the decorations that Emily had cut to create voluminous shapes that would spin from the ceiling.

So the day passed, with hard work and laughter throughout. By the time that Katherine returned to her rooms to dress for the evening, the house was so full of sound and happiness that, for the first time, it did feel somewhat like a home.

Her gown was a pale pink with raised capped sleeves and a lace-and-tulle overlay. It was soft and romantic, almost ethereal in the way that it flowed from her body with its short train. The wide satin belt accentuated her waist in the empire style and set her form to perfection. Mrs. Davenport took extra care with her Lady's hair. Katherine's curls were pinned in a loose technique that left a fine spray of ringlets framing her face. To complete the look, two silver combs were tucked at the crown of her head so that they gave the appearance of a single arching piece. The glittering effect of the pale jewels captivated Katherine as she stared at the completed work in the looking glass.

"My Lady," Mrs. Davenport breathed. "You look like something sent from the heavens to bless us."

Katherine gave a half smile but could not disagree. She hardly recognized herself in the mirror. She pinched her cheeks for a bit of color that she might not look so pale and other-worldly. With a nod, she declared the preparations complete.

The guests had gathered below and were milling about with loud voices and shouts of greeting. She slipped from her room and moved to join her husband at the top of the stair, from which they would make their entrance. He was seated in a small alcove that overlooked the gardens but stood when she approached.

"You look…" He shook his head in search of words.

"Perhaps I allowed Mrs. Davenport to go too far." Katherine blushed and shook her head. "Is it too much? She seemed to be having such fun."

"No," he replied with a firm confidence. "It is perfection."

She released the breath that she had not known she had been holding. For whatever reason, one which she refused to consider, her husband's approval had begun to matter.

"Shall we?" She gestured toward the balcony and offered her hand that she might place it upon his arm.

"A moment, please," he fumbled with something in his pocket and appeared all thumbs before pulling out a small box which was presented to her.

Her mouth formed a circle as she looked down at the gift. She looked up with wide, remorseful eyes and admitted that in the chaos of the preparations, she had failed to procure a gift of her own. He assured her that it was not necessary.

"I know that I said that I would not." He shrugged. "But I could not deny you some small token. I only hope that you might accept it."

He waited for her refusal while Katherine pressed her lip between her teeth and considered the offer. What harm could come from accepting a gift from one's own husband? It was not improper.

With a slow motion, she lifted the lid from the box and peered inside. Her gasp was barely audible, but her eyes as she glanced up at William revealed her instantaneous love for the object.

A petite knotted heart, smaller than her fingernail, was threaded on a fine gold chain. Her hand flew to her waist where the brooch from Anne had been centered on her belt. The two items were a pair, matched as if they had blossomed from the same gilded branch.

"You wear that brooch every day." He shrugged. "So I had a necklace commissioned to match. It is just a small thing, nothing really." She wondered that he had taken note of such a small detail.

"No," she disagreed. "It is more beautiful than anything I deserve." She thanked him whole heartedly and turned that he might secure the clasp at her neck. He moved with precise motions such that his fingers never came into contact with her skin, as if he were afraid of the sensation. Still, Katherine could almost sense every movement in her mind's eye despite the distance.

When he stepped away, she turned to face him once more and smoothed her hand over her collarbone where the necklace lay.

"William, I…" She did not know what she wanted to say. Instead, she stood there with her head moving from side to side as she searched for the proper response.

He laughed.

"What?" She was confused by his amusement.

"You used my Christian name," he pointed out with a sure smile.

"Well, do not let it go to your head," she retorted with pursed lips and a smile that she struggled to contain. He had donc her a service by lightening the mood and allowing her to tease. "Come now, the guests are waiting," she said as she placed her hand on his arm.

Together, they made their way down the elegant arch of the staircase. Each room was brimming with people, and Katherine doubted that a single guest had declined the invite. Perhaps they had been curious about the new marriage and had come to observe the couple. She found that she did not care; she was determined to enjoy the evening.

"Shall we open the floor?" William asked as he led her into the first of the two enormous ballrooms.

Katherine allowed herself to be taken into his arms as he gave the nod to the instrumentalists, and the music began. Somewhere in the distance, the music must have begun in the other room as well, but Katherine had to struggle to hear it. She complimented the layout of the estate that allowed such duality to exist.

All of the usual diversions of conversation eluded Katherine, for she could not compliment the skill of the hostess, the finery of the home, or the number of guests in attendance. Having never hosted her own event, she was loath to find something to say that would distract her mind from the gentleman at hand.

Katherine elected to remain silent, but that too presented its own series of problems. She became too aware of the ease with which William spun her about the room. The small of her back tingled and burned beneath the wide splay of his fingers, and she felt a severe lack of breath for so early in the set. She did her best to appear pleased with the activity, for she was well aware that, even though several other couples had stepped to the floor, the marquess and his new wife were the ones to observe.

Katherine struggled against her own confusion. How was it that this gentleman that she hardly knew, albeit her husband, could elicit such an array of tempestuous emotions? Her inner voice corrected her. She had come to know him, in some small way. His letters had accomplished that much. She even found that his admitted failings were not held against him. In fact, his ability to express his faults was a quality that she had come to admire.

She chanced a glance up at her partner, and the motion drew William's attention, and he looked down upon her.

Her cheeks burned under his gaze. She would have turned away, guarded her embarrassment from his view, but instead he hauled her closer so that he might tilt his head toward her ear and express his concern.

"Are you all right?" he asked. The roughness in his voice revealed that he too might be struggling with the same discomfort.

"Of course." She nodded, but the crack in her voice gave the truth away. "I am fine."

She could tell that he wanted to press the issue, but the song ended, and Katherine shuffled away, all the while pretending that she did not hear his soft call of her name as he attempted to stop her without drawing attention.

"Oh, Katherine…" Anne grabbed her arm and followed her cousin into the hallway as she raced from the room with as much decorum as she could muster. "You DO love our William. At first, I was certain that you were still angry, but your blush tells all. When did it happen?"

"I do not love him," Katherine hissed. Her determination to squash her cousin's assumption made her words harsher than she intended.

Anne raised one perfect eyebrow and hummed.

"I meant it, Anne," she pressed. "It is all an act."

She lowered her voice and pulled her cousin close in a conspiratorial way, glancing about as if to ensure that they would not be overheard.

"We have a terrible foe, Lady Isobel DeGent," she murmured. She could not say what caused her to make more of the story, but any misdirection from her cousin's observation seemed necessary. "She is determined to find us out, and we must ensure that there is no cause for suspicion."

"Oh," Anne replied and tilted her head as if considering the tale. "I became acquainted with her earlier. She did seem to ask an unusual number of questions about you and Mr. Singer. I had not thought much of it at the time."

"You see?" Katherine breathed a sigh of relief that her story was supported by Lady Isobel's actions.

"I do." Anne nodded. Then, with a firm scowl that was reminiscent of her father's brow, she continued. "If you asked me, however, I would say that your acting has improved greatly since our last meeting."

Her knowing grin made Katherine bristle. Of course, Anne would not be put off so easily.

"Then it is a good thing that I did not ask," Katherine said before she made an excuse to hasten away and check that the servants were monitoring the level of the punch bowls. It was too early to be necessary, and she had no lack of confidence in the serving staff, but she was grasping at excuses this evening. Anything that would prevent her from evaluating the strange influx of emotion that had presented itself without cause.

. . .

Katherine spent the next few hours keeping herself busy with the duties of the ball, all the while practicing covert avoidance of her sisters, her husband, and Lady Isobel. She mingled happily through the crowd, ensured that all of the needs and wants of the guests were provided, and did her best to appear happy and unruffled.

No expense had been spared to ensure that the evening would be a success, and the entire atmosphere was as gay as any party she had ever seen.

"I was hopeful that I might catch you away from the throng," said a masculine voice from behind her. It was not William. How was it that she knew his voice so intimately already when his most intimate thoughts had come by way of letter?

Katherine had been tidying the table of card-making supplies, a fun activity for the guests that had been Lady Agnes's idea.

She turned to see the most unexpected face.

It was none other than Colonel Markey.

"Jon!" she exclaimed without any thought to formality.

"I had guessed that you were unaware of my invitation," he laughed. "I believe that I had been an addition on the duchess' list since her party had been disbanded."

Katherine felt her heart leap to her throat. If it was because she was pleased to lay eyes on the gentleman, or shocked at the sight of him, she could not say.

She glanced around for the sight of her husband, but he was nowhere to be found. She wondered why that had been her first thought. Did she expect William to be jealous? Did she want him to be? No, she decided, but she also did not want to throw the colonel's presence in his face when he was well aware of her history with the gentleman.

"How have you been?" she asked, hopeful that he had positive news to share.

"As well as can be expected." The colonel shrugged, his eyes lingering on Katherine's form. She shifted under his stare and wondered what he meant by the statement. "Dance with me?" he asked.

After a moment of hesitation, Katherine agreed. What harm could come of it? Besides, she could not dance every dance with her husband, and what better opportunity than to dance with the gentleman that she had fancied herself in love with? At least, she had thought it to be love. Now, however, she was not so certain.

Katherine thrust that thought aside. Certainly, her recent experiences could not have changed that evaluation so much. She had been in love with the colonel, had she not? With a firm shake of resolution, she decided to find out. She accepted the gentleman's offer and allowed him to lead her to the floor.

The music, which might have been of Italian origin, began with a gusto. Katherine was pleased to find that the set was meant for two partners alone. This would give her the opportunity to evaluate her true feelings for Colonel Markey. She was certain that it would prove that her depth of emotion for the colonel was much greater than that for the marquess. Not that there was anything to be done for it, she reminded herself, but it would give her some validation for the anger that she had been struggling to maintain in recent days.

The music was romantic, as the occasion permitted. Katherine allowed Colonel Markey to take her into his arms and guide her through the slower-moving steps before the upbeat movement began.

She closed her eyes, willing that tingling sensation to come upon her. Wishing that the shortness of breath would appear despite the lack of endurance required for the dance.

"I had hoped to see you again," he admitted with a voice that had dropped to a mere whisper.

"Yes," Katherine agreed. "I am pleased that we might still be friends after all."

She wanted to tell him to remain quiet. Certainly, the reason that the symptoms had occurred with Mr. Singer were a result of prolonged awkward silence.

"I had never wished to be your friend, Katherine," the colonel muttered. "I had hoped to be something more. Much more."

Now, the color rose to Katherine's cheeks, but not for pleasure at his words but rather mortification at the audacity of the man.

"I am a married woman," she replied, "as you are aware."

"Yes," he mused. "It is only that I cannot bear to be without you, to see you with another." His lip curled and he scowled. "I despise him."

"Colonel, this is a wholly inappropriate conversation, and I cannot allow it."

"Tell me that you love him," he pressed. "Tell me so, and I will away with the pieces of my heart. Tell me in truth and I will believe it."

"Then I love him," she replied with a burst of frustration. Her body was tingling now, but not in the way that she had expected. Instead of the flutter and flurry of passion, she was feeling a strong bout of annoyance at the impropriety of the gesture. She should have been flattered—many ladies would have been—but instead she was insulted that he would be so presumptuous as to assume so much upon a married woman, one newly so at that.

Colonel Markey sighed. "Ah, but you do not sound sincere." He pulled her closer. "I had guessed as much."

"I assure you that I love my husband," she repeated with attempted sincerity, but the words fell dead at her feet. She had been so determined to refuse the issue all evening that she could not lie even if the situation called for it.

"Yes, my love," he whispered. "You are right to maintain appearances."

"Colonel Markey!" Katherine ground her heels into the floor so that they were forced to come to a halt. "There are no appearances to be kept. I mean every word when I assure you that I am in love with my husband. He alone."

Somehow, in the course of the conversation, Colonel Markey had transformed from the definition of her ideal man to the lowest of scum that walked the land.

He had the gall to wink at her, and Katherine wrenched her hand from his grasp and stormed away. His laughter, a thrill at the challenge that she had presented, followed her from the room.

CHAPTER 23

Katherine paced with mindless determination through the hall, seething, unsure of where she was going. It was not until she found herself in the opposite ballroom standing in front of William that she realized what she had been looking for—her husband.

"Come," she offered her hand. "Please," she offered in a belated sort of way.

Without question, he offered his apologies to the couple with which he had been speaking and placed his hand in hers.

"Where are we off to?" he asked with an amused grin.

"Do not speak," she commanded as she dragged him toward the floor.

He obeyed but shot her a questioning glance.

She pulled him into formation and placed her spare hand on the outer edge of his shoulder. The music played on, and she allowed herself to be lost in the sound.

"I think I like you when you are angry," he whispered after several minutes had passed.

"I am not angry," she retorted, but the fire in her voice gave the truth away.

"Well then, bold," he said, his eyes dark with passion.

She blushed but could not deny her actions had been bold.

"To what do I owe the honor?" he asked.

"Shh," she glared.

William pressed his lips together, but there was humor in his eyes. He obeyed. He was enjoying the moment.

Again, he fell silent, and she was in the process of calming her nerves when she felt something that sent the breath from her lungs and her eyes wide with shock.

His thumb was rubbing barely noticeable circles on her lower back. An observer would never take note of the indiscretion, but Katherine felt every change of direction like a signal to her soul. Her mouth ran dry, and her breath came in short gasps. Somehow, she moved closer to him. In a moment, she realized she clung to him. The action of his thumb circling continued, and she wondered if he were aware of the turmoil that he was causing. She refused to look and find out, afraid of what she might see in his eyes.

Why did she not feel such unruly exaltation with the colonel? Had he not spoken such inappropriate thoughts she might have been able to enjoy at the moment?

No, she admitted. She had felt none of this with the other gentleman. Even if he had been a total gentleman, the water had been tepid.

She wanted to tell William to stop, yet she wanted to sensation to continue. A slow heat had begun to burn deep within her, a spark like flint to tinder. Oh, Katherine felt an inward groan, what had become of her? These conflicting emotions would tear her to pieces if she did not learn to control them. Instead, her body betrayed her, and she leaned into him, accepting the liberation that he offered.

"It will be all right," he promised, his voice a soothing murmur in her ear. Although he could have no way to know her concerns, she felt at the same time calmed and energized.

He murmured soothing nothings into her ear until Katherine relaxed beneath his fingers. She closed her eyes and let the music flow around her. William guided their steps, and she allowed herself to be shepherded by him. They were dancing. It was a slow dance as old as the first lovers. A new sensation revealed itself. All nervous tingle subsided into something that was more dangerous than the first. Comfort washed over her. Calm. There was a rightness in this. She wanted him to hold her. She wanted him to touch her. She wanted *him.*

His words and motions soothed her ragged soul and eased the anger that had brought her to his side. Inside of her began a slow flame, like a warm hearth on a winter's night, but she knew only a breath could bring that flame to life.

The song continued, and neither said a word as they moved to the rhythm and shared in the moment that was devoid of outside influence. When the last notes sounded, Katherine drew away and looked at her husband with new but guarded eyes.

"Thank you," she murmured, and she meant it.

He nodded but did not speak.

"Katherine!" a voice called from a distance.

She looked over her shoulder to see Georgiana waving for her attention. Katherine smiled at her sister and excused herself. Again, William seemed unwilling to let her flee, but this time he nodded and made no attempt to restrain her.

KATHERINEHAD NOT KNOWN THAT GEORGIANNA WAS downstairs. Her sister was not out yet, and it was not appropriate for her to present, but Katherine supposed she and William were not in the midst of the ball. She could not blame Georgianna for wanting a peek at the festivities.

It was soon revealed that Georgianna had been beside herself with pleasure upon discovering the beauty of the pianoforte that stood in the adjoining music hall. She begged her sister that she might visit often and be allowed to play upon the piece.

"Of course, you may," Katherine promised. "I should like nothing more." It was decided that Georgiana would stay for at least a month of the summer and enjoy all the fine offerings of Winebury's musical collection. Katherine was sure that Claire and Caroline would be glad of her company

"Oh, Katherine," Georgianna gasped. "You are so fortunate to have made such a match."

"I would not call it fortunate," Katherine replied with a dry implication that the events had been anything but ideal.

"Fortunate indeed," Georgianna pressed. "You shall want for nothing, be honored by all, and have the eye of a gentleman that most ladies would die for." Her voice dropped so that only her sister might hear. "I know, for I have overheard the whispers of disappointed hearts."

Katherine laughed. "You are naïve," she replied, "but I shall allow it." In order to change the topic, she elected to be a proper chaperone and order her sister back upstairs.

Katherine abandoned the party in search of a breath of air. It was far too wet to venture outside, so she slipped up the staircase and into the quiet of the second-floor hall. The balcony that overlooked the main hall was the perfect vantage point from which to observe but maintain her peace.

She stood at the rail looking down upon the guests as they passed from room to room with raucous laughter. It was a party that would be talked about for ages.

"Are you not enjoying the ball?" a warbling voice sounded from behind her.

Katherine smiled, not needing to turn to know that it was the countess who approached from the darkness of the hall.

"I am," she admitted. "I only needed a breath before returning to the excitement."

"I see," Lady Stratton replied.

Together, the ladies stood at the rail and watched the activity unfold beneath them. Mr. Singer and Colonel Markey passed before them several times. Both appeared to be searching for something. Katherine wondered if she might be the target of their quest.

"I would not fault you to say that you were ruffled at the sight of your former beau," her new mother observed.

Katherine was unable to practice falsehood with Lady Agnes. The Lady's ability to perceive the truth was without flaw.

She shrugged.

"Ruffled is a good word for it," she admitted.

"Is it still so hard to forego that future?" Lady Stratton asked.

Katherine turned to the elder woman and decided to bare her truth.

"I harbor no loss for that future," she admitted. "Not any longer."

"Then, what is it?"

Katherine had no idea how to express the truths that she had learned this very night. How could she explain that she had been hopeful for the promise of love that she had expected from Colonel Markey, only to find it dashed by the disgrace of his approach?

"I am loath to admit it," she began, "but I do not believe the colonel to be the gentleman that I had thought I cared for."

"What is it, child?" Lady Agnes's voice was coated with concern. "Has he done you wrong in some way?"

"No," Katherine admitted. "Not at all." In truth, he had not. Though his words had caused her disgust, she had been left wholly unharmed.

The countess wrapped her arms around her new niece and held her as they looked over the celebration below.

"It is only..." Katherine could not put it to words. "It is only that I have discovered that he is not what I had once thought. Perhaps he has changed since I last met him. Perhaps he was never what I had thought."

"Perhaps it is *YOU* who has changed," Lady Stratton offered.

Katherine shook her head. She had not considered that option, refused to consider it. She could not have changed so much in so few weeks. Even if she had, there would only be one reason for it... one which she still refused to consider.

At that moment, as if the devil himself had willed it, William stepped into the hall trailed by none other than

Lady Isobel DeGent. They appeared to be having a disagreement, one which William was attempting to escape.

The countess stiffened as she watched her son try to shake the persistent tail. Lady Stratton hissed when Lady Isobel scanned the lower hall for watchful eyes before attempting to wrap herself around Mr. Singer.

Katherine hushed her elder, not wanting to be discovered.

William extricated himself with difficulty. Lady Isobel's arms snaked around his neck and attempted to pull his mouth down toward hers, but he grasped her arms and set her aside with a gentle but firm resolve. He offered what appeared to be words of consolation but was only met indignation and persistence.

With a stern expression, he continued to put the Lady off until he could take his leave and disappear beneath them to the more remote areas of the house. Lady Isobel patted her strawberry curls and ran her finger along her brow as if ensuring that all were in place. She straightened her shoulders and sauntered back into the ballroom with a devilish grin.

"We have yet to see the last of her," Lady Stratton spat.

"Your nephew handled her with skill," Katherine offered, though she was surprised by the exchange.

Lady Stratton seemed unconvinced that it would be enough and said as much.

Katherine offered to usher the countess to her rooms. The elderly lady seemed tired and ready to retire from the ball.

Lady Stratton accepted the offer with thanks and accepted Katherine's arm that she might guide her down the hall.

"There is no cause for alarm," Katherine promised. "She shall not succeed in her ploy."

Lady Stratton patted Katherine's cheek with one hand and kissed her brow. "Bless you, child," she said before stifling a yawn.

When she had deposited the other Lady behind the door to her chambers, Katherine turned with purposeful resolve and hastened down the stair.

CHAPTER 24

Long ago, Katherinehad discovered the respite of Mr. Singer. She had never invaded the space, as of yet, but had known that it was where he could be found in times of trial and frustration.

Katherine slipped down the staircase without notice. Her knowledge of the house allowed her to move without discovery by guest or servant.

The door to the library was shut tight against the world. Any who might attempt to venture within would find only what appeared to be a darkened room with bare leather furniture and a wide moonlit window. Her knowledge of the space allowed her to spy a figure at the edge of the window, looking out upon the grounds.

William was within, as she had suspected.

"I had thought to find you here," she said loud enough to announce her presence as she slipped into the room.

She moved through the relative darkness of the room with ease. Strange how she had found her way in the large edifice. Her pink gown reflected the pale beams of light that filtered in through the window. He did not turn to welcome her, nor did he stiffen as if he wished to be left alone. Instead, he stared out the window as if lost in some thought that he could not escape.

Katherine came to stand at his side. Together, they observed the grounds, devoid of life in the waning light. "What troubles you?" she asked at last.

"Lady DeGent has the single-minded purpose of finding us out," he said after several moments of companionable silence.

"I know." Katherine turned toward him and pressed one hand on his should so that he might mirror her move. "She made that clear upon our first meeting."

"Why did you not tell me?" he asked with an expression of concern.

"I do not fear her," Katherine replied.

"You should." He shook his head. "She is a force to be reckoned with. She has resources, power, and determination to have her way no matter the cost. She shall stop at nothing to have her way."

"You need not be concerned." Katherine gave a half-hearted laugh. "You shall not be the one to bear the shame."

"I know." He raised a hand to her cheek and looked down at his wife with such softness that Katherine felt her breath catch in her throat. "That is the worst of it. If I could carry that burden, I would."

Katherine covered his hand with her own and pressed her cheek into his palm. She closed her eyes, turned her head, and pressed her lips to his palm.

"For that, I am thankful," she murmured against his skin.

Katherine was still confused about her emotions. She did not love her husband. Not yet at least. However, she had grown to respect him and realize the true value of his character. It was more than she had anticipated. It was more than she deserved.

William's hand slid from her cheek to the back of her neck, his thumb prompting her face to turn back to him. His eyes searched hers, asking a question that she dared not consider. He was hesitant. She had put him off before, and Katherine was not surprised by the current level of his confusion.

He opened his mouth to speak, but she did not wish to hear what he had to say. She did not want to think about anything but the moment, certainly not what all of this might mean for the future.

Instead, she stole the words from his mouth with a kiss. She rose to the tips of her toes, her satin slippers brushing against the shining leather of his boots. Her fingers wrapped around his lapel and pulled him forward, that he might bend closer to her.

Katherine had never imagined that she could be so lacking in inhibition, but it seemed that all sense of propriety had abandoned her upon her marriage to Mr. Singer.

She wanted more. She allowed herself to explore his mouth with her own. Every sensation was new to her, foreign, and yet somehow innate. Sparkles of longing ran through her, although she was not sure what to call the feeling. She could tell that William was holding himself back, anticipating the moment when she might come to her senses and renew the wall between them. That feeling of mortification was certain to come to pass, but for the moment, she reveled in the glory of her passion.

It was not wrong that she should kiss her husband, and after Lady DeGent's assault upon him, she felt in some primal way that she should stake her claim. He was her husband. No matter that she was a wife in name only; he was hers.

The slam of the door against the wall caused both of them to startle and peer into the darkness at the figure that stood silhouetted by its frame. Katherine could not make out the person, only that it was male and had been taken by shock at discovering the pair wrapped in their embrace.

Her cheeks grew hot with embarrassment, not that her reaction could be seen in the darkness of the library.

The figure leaned to the side and pulled the door closed between them, perhaps embarrassed themselves by the scene that they had not intended to happen upon. Maybe it had been some erstwhile servant. In any case, the person left the couple alone once again in the silence of the room.

The interruption had dissipated the passion that had overwhelmed Katherine only a moment ago. She pressed her hands to her cheeks and laughed with hysteria.

"Oh dear," she breathed.

William did not seem at all put out by the encounter. Rather, he laughed as well, amused by his wife's innocent nature.

"Come," he offered his arm. "We shall take that as a signal to return to our guests."

As they walked, he made the casual suggestion that they might have a discussion about this event at a later time.

"Oh, no." Katherine shook her head and continued to repeat the word with each move. "No. No. No."

Rather than be put off by her reaction, William laughed with gusto. He shrugged as if resigned to whatever pace his wife set for their development. Though Katherine did her best to renew her resolve against him, she knew that his patience would only draw him to her more. Blast the man, she thought, as she schooled her features to reenter the party. She was beginning to realize that this marriage was going to be more complicated than she had thought.

CHAPTER 25

It was not until the end of the evening, when Katherine was alone at the punch table soothing her throat that had become parched from the constant amusement of her sisters and cousins, that Colonel Markey sought her out once more.

"My Darling," he cooed.

She raised her eyes to him with a glare but said not a word.

"Please allow me to renew myself to your good graces," he begged. "I behaved abominably and cannot bear to think that you might be cross. Please allow me to explain my behavior."

Katherine blew out her breath. She was inclined to think well of Colonel Markey. After all, he had only ever behaved with perfect decorum prior to this event. Perhaps he had been beside himself upon seeing her in the flesh for the first time since her union. She wondered if she had been too hasty in her judgement.

"I shall hear it," she replied with a sigh.

"My dearest Katherine," he began. "You must understand the turmoil that I have felt upon hearing of your union. Though I did my best to offer my congratulations, I must admit that I had come here this night to observe your partnership for myself."

Katherine nodded. She could not blame the gentleman for being shocked at the speed of her union or abandonment of his affections. Many would be surprised by that same fact. It must be all that much more difficult for the colonel to stomach, she realized.

"I wish you only happiness in your future," he groaned. "I must admit that in my heart, I do still believe that your affection lies with me. All paths indicated our futures combined, not this. Due to the discrepancy of our ages, I had intended to wait to present my offer, but I see that I was wrong in doing so."

Katherine pursed her lips and did her best not to reveal the truth of his observations. Her marriage was rushed. Colonel Markey had every right to be muddled by the turn of events.

"Had I been so wrong in my estimation to think that you would not have declined?"

Katherine was torn between the truth and what she knew was meant to be said. She decided to settle somewhere in between.

"I never meant to mislead you," she avowed. "You did not misread my intentions at the moment of our last meeting.

However, it was at that very party that I first came to know Mr. Singer. Upon our meeting, I discovered that my attachment to William was greater than I could have ever expected. While you were away, that fondness grew until we could no longer bear but make our union official."

"I cannot believe it." He shook his head, but rather than anger, his voice was filled with sadness. "I cannot believe that we were not meant to be."

"I am sorry for your hurt," she offered, "but it is so and cannot be otherwise."

"Something other than fate must have come between us," he cried. "Was it his income? I admit that I am but a lowly colonel compared to Mr. Singer, but I could still have given you a life to be proud of. If it was his title, I cannot hope to best that, but even he is only destined to become an earl at the death of his uncle. Give me some word of where I went wrong?"

"There is nothing to your name that could have been corrected," she assured him. "I can only say that I wish you every happiness and am truly sorry for any pain on my behalf."

He grumbled and pulled an intricate foiled card from his pocket.

Katherine reached forward and closed his hands over the offering before he could present it to her. This should not be mine," she said.

"There can be no other," he whispered. "Only you."

Her heart broke for the gentleman as she watched him walk away with his head hung low. It was not until he had disappeared from the room that Katherine realized that Lady Isobel had been standing not five feet away. There was no way that she could not have overheard the conversation. In fact, Katherine would have wagered a fair amount to say that the Lady had gone out of her way to do so.

Lady Isobel arched an eyebrow and blinked her long-lashed eyes once before turning on her heel and sauntering from the room.

Let her be smug, Katherine thought. She had handled the situation with decorum and civility. There was nothing about the conversation that Lady DeGent could find fault with. In fact, Katherine smiled to herself, she had shown the appropriate level of devotion to her husband, as a happily married lady would.

"Let her best me now," Katherine muttered to herself as she went to say her farewells to the guests.

CHAPTER 26

A month passed, and the house settled back into the quiet of its daily routine. Katherine was glad for it, though she had been afraid that William might find the opportunity to press her further about whatever strange emotions might be developing between them. She had managed to put them from her mind and focus on her paintings and household duties.

To her relief, and conflicting disappointment, he was called away again and again, this time to Lincolnshire to inspect a property that was for sale and worth considering for purchase. Katherine made use of the time by entertaining her sisters and cousins as well as William's sisters. Somehow, they had a full house, although they had no children. Georgianna, who could not wait for the summer, spent hours at the instrument while Jo explored the stables, and Anne sent over several new gowns for the upcoming season, saying they had grown too small for her. The atmosphere was lively. Days were filled with familial nonsense, and even Lady Stratton declared herself quite ready to adopt the unmarried Westlakes just to keep the house filled with their laughter. Anne was welcomed too but was a hard sell to be torn from her husband for more than few days.

William had been gone for nearly a fortnight, and her sisters returned to their homes, when a rider arrived with a haste that sent the house on end.

"My Lady…" Jasper, Mr. Singer's personal groom, leapt from his mount and raced to greet the women at the steps. "Mr. Singer has fallen ill, and I have been sent ahead to warn of his arrival."

"Ill?" Lady Stratton gasped. "What ails him?"

"The ague, I am afraid," Jasper revealed. "We had not expected such now that the warmer weather has arrived, but the air has been noxious there for several weeks, and there was nothing that could be done. The ague is rampant."

Lady Stratton called to the servants and began marshalling them into action to prepare for their Lord's arrival. Katherine pulled Jasper aside and asked if he had the stamina for another expedition. When he confirmed that he did, she began to issue her own requests.

"Ride for the doctor—if that failing, the apothecary. Make him aware of the circumstance, and have him brought immediately," she began. "Then, you must off to the village and arrange for the employment of several additional laundresses. We shall need to make use of their services at all hours. Have the largest bathing basin brought directly to his rooms. Lady Stratton is already putting the others to tasks, so you must waste no time and leave at once."

Jasper bowed low and tipped his hat to his new Lady. His grin revealed that he was impressed with her fortitude and ability to manage the situation. With a spray of mud, he was off to do her bidding, and Katherine returned to the house to help in whatever way possible.

"We should send the girls to Sandstone," Lady Stratton demanded. "We do not know if the ague is contagious. Remember when the influenza went through the village?"

William's two sisters blanched white. "I'm not leaving," Caroline declared crossing her arms over her chest. "They demanded we leave Mother, and the next thing we knew they were telling us she was dead." She stood determinedly shaking her head.

Caroline broke into sobs. "William can't die. He just can't."

Katherine's heart went out to the two girls. She knew they wanted to stay, but if William was all right, and either of the girls grew sick or died, he would never forgive her for putting them in danger.

Katherine reached out to embrace them both. Somehow, they had become her true sisters.

"You may stay," Katherine said, for the first time countermanding Lady Stratton. "But you must move to the other side of the house. You will not come into this wing. I will send word daily of your brother's condition, and it might not be as bad as all that. We shall pray."

William arrived several hours later, by which time Lady Stratton was wringing her hands and pacing a ragged trail into the carpet. He attempted to climb from the carriage himself, but when Katherine saw the grey pallor of his skin, she tucked herself beneath his shoulder and allowed him to use her as a crutch. She had told the girls that it might not be that bad. It appeared to be much worse.

"Whatever made you so daft as to think travel was a good idea?" she scolded.

"I prefer to be here." He groaned as a wave of nausea had him curled at the waist.

"You should have stayed put and been seen straight away," she argued. "Honestly, you shall be the death of me and my nerves."

He had the gall to laugh, which turned into a rasping cough. "I shall be the death of myself, I am afraid."

"That is not funny," she snapped. "Leave it to you to make an attempt at humor when you can barely see straight for the fever. You should be in a bed."

He laughed a deep sound, which rumbled into a cough. "Now, she wants me in bed," he said, and she blushed. "Undoubtedly you are mad with fever," she said.

She stopped and redirected his path, for he had begun to wander away from the door. "You have already soaked my gown straight through with your melting."

"I am glad you learned proper wifely scolding while I was away," he muttered, but his tone was amused rather than harsh. "You would not be worried about me, would you?"

"Be quiet," she demanded. "Do not allow it to swell your brain. Anyone with half a heart would be worried at a time like this."

"That's sweet," his words began to slur.

"Jasper!" Katherine cried, and the groom appeared just in time before William' unconscious weight overwhelmed her small frame.

The apothecary was waiting in the room prepared for William. The others were instructed to wait in the parlor while Mr. Singer was bathed in a chilled bath then dressed and set with cool compresses. Still, the fever burned.

When the apothecary applied a series of balms and forced several tinctures down his throat, only to have them reappear several moments later by the rejection of his stomach, the man revealed that there was naught more that could be done until the morning.

"Give him some broth, if he can stomach it," the man informed them, "and if he is not improved by morning, we shall be forced to let the disease from his blood."

The apothecary seemed weary. Hours of working on his patient had yielded little result. As the invalid drifted off into a fevered sleep, the house quieted to get what little rest could be had. Katherine, however, could not calm her mind.

She wrapped a robe around her waist and crept down the hall to her husband's room. Inside, a servant changed the compress on his forehead and gathered another collection of soiled rags.

"My Lady." She bowed before her mistress. "He is not much improved."

"I see that." Katherine nodded with a solemn frown. "Would you have some broth warmed and brought up?" she asked. "I shall sit with my husband for now." Husband, she thought. How strange that sounded on her lips.

The servant girl nodded and slipped away, likely relieved to be away from the sickbed.

Katherine perched herself on the edge of the bed and pressed the new compress to his forehead. He did not stir.

Over the course of several hours, during his few waking moments, Katherine was able to coax several mouthfuls of broth down his throat. Though he was never fully aware of her presence, he did do his best to obey her commands. Only once did a cough send the liquid spraying back at Katherine, to which she wiped away what she could while praying for strength and continuing her ministrations.

The next day was no better, nor the day after that. The bloodletting yielded no change. In fact, the apothecary had begun to fear that the fever had taken a turn for the worse.

"There is naught else that can be done," he informed Katherine one evening as he took his leave. "You might do your best to make him comfortable in his passing hours, but you can hope for no more. Perhaps you should send for the vicar."

"No!" Katherine snapped. She would not have that hypocrite in her house. Her house, she thought. When had it become her house? She had too much to share with William to give up now.

"Surely, there is something that we have missed," she pressed. The apothecary's tone informed her that he had no intention of returning. He was exhausted, as they all were, and he had run out of solutions for the illness.

"My Lady, you are young." He pulled her aside so that they might not be overheard. "A widow of this position has much life and promise to her future. Perhaps it would not be so terrible to allow nature to take its course."

"How can you say such a thing?" she gasped.

The apothecary shrugged and revealed a weak but knowing smile. "Your marriage was sudden, and I might venture a guess that you knew little of your husband before the event." He raised his hands between them as if he did not care to know any further details but had felt obligated to say his piece. "For one so young and beautiful, you shall be left without any care in the world. There is nothing that can be done to save Mr. Singer. I suggest you prepare yourself and perhaps take what little blessing you can from the event."

He left the estate without another word as Katherine stared after him in shock. Of course, the man would have preferred to keep his patient alive. She had no thought that he was at all pleased with the outcome. Rather, he had accepted the fate and asked her to do the same.

Fate had given her an out to her torment. In such a strange and unpredictable turn of events, all her wrongs might be righted with the death of her husband. Was this not the only way free of the forced marriage?

Why, then, did Katherine not feel relief? Why did she feel so bereft?

She clenched her teeth and with two thrusts shoved her sleeves up to her elbows.

She rang the bell. The footman came running and flew to a halt at the top of the stair where she met him nose to nose. "Go and find Jasper," she said. "Tell him to ride to Northwick. Find the physician, Doctor Larkin. I don't care where he is. Find him. He will know the newest procedures."

The man bowed and raced from the hall without another question.

"This shall not be the end of it," Katherine resolved. With a renewal of determination, she returned to the chamber to bolster the forces. Like a general marshalling her army, Katherine ordered that all preparations must be made for the arrival of the doctor. "I want every inch of this room scrubbed and changed," she shouted. "Dispose of all old broth and tell the cooks to boil a new batch. Change the water in the basin and bring in fresh. Bring fresh blankets and open the windows."

"The windows?" the maid said appalled. "I've never heard of such a thing. He already has a chill. Do you wish to kill him?"

Katherine had a moment of hesitation but remembered her grandmother's old tales, telling of opening all the doors and windows and cleaning which seemed to dispel the miasma of many sicknesses. She hoped it worked.

She tucked the blankets close around William, although he seemed to be burning up and he kept pushing the blankets away. The fresh air in the room brought the scent of lilacs on the wind, dispelling the scent of sickness. When it turned damp in the evening, she would close the windows, but right now, the fragrant air was a balm to her soul.

Lady Stratton came into the room and stared at her with wide eyes. "Is there hope?" she asked as she watched the maids carrying away the soiled, sweat-soaked bed linens.

"No," Katherine revealed, "but we shall not go down without a fight."

Tears welled in Aunt Agnes' eyes at her understanding that Katherine, of all wives, had no reason to put forth such effort. Katherine laid her hand on the elder woman's own wrinkled knuckles and told her to have faith.

"The Lord brought me here for a reason," she said with all the strength that she could muster, "and that makes no sense if William does not stick around long enough to find out what that reason is."

Lady Stratton put aside her exhaustion and straightened her shoulders. With one nod to Katherine, she raced to the laundry to direct the team of woman whose fingers had gone raw with scrubbing and lye.

CHAPTER 27

When Doctor Larkin arrived, he raced up the stairwell with nothing but a nod to the butlers. Without a word, he set to work, listening to Katherine's explanations and description of events as he did. Every so often, he nodded his greying head or asked a question about some procedure or other.

"This is Cinchona Bark." Doctor Larkin held up a glass vial with the medicinal product and passed it to Katherine. "It has been used with great efficacy in some of the southern colonies. I think this may be more than a simple ague, but there is hope. We shall extract the solvent and prepare a tea and a rub to treat the malady. It is extremely important that we do so right away before the fever progresses beyond repair."

Katherine set about following his instructions as they worked together to complete the task. He agreed that the maids should open all of the windows, as long as it was not damp or raining, to leave in fresh air by day and be closed by night. Katherine had wondered how the fever could go down when it was so stifling in the room and yet she didn't want William to get a chill. At this point, she was ready to try anything.

By the time they were spooning the liquid down her husband's throat, she was beginning to feel as if even this plant, however magical, would do little to change the tide.

Hours passed without change, and what little energy she had begun to slip away. Her gusto and resolve turned to frustration and anger at the Lord for the grave injustices that he had sent upon this kind gentleman who had done no wrong. Why was it that the wicked continued to live in luxury when men of honor suffered? She prayed, but her prayer had taken on a bitterness. She no longer cajoled; she ranted. She demanded, and then she cried.

The room had cleared, and she had fallen asleep in the chair beside the bed, her arms folded beneath her head as they rested on the coverlet.

A noise woke her from her dreams, and she looked around the room in search of the source. The darkness outside the now closed window told her that the servants and physician were not set to return for several hours.

Again, the noise sounded. This time, she recognized it as a weak, choking cough from the pillows above her head.

She looked up to see the wakened grey eyes of her husband looking upon her.

"Spare me a drink?" he croaked.

Katherine gasped, and without thought or hesitation, flung herself upon him. The wheeze that burst from his lungs had her drawing back with apology.

He licked his lips, and she recalled his parched request.

With trembling hands, she pulled the kettle from where it sat at the edge of the fire and poured it. She then seated herself upon the edge of the bed and held the cup to the cracked skin.

"Slowly..." She coaxed the liquid down his throat. He attempted to steal more, but she pulled the drink away. "Slowly," she repeated. "Doctor Larkin said that your stomach might not be able to handle much at first."

"Doctor Larkin?" he asked.

"Yes." She nodded. "I sent for him when the apothecary could do no more. Even Dr. Harding had no more ideas. Third time was the charm, apparently," she quipped.

He nodded but did not reply. His eyes followed her throughout the room as she went about fulfilling his immediate needs. The balm was reapplied and more tea offered in sips and starts. His gaze was like fire upon her skin. Had she not known better, she might have thought that she had acquired a fever of her own.

Once he was comfortable, she raced to the door and made her excuse to leave. Too heavy was the relief that she had felt at the opening of his eyes and the sound of his voice. The house must be informed that he was awake, the doctor awoken, and his aunt brought to his bedside. They were not out of the storm yet, but for the first time since his return, Katherine felt as if the sky was clearing.

Despite the hour, the house awoke with a cry of jubilation. Katherine took that moment, with William so overwhelmed by well-wishers, to steal a few hours' sleep to relieve her exhaustion. She hated to admit that after the threat of his death had hung over her like a pall for several days, she was unable to face him. Now that there was hope to be had, she felt the weight that she had been carrying all this time begin to crash around her. She had been so terrible to him.

Tears welled in her eyes, and she found herself sobbing without control. She lay upon her bed with her body convulsing and gasping for air, unaware of how much time had passed or that a visitor had entered her chambers.

A wordless form crawled onto her bed and lay a head on Katherine's shoulder, and then another came to the other side. Hands combed through her hair, rocking her through the weeping.

"Don't cry," saidClaire. "Doctor Larkin says the worst is over."

"Aunt Agnes told us," saidCaroline. "You saved him."

"I only did what had to be done," Katherine replied.

"But you stayed with him," said Caroline. "He was never alone."

Katherine wrapped her arms around the two girls, and they snuggled in on the one bed. Exhausted, they slept.

. . .

THE NEXT MORNING, KATHERINE AWOKE WITH NERVOUS energy that only increased as she discovered that William was even more alert than when she had left him on the previous evening.

She knocked on the door. Suddenly, the room she had remained within for days on end felt foreign and frightening. He was no longer a sick man, a patient for whom she had to care. He was a man, her husband. Butterflies assaulted her. She poked her head inside to find William speaking in low tones with Aunt Agnes and Uncle Cecil.

When they saw Katherine, Uncle Cecil stood and gave her a slight bow. "We were just leaving," he said taking Aunt Agnes' arm. "I've said my piece. I was just telling he him had a right nerve trying to die before I have my heir." He leveled a look at Katherine, and she blushed to the roots of her hair.

"He doesn't mean it, dear," said Aunt Agnes.

"I bloody well do mean it," said Uncle Cecil. "Don't put words in my mouth, woman."

Lady Stratton smiled at her husband's bluster. She squeezed her nephew's hand and nodded at Katherine as she exited the room. "I shall return," she called over her shoulder.

Although his eyes were alert, William still moved as if each motion was a great exertion of effort.

Katherine stood inside the door and entered no further until William patted the bedside with one weak hand. She obeyed his silent command and moved to the side of the bed. Again, he patted the coverlet. With a sigh, Katherine sank down beside him so that they faced one another. She left one foot on the floor as if it would keep her anchored while the world spun around her.

"I am told that I have you to thank for my recovery," he said.

Katherine shook her head. "Everyone…" she began, but he raised one hand to stop her.

"No," he continued. "Every person in this house that I have encountered since I woke has said the same thing. That all was lost until you refused to give up."

"You are still so weak," she observed, as if it lessened her role. "Your color… faded."

He gave a pained laugh. "Doctor Larkin tells me that my recovery will move quickly now that the fever has broken. It will not be long before I am set to rights."

Katherine leaned forward and pressed her forehead to his shoulder.

"You could have let me pass," he whispered. "Then you would be free."

Without removing her head from its guarded position, she shrugged.

"Now you are quiet and demure. Though I am told you are quite the commander," he replied. "And in fact, I've heard you giving orders with my own ears."

Again, she shrugged. She felt shy. No man wanted a commander as his wife, and suddenly it mattered what this man thought of her.

"I do not mind," he said. "In fact, I like when you are bold."

When his hand snaked beneath her chin and lifted her head so that she must look at him, she did not resist. So great was the emotion that welled within her that she dared not put a name to it.

"Thank you," he said with sincerity. "I cannot thank you enough for helping me and taking care of my sisters."

"Just promise me that you shall never do that again," she murmured.

"What?" He laughed. "Travel?"

"No," she shook her head. "Nearly die on me."

"I promise," he murmured. "I already promised Uncle Cecil. He promised to haunt me if I died before him. I told him that's not how it works. Hauntings."

Katherine chuckled and lay her head on his shoulder.

No further words were exchanged. The brief conversation seemed to tax him, and William's even breathing told her he was asleep.

Katherine was glad for it because she could hardly handle the new bond that seemed to have sprung up between them. Whether it be friendship, companionship, respect, or more, she did not want to evaluate the depth of feeling. Instead, she allowed herself to be happy for his recovery without thought to her motivations. Someday, she might think on it, but until that day arrived, she was pleased to just be rid of the anger and injustice that had once poisoned her soul.

CHAPTER 28

It took a week longer for William to make a full recovery, less time than Katherine could have imagined possible. Doctor Larkin declared the patient healed and gave his card with the promise to check in on the couple at regular intervals. He was extended an open invitation to their home at any time.

On the morning of the Tuesday following, William found Katherine had returned to her painting, a sure sign that she was also beginning to feel back to sorts. Life at Winebury was making its slow crawl back to normalcy, and William was busier than ever making up for lost time in his management of the properties. As such, there had been no opportunity to speak on her growing affection for her husband. Though her heart told her that she was in the beginning stages of love, she was afraid to say too much at present for fear that her words might stimulate a relapse in his state. Of course, she was overreacting, she knew as much, but any chance to prolong her declaration was grasped with vigor. Perhaps it was her state that would suffer a relapse if she examined it too closely.

She had no doubt that William was attracted to her. She also knew that, at present, he was overcome with gratitude for the role that she had played in his healing. However, she had no illusions as to the fact that he had married her in response to a call of honor, not love. To guess that William might love her in return, out of passion rather than convenience or duty, was a gamble. He was devoted, no doubt, but only because it was required of him as her husband.

Did he truly love her? She could not say.

HE WAS OUT OF THE HOUSE TRYING TO CATCH UP ON things which needed his oversight during his convalescence when the letter arrived.

It was addressed to Katherine, and she accepted it without thought that it might be anything but some regular correspondence from her siblings. It was not until she had finished the last strokes of her paint brush that she picked up the folded paper and perused its contents.

The feminine shape of the letters was unfamiliar at once, and she raced through the contents before returning to the start to read at a slower pace.

It had been sent by none other than Lady Isobel DeGent.

To Katherine's shock, the Lady expressed her heartfelt sorrow at her abominable behavior. Her admission to jealousy brought truth to the matter. She had only begun to realize that her attempts and suspicions were unfounded when she witnessed the true depth of affection that flowed between the couple

Katherine was both stunned and relieved. So, her refusal of Colonel Markey had been an effective maneuver. When combined with her husband's refusal of Lady Isobel's advances, their behavior had painted a convincing picture.

She smiled and read on.

In proof of her humility, Lady Isobel asked Katherine to do her the honor of hearing her apology in person. They were to meet at an abandoned greenhouse that stood between the two properties.

"It will be the perfect symbol of our midway meeting that we might build a friendship from the rubble of our experiences," the lady had written. Katherine was enraptured with the symbolic reunion. Her heart leapt that all might be right in the world with this one reparation.

She raced to put on walking shoes and cross the pastures at once. She had abandoned the letter and moved quickly, for while she had painted, Lady Isobel might already have been waiting for some time, an event that might be taken as a refusal.

She tucked the letter in her pocket and ran out the door without a word to anyone in the house. Her new friend awaited, and the sun was shining bright in the blue globe of a sky. What a beautiful day it was!

The greenhouse was not far, a quarter hour walk at most. William had shown it to her soon after her arrival at

Winebury when he had taken her for a riding tour of the grounds. He had been true to his word and found her a docile mare. She had been sure to put the path to memory, for she had decided to paint the scene with Claire and Caroline when it had become overgrown with wildflowers in the bloom of summer, which was fast approaching. She thought she would assess the state of the flowers on her way.

A figure stood shadowed by the hazy panes of glass that had weathered over the years. An elegant travel carriage with paneled windows and arched doors stood a few feet away, as if Lady Isobel had settled herself in for a long wait.

Katherine smiled at the thought that the Lady had been willing to give her time to make her decision about accepting the meeting. That spoke volumes about the sincerity of her letter. Katherine hastened toward the coach and waved at the driver, who was the figure that she had seen without.

"My Lady is inside." The man bowed low and gestured toward the vehicle. A brisk chill blew against her gown, and Katherine was glad for the cover.

"Thank you," she said as she allowed herself to be handed into the carriage.

The vehicle was dark, the windows drawn against the light of the day, and Lady Isobel sat in the far corner cloaked in the shadows of the darkness. The door shut behind her, and Katherine took a seat. She had decided to allow her counterpart to say the first words. She had, after all, been the one to initiate the conversation.

At once, the carriage began to move.

Katherine could not contain her surprise and demanded an explanation of her partner.

The shadow turned toward her, and the grimace that smiled back at her was not the feminine features of Lady DeGent at all. Instead, the drunken gaze of Colonel Markey hit her with a force that drew the air from her lungs.

"You!" she cried.

"You!" he mimicked in a high-pitched voice. "Of course, you would be surprised," he growled. "After all that passed between us, you think it so easy to simply charm another man and be done with it? Is he dead?"

Katherine swallowed deeply. "No," she blurted. What was happening? She asked the question of the gentleman. No—she rephrased her thoughts—the scoundrel. How did he even know that William was sick? She supposed he may have found out from someone in town, but he denied it.

"He should have died of the tertian ague. He was drinking the tainted water for a week. Most everyone on the ship is dead."

"You!" Katherine accused.

He lurched over to the bench upon which she sat and grabbed her wrists with such strength that she was certain that there would be bruising. "Yes. Me," he said. She tried to tear away from him.

What would a bruise to her wrist matter, she lamented, if she were left ruined or murdered upon some side of the roadway? That thought spurred Katherine to fight back, but she was soon overwhelmed by the colonel. Her wrists were tied together and fastened to the handle of the coach door. With a sinking feeling and a laugh from Colonel Markey, she grasped at the latch only to discover that it was locked from the outside.

"William will come for me!" she cried. "My father, our friends, they will all come."

"Nonsense!" The colonel laughed, and the sound made bile rise in Katherine's throat. How had she ever found this man appealing? "No one shall come for you once they read the heartfelt, and might I add very convincing, letter about how you simply could bear your life with Mr. Singer any longer. You have run away with your one true love, and if any try to stop you… then there will be nothing left for you in this world but to end this life of suffering."

Katherine's eyes grew wide with fear. Little did the colonel know it, but his words would ring all the more true to any who knew the circumstances of her union. She had done such a thorough job of appearing aloof and miserable that many would believe that she could no longer bear to suffer in silence. With a groan she recalled the moment when she had told William that she would rather die than be with him.

No, she realized, no one was coming.

CHAPTER 29

The carriage lumbered on, making poor time for its size and avoidance of the main throughways. Katherine drifted in and out of sleep in her boredom. She thought that she overheard the driver talking as they stopped to exchange the horses. As best she could tell they were on their way to Scotland, and this far north, Scotland was not far enough away. She was already married, she argued, but Colonel Mackey would hear none of it.

"And who witnessed it? One or two men, easily dealt with."

"Dealt with? Whatever do you mean?" she asked, a chill running down her spine, but he did not answer.

Her heart dropped. She knew there would be no hope once the border had been crossed. She had to find a way to escape, else all was lost.

The interior of the carriage darkened further as night began to fall. Lamps were lit and provided a flickering sort of light that made Katherine think of dangerous and terrible things that might be to come.

“What has Lady Isobel to do with this?” she asked after a long while. She had not even known that the colonel and the Lady were acquainted.

Colonel Markey laughed. “Oh, smart as a whip is she,” he replied. “*Your* letter was written by her maid’s hand that it might have a feminine look that I could not hope to supply. She is determined to have Mr. Singer and was all too happy to discover that I was determined to have you. Our purposes suited one another, and she offered me a hefty sum to ensure that we were not too put out in our new life.”

Katherine groaned and knocked her forehead against the side of the carriage several times as if she could beat the horror from her brain.

“Stop that!” he growled. “I shall not have your beauty marred by such action. You must forget the past and forge a new life.”

His voice took on a new tone, as if a second person lived inside him. He was all of a sudden soothing and kind.

“It shall all be well,” he promised. “We shall be happy together and want for nothing. This is how it was meant to be. You know that.”

“I do not,” she spat. “You are a vile, disgraceful man, and I demand you set me free.”

His voice reverted to its previous growl, and he pressed his face within an inch of her own.

"It is too late for that, *Ducky*." His breath smelled like the liquor from the flask he had ben sipping all day. "You are mine now. You had best get used to it."

Katherine struggled against the restraints, but just as every other time she had done the same, they did not budge. His laughter sent a trail of ice coursing through her veins.

"I cannot tell you how green I felt when I saw you kissing that fiend," the Colonel mumbled with a glaze to his voice, as if he were stuck in a memory rather than present in the moment. "I do not see how you can bear be near him, unless the appeal is that he is titled and fairly flush in the pockets. Lawks! Never have I been more tempted to darken someone's daylights, but I played my part for the time. I played my part…"

Katherine recalled the intruder that had happened up them during their private embrace at the ball. The door had swung open with a bang. She had thought it an accident but now realized that it had been the brief moment of anger that Colonel Markey had been unable to control. Then, he had slipped away without identification… to make his plot and destroy them.

She felt ill with the thought. The matter was not lessened by the hunger that had begun to gnaw at her, or perhaps it was just worry growing in the pit of her stomach. She urged him to stop, thinking not only to refresh herself, but that it would allow rescuers to reach her, if any were coming to her aid, but the colonel would stop for naught but a change of horses. She had not laid eyes upon the world outside of the carriage since she first took her seat so many hours before.

"Ho!" the driver called from without. "Wha's the meaning o' this?"

The vehicle shook as the horses were pulled to a halt. Katherine peered through the gap of curtain that Colonel Markey had pulled back but saw nothing but fields and forest beyond.

"Drive on," he demanded.

A crowd of voices called out, and the driver began to holler obscenities in response, ordering the mob to clear the way for his passage. He was refused.

Katherine looked up to see fear in the Colonel's eyes for the first time. He ripped her bindings from the handle and held them like a leash as he pulled her across the carriage to sit beside him.

"Not a word," he breathed into the curls at her ear. Katherine felt nauseous at his stench. He was drunk as a wheelbarrow, no doubt.

The hand the held her bindings rose to cover her mouth. She was too afraid to scream even if she could. Who was outside the carriage at this hour? Bandits, or worse? She could hear the angry mob surrounding the carriage and making demands that those inside make their appearance. The colonel did not respond.

A metallic click sounded in the quiet of their confines and something pressed to the back if Katherine's ribs. She need not guess twice to know that it was the barrel of a pistol that would have no chance to miss its target.

A sound at the door revealed that the locks were being pulled away.

"Away with you!" Colonel Markey shouted to their attackers. "Away or she's dead!"

Katherine was confused. Why would bandits care whether or not she lived? She was not worth a bargain, except perhaps as a diamond of the first water. Those outside had no way of knowing that worth.

"Come out, Jon," a cool voice spoke when the others settled. "Surrender. Your plot has been sprung."

Katherine squealed against the hand at her mouth. William! Of all the voices, she had expected his the least. How had he tracked her or challenged their progress? Then, she recalled how cumbersome the coach was. Single horse riders could give chase and surpass the abductor's progress with ease. Yet, where had he found the men to help him?

"Tell your cronies to stand down," Colonel Markey snarled. "Or there will be nothing but a limp doll left of your wife."

Katherine sent a prayer of thanks to the heavens. He had come for her. Perhaps he loved her after all.

She bit the hand at her mouth and Colonel Markey released a long strain of curses. Once he had again contained her flailing, form the barrel reappeared, this time at her temple.

"I would think twice before doing that again," he breathed venomous air against her cheek.

"Come out, Jon," William repeated. His voice was calm. Too calm. While Katherine's heart felt near to an explosion of fear, he sounded as if this were nothing more than a simple discussion over tea.

"You'll have to pepper the carriage and take us both!" Colonel Markey replied.

His voice was crazed and feverish. Katherine believed him. Katherine cried out as best she could, but the sound was muffled and weak.

"We shall be together yet," he whispered. "For all eternity, My Love." He reached his hand into the air, raising the gun to the roof of the carriage, and released a bullet. Katherine knew that he intended to bluff her death, but she did not know for how long that bluff would hold nor if she would be granted another moment without the gun directed at her own body.

She did not know enough about guns to know if it was a two-shot pistol or not. Before he could lower the gun, she threw herself across the carriage into the forward most seat and rolled onto the floor and under the opposite seat. She screamed at the top of her lungs.

"Shoot high!" she screamed. "I am on the floor."

Before she had finished the first sentence the back portion of the carriage was riddled with bullets. She curled herself as small as possible into the safety of the corner and covered her head with her arms. She waited for the pain of a shot, knowing full well that bullets often went astray, but there was none of it.

Silence fell, and she remained huddled against the sight she knew waited on the far side of the coach.

She heard her husband berating someone, "Edmund, you bloody idiot, you could have shot my wife!"

"I'm all right," she whispered, but her voice seemed to have no volume.

The door creaked open, and a soft voice called her name. She could not bring herself to reply, but her whimpering revealed that she was still very much alive. Firm arms wrapped around her and lifted her from the seat. Like a child curled into a small protective ball, she remained as she was carried from the wreckage. She never caught a glimpse of the dead body of her abductor, and she was overcome with relief for that.

Soothing words were whispered against her hair, and someone wrapped a blanket about her shivering body.

"We'll take care of this mess, William," a young male voice chirped at her side. "You get your Lady away from here. She's seen enough for one night."

"Thanks, Alex," William said. "And thanks to you too, Edmund. Reckless though you are, you have ended this mess."

William pulled her onto his horse with him and held her close. It seemed only a moment had passed before they arrived at the small inn where the found some repast in a back room that offered a little privacy. It might have been hours because Katherine did not begin to make sense of her rescue until well into the meal that had been placed before her as she comforted herself sipping the hot tea.

William carried a second tray into the room and sat beside her at the small table in the plain room.

She looked up with wide, startled eyes and found her husband.

"I did not run away," she stated. Of all else, that was all that she needed him to know. How might she convince him to believe her?

"I know," he said, pulling a napkin from the tray and shaking it loose. As simple as that?

"You know?"

"Yes." He smiled with sad eyes and put the napkin aside. He crouched before her that he might push the curls away from her tear-soaked face. "Not at first, but it did not take long for me to see the truth."

"How?" she gasped. "I have been awful." It was true. She had not been the kindest wife at first. Yet perhaps the changes that she had made in recent weeks had been enough to convince him.

"Perhaps a bit," he laughed.

She would have gasped at his teasing, but she had not the strength to do so.

"Aunt Agnes never doubted, but I must admit that I believed the note at first," he revealed. "I would not hear her reason. She was adamant that you had grown to care more than you had come to admit."

"I had," Katherine admitted in a small voice. She raised her eyes to her husband that he might understand. "I have grown to care… about you. Very much so."

He released a breath as if relieved to hear the words at long last.

"How did you come to believe?" she asked.

He laughed. "It was that darned cat," he revealed.

"Patches?" Katherine felt a surge of crazed laughter.

"Yes," he confirmed. "I knew that you would never leave her behind, and when I saw her pacing in front of the door to your rooms, I knew that something had gone wrong." He then revealed that he searched her room to find nothing amiss. "I hope you do not mind the breech of your privacy."

"You are my husband," she said, burying her nose in her soup bowl as she felt the blush warm her cheeks.

"The brooch from your sister was still at the dressing table… all signs that you had intended to return."

"Except this." She put down her spoon and placed her fingers to her neck where the necklace he had gifted her still hung.

"Yes," he nodded. "That would have been a strange item for you to take along for an intended escape."

"I never took it off," she confirmed. "I promise that I truly believed that Lady Isobel had meant her words."

William was confused by this piece of news until Katherine pulled the note from her pocket and revealed the ploy that had drawn her away from the safety of Winebury and into the clutches of Colonel Markey.

William clenched his teeth as he read. "This cannot be allowed to stand," he said. "This news must be passed to the proper authorities. Lady Isobel will not be free of her involvement in this."

Katherine found that she did not care what happened to Isobel. She just wanted to go home with her husband. "Finish your dinner," Katherine suggested. "And then we will go home." Home. It had such a wonderful sound.

"Are you sure?" he asked. "After your ordeal…"

"After my ordeal, I want to go home," Katherine said firmly.

CHAPTER 30

William gestured to a servant from the inn who came at his call. He gave instructions that a rider be sent to catch up to the Duke of Bramblewood. It was imperative that this note be passed to the proper authorities immediately. Lady Isobel would not be free of her role in this. That completed, he turned his attention back to his wife.

"Eat," she urged. He saw a shadow of the commander who had marshalled the forces and saved him. "You are too newly out of the sick bed to miss meals. You need your strength."

"Oh?" he said, and she blushed so prettily that he knew that he would indeed need his strength this night. He had no reason to argue, even if his wife was being demanding. He tucked in, anxious to eat and be on their way.

The promise of a warm bed was now an even more welcome thought, but at first bite, he realized Katherine was right. He was hungrier than he had thought he was. His worry for his wife seemed to have driven all else from his mind. His wife. He found at this moment he did not care what else happened in the world as long as this beautiful woman was by his side. Forever. She was his. There was no rush.

Katherine reached across the table to clasp his hand in a most intimate gesture. She thanked him for saving her, and at the same time promised that she would need saving no more.

"I think we have saved each other," he said.

That lovely blush crept up her neck, and he wanted to place a kiss right there at the base of her neck where the tiny hollow was. "I will always be there to save you," he promised. "I will supply your every need, Love."

"Right now, I think I will need a horse," she said with ultimate practicality. "Unless you want me to ride with you the entire way home." Her face flamed in embarrassment.

He gave her a cheeky grin before he spoke to the innkeeper about the loan of a gentle horse for his wife.

Nothing could come between them anymore. Katherine had rescued him, against all odds. William had come to her aid when she needed it most, and now, they were going home.

As they arrived at Winebury, they were accosted with people anxious to know the story, but William deflected their questions. “Morning is soon enough to satisfy all of your curiosity,” he said. “We are home. We are safe. We are tired.” Without further ado, he marched her up the stairs. If it would not have scandalized the servants, Katherine was quite sure he would have picked her up and carried her the full flight of stairs. As it was, he kept his hand warm on her back, guiding her.

When they reached the landing, Katherine turned to him, a question in her eyes. “Where is Patches?” she asked since the cat was nowhere in sight, and usually, she was at Katherine’s heels.

“About that,” William said. “I hope you don’t mind. I didn’t want to take her off of your bed.”

Katherine pulled back alarmed. “Is there something wrong with her? Why is she on the bed?” Indeed, why was she not purring and winding her way around Katherine’s ankles.

“She has kittens,” William said matter-of-factly. She birthed the things on your bed while I was frantically searching the room. I didn’t have the heart to move her.”

Mr. Singer shrugged. “My sisters have laid claim on two of them. I told them they would have to ask you. You are the Lady of the house.”

Katherine threw her arms around him. Not only did he save her, but he had the kindest heart in the world, and he was hers. A that point, he scooped her into his arms and took the rest of the stairs to their chambers two at a time. He shifted her in his arms as he reached for the doorknob.

"I love you," she said as they paused in the corridor. She had no care for what he might think. She would show him her love until he might begin to feel the same, she decided. However, the thought was without need, for the moment the words crossed into being, he pressed his lips against hers. Without a word, he had conveyed his undying commitment to always come to her aid, and she felt completely loved, even with all of her foibles.

Katherine leaned into the kiss and murmured the words again, words that she had been waiting to say for longer than she had ever realized. "I love you, William."

He kissed her deeply, longingly, and then as if he only then realized what he was doing, he stopped and would have put her on her feet so that he could actually open the chamber door.

She snuggled against his neck and whispered. "You know, you never did carry me over the threshold. I think it is high time you did so."

William needed no more encouragement. He kicked open the door and stalked across the threshold.

Mrs. Davenport was in her room, straightening items on the dresser, but William was curt. "Your lady won't be needing you tonight," he said. "Take the night off."

The maid curtseyed and scurried from the room, a knowing light in her eyes.

William turned to put Katherine on the bed, but there was Patches calmly licking her five multi-colored kittens. Without missing a beat, William turned and pushed open the door between their bedrooms.

If Katherine had wanted to notice, she would have seen that the room spoke strongly of William's character—efficient, well-ordered, and masculine. It smelled faintly of his cologne, but Katherine's attention was wholly upon her husband.

He placed her reverently on the bed and knelt to pull off her shoes and stockings with worshipful care while Katherine blushed furiously.

"As I recall," he said, "There is a scratch on this leg that needed kissing well again."

"It's all healed." Katherine giggled.

"I think I need to see for myself."

And so, he did.

Although their love had blossomed late, and only after great difficulty, it was no less potent than any of the dreams that Katherine had once imagined. In fact, it was more… So much more.

William Singer had wanted to marry for love. He had his aunt and uncle's marriage as an example. He knew he wanted Katherine, prized her, and cherished her, but he had not expected a love so deep when he had offered for her. Perhaps, as Aunt Agnes said, Fate takes a hand in these things. He knew no one was as fated to be his dearest love than his wife, Katherine Westlake Singer, one day in the far future, to be his countess.

If you enjoyed reading Rescued by Ruin, please consider leaving a review.

Continue reading for a sneak peak into Lady Arabella and the Baron, Book One in The Sedgwick Ladies series.

LADY ARABELLA AND THE BARON

Lady Arabella Sedgewick, the eldest daughter of the Earl of Ashbury, tossed a letter disdainfully onto the glossy writing desk, barely resisting the impulse to crumple the costly, delicate parchment. The pages scattered, mingling with previously discarded correspondence. She stalked momentarily away from the mess to stare blindly out of her chamber window where the trees of her father's estate grew lush and green. She brushed back a blonde strand of hair which had divested itself from the pins and uncurled from the complicated updo that her maid had labored to create. She tucked the errant lock carefully behind her ear, hoping she didn't look untidy. Her hair, straight as a pin, often divested itself from every fastening her maid tried, much to Arabella's dismay.

The estate below bustled with activity; the grounds perfectly manicured, but her father, the Earl of Ashbury, was nowhere in sight. Arabella knew that Wilkins, the head gardener, had most likely worked his fingers to the bone in order to have everything presented so flawlessly, with as little notice as the Sedgewicks had given of their return home. The roses were in full bloom this late in the summer and were lovely enough to make even the Dowager Mayberry green with envy. The scent of them wafted to Arabella on a light breeze, and she closed her eyes in bliss. The breeze felt heavenly. How could she possibly be discontented in such lovely surroundings?

The lawns were trimmed to perfection, and as far as the eye could see, the lands of the Earl of Ashbury spread out in pastoral beauty. To the north, via the North Road, was the town of Northwickshire and to the south was the village of Knoxington, about an hour's ride by carriage, less on horseback. Further south, of course, was London. Arabella breathed deeply as a summer breeze again picked up a few stray blonde strands and continued to destroy her maid's work. The respite was welcome. Lady Arabella was monumentally glad to be home. No one here in the country gave her appearance any mind. No one here cared if she acted the lady, although such actions were not really an inconvenience. She enjoyed being in charge of her father's household. It was a burden she had taken on as a young girl when her mother passed, but there were certain responsibilities as a member of the Ton. Certain niceties were to be expected.

Really, they ought to have remained in Bath another fortnight, at the least. The little season in Bath was not over, but when Lord Ashbury announced his desire to cut short his family's holiday, it occurred to no one except his youngest daughter Daphne to voice an objection, and he had summarily ignored her protests. Privately, Arabella thought that his gout had flared up, as evidenced by his notice to the doctor once they arrived home.

When Arabella suggested this to her younger sister, Daphne, in the hopes that the girl would have some compassion for their father, the girl exploded with frustration and threw up her hands in exasperation.

“It’s Bath,” she cried, voicing an expletive that had Arabella raise her eyebrows. “The whole reason to go there is to take the waters and be cured! I don’t know why he couldn’t soak his toe,” she muttered in a pique.

“Surely not the whole reason to go to Bath,” said Arabella, thinking of the continual round of balls, soirées, and suitors, but Daphne stomped from the room undeterred in her ire.

Arabella, as the Earl of Ashbury’s eldest child, might have been expected to have some influence over her father, but she did not complain. Daphne had certainly seemed to consider her a traitor for not sharing her outrage at the truncated holiday, but Arabella rarely ventured to say anything that might displease Lord Ashbury. She never wanted to add to the burden of sorrow that her father had carried ever since the untimely death of his wife eight years ago. Besides, Arabella was heartily sick of Bath and had been well enough pleased to return to the Sedgewick family’s country estate, although the trip home from Bath was long, hot, and tedious.

Turning away from the window to pace the length of her chamber, Arabella fought against the growing sense of agitation that threatened to well up within her breast. It had been a foolish, childish hope; the idea that she might fall in love that summer. She sighed. She wasn't going to waste any more time on such romantic nonsense. There had been suitors a-plenty in Bath, just as there had been in London for the last two Seasons, and each and every one of them had left her utterly indifferent.

"Goodness, did someone sneak into your chamber and disorder your correspondence?" Marianne, the middle Sedgewick daughter, asked laughingly from the doorway, startling Arabella. "I don't think I've seen such a mess dare come anywhere near you since you were ten-years-old."

"Don't be ridiculous," Arabella replied, flushing with annoyance as she hurried to gather up the scattered papers. Arabella was fastidiously neat, and Marianne, who was more of a free spirit, constantly teased her about her obsessive tidiness. Arabella loved Marianne, but she had wanted to take just a few brief moments for herself, without having to play the role of the cool and composed eldest daughter, even if it was a role that Marianne generally saw through with disconcerting accuracy.

"I was only teasing. You do know it isn't exactly a cardinal sin to have a few papers strewn about, don't you?" Marianne said as she entered her sister's room. "In fact, you could blame it on the wind," her sister suggested as another errant breeze ruffled some of the papers, making the piles more askew. "Are they all letters from your many admirers?" Marianne continued as she caught up a page at random and lifted one eyebrow at the contents. "This gentleman certainly seems to be of the opinion that you are *perfection incarnate*," she quoted.

"That must be from Lord Hilliard's last letter, I'm missing a page or two," Arabella said, taking back her correspondence and fixing it into a neat stack. She searched for the missing pages which had fallen beneath the bed. "Ah! Here they are," she said triumphantly.

"No, it's not from Hilliard. It's signed Yours Eternally, Sir Giles Fenwick," Marianne replied.

"Oh well, they all sound precisely the same, don't they? That's the whole problem." Arabella gave up the pretense of composure and smoothed her dress so as to not wrinkle it. She sat down with a disgusted sigh. "How on earth am I supposed to choose a suitable match when I can't even tell one gentleman's letter from the next? There has to be something wrong with me, Marianne," she said as she attempted to re-pin the errant strand of hair that fell over her cheek. "I simply cannot seem to feel *anything* for any of them."

"I wouldn't judge yourself too harshly on that point, dearest," Marianne soothed as she pinned her older sister's hair for her. Marianne was also blonde, but her hair stayed obediently in neatly restrained curls.

"Thank you," Arabella said, feeling much more settled now that her hair was in place.

Marianne paced across the room and looked through the pile of correspondence. "Several of these letters look to be copied from the same collection of *Model Correspondence for Young Gentlemen*, unless I am very much mistaken."

"You made that up. There isn't any such book." Although, if there were such a book, Marianne would surely know of it. Arabella smiled in spite of herself.

"Oh, I daresay there is, or something very like it," Marianne said sitting beside her sister on the bed. "Even if there isn't, no one could blame you for being unmoved by such bland love letters as these." She waved the offending piece of parchment above her head. "My question is, why are you in such a rush all of a sudden to make some unimaginative gentleman's most predictable dreams come true?"

"It's foolish; I'd really rather not say," hedged Arabella, nipping sheets of parchment out of her sister's grasp in a futile attempt at distraction. She straightened them, precisely matching the corners.

"You'd really rather I go away and leave you to compose yourself, too," Marianne laughed. "You forget, I'm one of the few people in this wide world who knows that you aren't nearly so icy as you choose to appear. And as such, you must know I am wrung out from the trip north."

"It was uncomfortably hot in the coach, was it not?" Arabella agreed.

"You shan't get rid of me by talking about the weather," Marianne pronounced. "I know you. You are vexed with the monotony of the suitors, but you are also bored to tears with inactivity; therefore, you'll have a terribly difficult time getting rid of me at present, so you may as well have out with it." Her sister shrugged with feigned nonchalance.

"Very well, have it your own way, then. I had hoped, foolishly, as it turns out, to meet *someone* this summer who might inspire my regard. Since I most decidedly did not, and since I have absolutely no desire to endure another Season in London, I have concluded that I must encourage one of these—" She waved a letter about distractedly and turned up her nose.

"Insipid fops? Vapid swains?" suggested Marianne helpfully when Arabella trailed off. "Vapid swains?"

"Ardent suitors," Arabella corrected with a frown. "And you aren't nearly so amusing or helpful as you seem to believe."

"I am marvelously amusing, I assure you," said Marianne with a toss of her strawberry blonde curls. "And as for helpful, why on earth would I help you to marry any of these imbeciles? In this particular case, it is my duty as your sister to be as *un*helpful as possible."

"It is my duty as *your* sister to make a good match with all due haste, so that you and Daphne can be out, unhindered by an unmarried eldest sister who is nearly a spinster."

"Oh posh. You are no spinster at age nineteen."

"Nearly twenty," Arabella broke in as she stood to straighten the mess of correspondence.

"Ah, yes. There's a grand age," Marianne teased. "And don't use either Daphne or myself as an excuse for this folly," Marianne protested, her lighthearted, teasing manner dropping away suddenly. "Daphne is scarcely more than a child, without the slightest notion of coming out. She would much rather muck about in the stable as settle to be fitted for a ball gown. As for myself, I cannot claim any impatience to participate in the coming Season. If I did, however, no one would object in the slightest to two sisters being out at once. Why, even our Great Aunt Myrtle isn't so old-fashioned as that!"

"All the same, people *do* talk if a younger sister is engaged or wed before the eldest," Arabella said stubbornly. "I won't do anything to bring even a whiff of gossip upon our family, you know that."

"And you think there is even the slightest chance that I will make a match before you?" Marianne arched a brow at her older sister, who was generally acknowledged to be the beauty of not only the family, but of their entire connection, although Arabella would not say it was so. She purported that her nose was too long and her hair was too straight. She much preferred her sister's riotous curls over her own lackluster straight blonde hair.

"Shall I fetch you a looking-glass?" Marianne asked. "Or perhaps we can sift through these letters and find a few of the odes to *your hair like satin or voice of an angel* or your *eyes the color of a summer sky*, and don't get me started on your *porcelain or is it rose-petal skin*?"

"Nonsense," Arabella impatiently brushed Marianne's words away. Far from being vain about her looks, she had always harbored a secret fear that she had inherited their mother's reckless and impulsive spirit, along with her pure platinum blonde hair and blue eyes. Besides, she hated for Marianne or anyone else to make comparisons. "You are twice the beauty I could ever be, especially when you can be bothered to remember to spend more than five minutes on your appearance. And anyway, that is all beside the point. I am nearly twenty years of age, and it is high time I made a match. I need to make this decision and be done with it."

"Arabella, the problem is, once you make this decision, you are most certainly not *done with it.* I mean, you will not be done with the man. He will be a part of your life for the rest of your life."

Arabella sighed. "Don't remind me," she muttered.

"If you were even the slightest bit excited by that prospect, Arabella, to say nothing of joyful, I would hardly feel so concerned, but you cannot expect me to encourage you in anything that makes you look so utterly miserable."

"I'm not miserable. I was simply taking a moment to set aside some foolish fancies I had been cherishing—a *private* moment, I might add. Any of these gentlemen would make excellent husbands, I am sure," she said, picking up two of the letters and perusing them. "It's simply a matter of deciding which one to encourage."

"That seems terribly cold," Marianne murmured, putting an arm around her sister and resting her reddish-gold head on Arabella's shoulder to take any sting out of the observation.

"No, it's merely logical. I don't wish to participate in another Season, or to be a burden of any sort to my family, and I have proven to myself that I do not have the type of nature that falls madly in love. If, indeed, falling in love even exists outside of novels. The logical conclusion, then, is to encourage the most suitable of my admirers without any further prevarication."

"I suppose it has taken a great deal of prevarication to keep all of these suitors at an arm's length without actually dashing their hopes," conceded Marianne, knowing from her sister's stubborn tone that any further argument would only serve to further entrench her opinion.

"An exhausting amount, really," Arabella admitted. "It will be a relief, if I could just make up my mind once and for all," Arabella assured her with a brief hug. "But I will never manage that if I can't have a few minutes of solitude, and you know we are going to be inundated with callers as soon as word gets out that we've returned home early."

"I hope you'll take more than a few minutes to make such a monumental decision," Marianne couldn't keep from saying disapprovingly. "But I will certainly leave you to it."

Arabella attempted to resume her tasks, but was soon forced to admit defeat, at least temporarily. Marianne's evident disapproval left her questioning her judgment, an annoyance since she had spent the entire journey home coming to her decision to choose a suitor and had no desire to revisit the question. It was very like Marianne, she reflected, to question the basic and unstated rules of society and knock her logic all askew. Marianne had a stubborn streak of whimsy that, combined with a keen intellect, had her always wondering *why* things had to be a certain way.

They had all coped with the loss of Lady Ashbury in their own ways, Arabella reflected, gathering up the scattered letters one last time and sorting them into orderly piles to be analyzed later. Her father's grief had manifested itself in a retreat from seemingly all emotions; Marianne had delved into books in a constant quest to understand everything, and Daphne's grief came forth in a fiery and willful manner that was often termed spoiled.

The thought made Arabella defensive, as always. Daphne was far from spoiled. The girl was generous and warm-hearted, with no tolerance for any perceived injustice. If she was a little headstrong, well, such could be expected from a girl who had lost her mother at such a young age, after all. Arabella and Marianne had done their best to nurture and guide poor little Daphne, but as they had been children themselves, reeling with shock and sorrow, their best had perhaps not been quite good enough. *That* idea stung particularly, as Arabella acknowledged that her own particular manner of coping had been to attempt absolute perfection in all things. Perhaps such a goal was unattainable, but that had never stopped her from striving for it.

With a sigh, she set aside the uninspiring missives from her suitors. They might seem more appealing in the morning, but even if they did not, she would proceed with her plan. Perhaps she might summon a little more interest if she made a list of ideal qualifications, she thought, only she would leave off any silly, romantic notions. It was all too plain that she would not find a man who could make her heart skip a beat or make her smile or sing just by thinking of him. Not a single one of the gentlemen that she had been paraded before in the past two years had even come close to such an accomplishment. She was quite sure her perfect gentleman did not exist, except perhaps in one of Marianne's novels.

ALSO BY ISABELLA THORNE

The Ladies of the North

The Duke's Winter Promise ~ A Christmas Regency Romance

The Viscount's Wayward Son

The Marquess' Rose

Rescued by Ruin

The Sedgewick Ladies

Lady Arabella and the Baron

Healing Miss Millworth

Lady Marianne and the Captain

Spinsters of the north

The Hidden Duchess

The Mayfair Maid

Searching for My Love

The Ladies of Bath

The Duke's Daughter ~ Lady Amelia Atherton

The Baron in Bath ~ Miss Julia Bellevue

The Deceptive Earl ~ Lady Charity Abernathy

Winning Lady Jane ~ A Christmas Regency Romance

The Ladies of Bath Collection

The Ladies of London

Wager on Love ~ Lady Charlotte

The Hawthorne Sisters

The Forbidden Valentine ~ Lady Eleanor

The Baggington Sisters

The Countess and the Baron ~ Prudence

Almost Promised ~ Temperance

The Healing Heart ~ Mercy

The Lady to Match a Rogue ~ Faith

Other Novels by Isabella Thorne

The Mad Heiress and the Duke ~ Miss Georgette Quinby

The Duke's Wicked Wager ~ Lady Evelyn Evering

Short Stories by Isabella Thorne

Colonial Cressida and the Secret Duke ~ A Short Story

Jane's Christmas Baby

Love Springs Anew

The Mad Heiress' Cousin and the Hunt

Mischief, Mayhem and Murder: A Marquess of Evermont

Mistletoe and Masquerade ~ 2-in-1 Short Story Collection

New Year's Masquerade

Stitched in Love

Collections by Isabella Thorne

Winter Holiday Collection